The Summer Of Going Topless

LIZ DAVIES

ACKNOWLEDGMENTS

I'd like to thank (in no particular order), my brilliant and supportive team of beta readers without whom this book wouldn't be what it is today.

Denise Vibbert
Melissa Palleschi
Jennifer Bourgeois
Shelby Calvert
Nancy Harrison
Sharon Rice
Kyla Blair
Veronique Dion
Ashton Andrews
Inés Hernández
Wendy Macmillan
Rachel Wilk

Thank you for your honesty, your insights, and your enthusiasm. I couldn't have done this without you!

My poor husband also deserves a mention. Not only is he totally and utterly supportive of this time-consuming job of mine, but he also helps in any way he can – including sweeping the kitchen floor at 6 o'clock in the morning and bringing me tea in bed every day.

CHAPTER 1

There was no other word for it, but saggy. Her boobs sagged, her stomach sagged, her knees sagged. The flesh under the tops of her arms swung, flapping like an old sheet on a washing line. And don't get her started on her face, Candice thought, with a shudder. At least the body parts were decently covered by clothes – most of the time anyway, and definitely when she was in public. It was a pity her face had to be on show.

Scrutiny over, she turned away from the mirror and hastily dragged on a pair of thick black tights (because she'd read somewhere that black made everything look slimmer) then yanked a jumper over her head. A below-the-knee pleated skirt and a pair of low-heeled, sensible shoes completed the ensemble.

She turned back to the mirror and let out a loud sigh. She looked as though she was about to attend a funeral, and a rather unfashionable funeral at that. The problem was, she always looked this way.

It might help if she didn't wear black for once, but most of the contents of her wardrobe were black, so she didn't have a great deal of choice. At least black went with everything, more or less, therefore she didn't have to dither or deliberate every morning. The few splashes of colour in her wardrobe were due to a pink cardigan (not that she'd ever had the guts to wear it), a summer dress in turquoise (ditto), and a beige coat which her mother had given her before she died, which possibly dated from the 1970s.

Candice shied away from beige – it was the colour old people wore. She remembered both her parents being a symphony in cream, stone, and beige, with the occasional brown sock thrown in for good measure, just to liven things up a bit. All her elderly parents' friends had seemed to favour the same shades, too.

So, she wore black. All the time. Everywhere. Except when she went to bed. Her PJs tended to be fluffy, pink, and with rabbits or lambs on them.

Once a month she put herself through the ordeal of examining her unclothed body in the mirror to check on the progress of middle-age. It had clearly arrived some time ago, creeping up on her like a stealthy ninja performing a slow, depressing ambush. By now she was well in the grip of it, with only the steady decline into old age to look forward to.

Great, she thought, she'd managed a new depth of depression before she'd even eaten her Weetabix or drank her morning cup of tea. It must be a new record, even for her.

She dragged a brush through her neat ash-blonde bob, thinking she should make an appointment to get it trimmed and coloured soon, because no doubt those dreaded grey hairs were starting to become visible. Putting the brush back on her dressing table, she stood for a second, listening to the sounds of an empty house. The tick of the clock in the living room, the click and tick of expanding and contracting pipes, the creak of a floorboard for no apparent reason, all of which used to freak her out once, but now she'd eventually grown used to hearing.

She missed the kids and their noise. It didn't matter if they would still have been in bed at this time in the morning, the house always felt lived-in when they were there. She bet they didn't miss her, though, now that they both had jobs and homes of their own. Of course, they visited, but the occasional lunch wasn't the same as having their large, noisy, smelly presences in permanent residence. Ivan had a business which took up all his time and more. Preston, her youngest, visited even less often than his elder brother because his job took him all over the world; he was hardly ever to be found in the tiny house he rented. She never knew where he was, often having to depend on Twitter to discover his location. It also didn't help that he could be a bit hit or miss on the tweeting front at the best of times. Days could go by when she believed he was in Bangladesh, only to finally see that he'd posted a photo of himself halfway up a mountain in the Himalayas.

Candice switched on the radio for company. She was forced to fiddle with the ancient beast for a few minutes before it settled down and stopped being temperamental. It was like her – getting on a bit. And no wonder! She'd bought that radio not long after she and Malcolm had got married. It was funny to think that the radio had lasted longer than their marriage. Actually, it wasn't funny at all – it was really rather sad.

Her husband had left her when the boys were fifteen and thirteen respectively. Roughly ten years ago, give or take a few months. She didn't know whether to celebrate their ten-year non-anniversary or cry about it, although she had a sneaking suspicion she'd do what she'd done every other year – pretend it hadn't happened. She'd become adept at ignoring the fact that he'd walked out without a backward glance, and that he'd happily thrown away fifteen years of marriage without a second thought. Yes, that's what she would do, treat it the same as if it were any other normal day. To do anything else might break her heart, even after all this time.

After breakfast was eaten, the dishes had been washed, dried, and put away, Candice gave a quick glance around her pristine house before putting on her shoes and lifting her mac (black, of course) off the peg in the hall.

Time for work, thankfully.

She didn't know what she would have done all these years without her job. At first, it was what other mums called "a nice little number" because it fitted in with school hours. Of course, the school holidays and the occasional Saturday which she was required to work were a bit of a nuisance, but Malcolm had always done his part, even after he'd left her (left her, not the boys, as he'd pointed out more than once). As the children had gotten older and needed her less, her hours had increased until she was now full time. She was very glad of it, too. Her job had been all she'd had when the boys were in university, and she'd continued to rely on it both for company and for something to occupy her days ever since.

As she did every day, she opened the garage and reversed her car out. At least it wasn't black, being the same silver colour that every second car in the country seemed to be. The Ford Focus was another survivor of her failed marriage.

Swinging the car out of the drive and onto the pavement, Candice groaned as the engine spluttered, before catching its breath and grumbling into life.

'Don't you dare cut out on me,' she warned it, as she pulled away from the house to make her way out of the village and onto the main road.

The car had been doing this a lot lately, and she had an awful suspicion it was on its last legs. The garage had informed her last time she'd taken it in, that it was only rust, dirt, and bits of string which was holding it together. She really, really didn't want to have to buy a new one. Not that she didn't have the money – she had enough, *just about* – but she was used to this one. It suited her perfectly, being a five-door hatchback with a decent sized boot. She didn't actually need a large boot now that she wasn't ferrying the boys and all their stuff back and forth to university, but it would always come in handy, like when she took the hedge cuttings to the recycling centre, or when…

Actually, now she came to think about it, she couldn't recall another instance when she'd used it lately. Although, if she gave it a bit of time, she was certain something would come to her.

The angry beep of a horn brought her out of her musings and into a world of annoyed fellow motorists. It took her a second to realise she was the cause of their ire. Or rather, not her, but her car.

She still had her foot on the accelerator so as far as she was concerned the car should have been tootling along at the same speed as it always did along this stretch of road – a nice, steady forty-five miles an hour, five miles under the speed limit, because sometimes a police speed van hid around the third bend and she had no intention of getting a ticket.

It was the car which was slowing down, not her. Candice pressed her foot to the floor, muttering, 'Come on, come on.'

No response. The car slowed even more, the speed dial dropping steadily – twenty miles per hour, fifteen, ten. While she still had some forward motion, she steered it into the side of the road, ignoring the flashing lights and blaring horns of those idiot drivers who had no manners, no patience, and next-to-no common sense.

The car, having finally come to rest, gasped, spluttered, and died. Taking a deep breath, Candice turned the key in the ignition. Not even a croak. She tried again. When nothing happened, she banged the steering wheel in frustration. Her faithful old car was dead. How on earth was she supposed to manage now, she wondered. She sat there, conscious of the angry glare of those motorists forced to queue behind her, who were waiting impatiently for a lull in the oncoming traffic so they could pull out and around her knackered Ford. As she caught the eye of an occasional irate driver, she found herself mouthing "sorry" at them, as if it was her fault her car had conked out.

Maybe it's not dead, she hoped, maybe the car was just resting. Perhaps all it needed was a bit of TLC, an oil change, a spark plug or two cleaned, and it would be as good as new.

She turned the key again, hopefully. Nothing, except a sort of wheeze, followed by a couple of clicks. Drat!

With a sigh, she reached for her phone.

CHAPTER 2

Mike the mechanic (yes, really, it made her chuckle, too, most of the time – but not today), tutted and shook his head as he came towards her. He was wiping his filthy hands on an equally filthy rag, but all the soiled piece of material did was to smear the grease from one place to another.

'It's not worth repairing,' he said. 'For one, you need a new starter motor, new plugs, new timing belt, the transmission's knackered, the camshaft is on its way out, and don't get me started on the suspension or the rust under the arches.'

'When you say, "not worth repairing", what exactly do you mean?' she asked. Surely any repairs would be cheaper than buying a new car?

He sucked air in through his teeth. 'The transmission alone will probably set you back a grand and a half, then—'

'*Fifteen hundred pounds!*' she shrieked. 'What's it made of, gold?' Candice, aware that if her voice went any higher she was in danger of attracting half of the dogs in the neighbourhood, lowered her tone. 'How much would you say the car is worth?'

'If it was in good nick, maybe five hundred pounds. You've got to remember it's fourteen years old and it's done nearly a hundred and fifty thousand miles, plus it's got a couple of scratches and the odd dink here and there.'

Mike shook his head sorrowfully. 'The minute you buy a brand-new car and drive it off the forecourt, the value drops, see. For your car, in this age and in this condition, you'd be lucky to get a hundred for it. A waste of money, are cars,' he added.

Which was ironic, Candice thought, considering that cars were what paid Mike's wages. They also paid for his nice detached house in the next village, a couple of holidays a year, and a wife who had the luxury of not having to work. Candice was in the wrong job. Or she'd married the wrong man.

Oh, she'd definitely married the wrong man, all right, but it had taken fifteen years, two kids, and him walking out on her to realise it.

'Want me to scrap it for you?' Mike asked.

'Now?'

Mike nodded. 'There's not a lot else you can do with it, unless you know someone who can do the repairs on the side, and that's assuming you can get your hands on some cheap parts from a scrappy.'

'Scrappy?'

'Scrap merchants. Car breaker yard. Where cars are stripped of anything still useable before the rest of it is crushed.'

To think that was the fate which awaited her poor Focus. It didn't deserve that, surely. But what else could she do? It wasn't as if the car was a departed pet who she could bring home from the vet to bury in a hole in the garden, with a little stone on top to mark the location.

'If you think it's for the best,' she said.

'Right then, let's get the paperwork done. Don't forget to let your insurers know that the car is being scrapped.' Mike led the way to his scruffy little office and offered Candice a seat.

She checked her watch. It was nearly lunchtime. She estimated that by the time the paperwork was sorted and she had walked to the nearest bus stop, there'd be no point in going into work because it would almost be time to go back home. She made a note to check the bus times from the village into town in preparation for tomorrow morning. Being without a car was going to be a damned nuisance. What was even more annoying was that without a car she'd have great trouble trying to traipse around garages to find another one. It wasn't as if car sales were normally located in the middle of the high street. It could take her all day just to get to one, and what if there was nothing there she liked, or could afford? Of course, she'd have a look on the Internet first, but she would have to test drive one eventually.

'Right love.' Mike interrupted her thoughts. 'All done. I'll offset the towing cost against what it'll fetch for scrap, so you don't owe me anything.'

That's that then, she thought, feeling a silly urge to give the old girl a pat on her dusty bonnet to say goodbye. Instead, she asked, 'Where's the nearest bus stop?'

'About a mile away. We're not on a bus route out here.'

See, that's what she'd been worried about. No car meant that getting to the various car lots was going to be a hassle. But first, she had to get herself home, which probably required a bus journey into town, then catching another one from town back out again. The transport system was like the spokes on a wheel, everything either going into or coming out of the centre, with little thought about connecting up the various villages scattered around the outskirts of the city.

She caught Mike giving her a sympathetic look. 'If you can wait half an hour, I'll get one of the boys to give you a lift,' he suggested.

"The boys" were all over forty and were as liberally smeared in oil and grease as Mike was. Still, it was kind of him to offer.

'Thank you,' she said, 'that would be lovely, but do you mind if they take me to the nearest place I can hire a car from?'

Another suck of his teeth. 'That won't be cheap. Isn't there anyone who could lend you one?'

She shook her head.

'Hang on, let me see what I can do. I'm not promising anything mind you, but I've got a few vehicles here. One of them might do you for a bit.'

She couldn't remember seeing any for sale, and she said as much.

'Nah, I don't sell 'em myself, at least, not to the public. But if I see a nice deal, I buy it and pass it on to a proper dealer.' He disappeared out of the door, returning again a few minutes later. 'Right, I've got an old Defender or a Mazda that I can let you borrow. It's up to you which one.'

'What's a Defender?' she wanted to know.

'A Land Rover. It's a bit scruffy, but I love old cars. Can't get enough of classic cars, I can't, and she's a real classic, let me tell you. She's a 1984 One-Ten, a bit rough around the edges, but once she's done up buyers will be snapping my hand off. They go on forever, do Defenders.'

'Okay...' She knew what a Land Rover was, but the image she had in her mind didn't match up with the reality of the vehicle Mike showed her. She'd been expecting the kind of Land Rover that the families living near her drove; newish, shiny, and looking more like a proper car than some kind of old farm-jeep-thing. This one was army green, with a torn canvas roof, and a tyre on the bonnet. A sheep wouldn't have looked out of place in the back of it.

She peered inside. It was rather on the basic side. But that was a good thing, she thought; at least she wouldn't get confused about which button to press or which switch to swipe. It had a steering wheel, three pedals, and a gear stick (all the essential stuff) but little else.

'Or, there's this.' Mike whisked a tarpaulin off a car which Candice hadn't really noticed before, since it was all covered up in a grey sheet. 'It's my wife's, or it was. She only went and bought herself a brand-new BMW M4, didn't she? Though why she needs a TwinPower Turbo inline 6-cylinder engine is beyond me. It cost a bloody fortune, too. She didn't even offer her Mazda in part-payment. I swear to God that woman thinks money grows on trees.'

Candice didn't say a word. Instead, she stared at a cute, curvy rear end, in a navy shade of dark purple. The colour reminded her of the foil wrapping on a bar of Cadbury's chocolate. In fact, as she strolled around it, admiringly, the car looked good enough to eat. Cute was most definitely the word for it. It was retro in style, all curves and rounded edges, without a straight line in sight. With its round headlights and an upturned mouth of a grill, Candice could have sworn the car was smiling at her.

'I'm not sure if I'd call this a middle-age crisis car,' Mike was saying. 'But you don't get many people with families buying this type of vehicle, because it's only a two-seater, see, and you won't get anything larger than a postage stamp in the boot. The insurance is sky high for a youngster, so it's usually middle-aged men who buy these. Or women like my wife. I haven't driven the thing myself, but she says it goes like a dream, so I don't see why she had to buy herself a BMW. Anyway,' he paused for breath. 'You can borrow this if you like. I wouldn't do this for just anyone, you know,' he added. 'And I'd like it back by the end of next week.'

Candice nodded. If the car's looks were anything to go by, Mike would be lucky if she gave it back at all. It was such a sweet little thing, low to the ground, almost moulding itself to the floor of the garage, like a water-worn pebble in a river. She imagined the air streaming over the bonnet and flowing over the curve of the roof. It was a sports car all right, but not an aggressive or in-your-face sort. Rather, it made her smile. It looked as though it had been designed by a woman, with women in mind. The car reminded her of something… she dug around for it. Ah, that was it! A jelly bean, the purple one. But what really made her day was that the roof came off.

'It's got a hardtop, see?' Mike said. 'You unclip here and here, slide it back, and it comes off. In here,' he pointed to what would have been the parcel shelf if this was a normal car, 'you'll find the soft top.'

The hardtop was the same colour as the car, but the soft, fabric roof was black, and she wasn't sure she liked it as much. Still, she saw the benefit of it, especially after Mike had shown her how easy it was to pull it up and put it back down again. When he asked her whether she wanted the hard roof put back on, she quickly refused. If she was going to borrow this (and nothing short of a small army could stop her now), she wanted to have five minutes of fun with the top down and the wind blowing in her hair. This might be the one and only time she'd get an opportunity to drive any kind of sports car. She was determined to make the most of the experience.

'Thank you so much,' she said. 'Do I pay you now or when I bring it back?'

'I don't want paying. Just bring it back in one piece, that's all I ask. If anyone wants to know which garage you use, tell 'em this one. It wouldn't hurt to mention how good we are, neither.'

'I certainly will,' she said, folding herself into the driver's seat with difficulty. She had a brief second when she wondered if she'd be able to get back out again, but she shoved the thought to one side. She'd deal with that particular problem if it arose.

'Good luck with the car hunting,' Mike said. 'If you want to bring it here for a quick once-over before you buy it, give me a bell. Just don't buy anything too exotic!' He chortled. 'If you stick to safe and sensible, you won't go wrong.'

Candice erred on the side of caution as she eased the little car out of the garage and onto the road, sensing a great deal more power under the bonnet than she was used to. With the clutch fully engaged, she gave the accelerator a quick tap and the roar from the engine made her jump.

Woah, she thought, she could do some damage with this if she wasn't careful.

Aware that she only had a short amount of time in which to enjoy Jelly Bean (yes, she named it, so what?) she decided she might as well start the car hunting now. The sooner she got it done, the sooner she'd get back to normal.

There were a couple of car lots on the main road from Evesham to Worcester, all grouped together as though they were frightened to be on their own. She'd start with those. If she didn't see anything in any of them, there were plenty of others around. Besides, she didn't have to decide today. If she saw something she liked and could afford, she could sleep on it and make a decision in the morning. Everything looked different in the morning, her mother used to say, and the familiar pang of loss stabbed her in the chest when she thought of her mum. It was two years since her mother had died, but it still felt like yesterday.

She knew her mother would have laughed her socks off to see Candice in such a dinky car. She'd have laughed even harder if she'd had to get in and out of it herself. Where other people might moan and groan about the car being so low to the ground, her mother would have made a joke out of it. Candice imagined trying to heave her hefty mum out of the passenger seat, and she gave a small smile.

The short journey to the first car lot was an absolute joy, though at first it felt strange not to have a roof over her head. She felt too exposed for a while, until she got used to having the sky directly above with nothing in between her and it. To her surprise, the wind wasn't a continuous stream of air in her face, but rather a flutter and snap of her hair, and a coolness on her cheek. It might only be late May, but it was a warm one, and this beat air con any day.

A toot and a wave from a car travelling in the opposite direction had her glancing in her rear-view mirror. It was from another Mazda MX-5, a gold one. The driver's hand waggled in the air, and Candice guessed that he or she probably assumed it was Mike's wife behind the wheel. Candice, herself, knew no one who owned a car like that. To be fair, she had trouble recognising cars at all – they all seemed to look more or less the same these days. They were either small, medium, or large, and came in assorted colours, though many of them tended to be silver. That's as far as she went with identifying car makes. Apart from the one she was currently driving, that is. Oh, and the Land Rover Mike had shown her had been quite distinctive, too, but for all the wrong reasons!

Marvelling at how light the Mazda's steering was, she turned a corner and floored it. Floored it? Ha! She recalled a boy from her youth saying that once. His name eluded her, but she remembered his car. It was a Mini, when Minis were really mini and fun, like dodgem cars, and not the middle-sized things they were today.

Candice pulled into the first garage with a bit of a flourish, rather too fast, feeling Jelly Bean's rear end wanting to fish-tail, but she held her nerve, gripped the steering wheel hard, and hung on for dear life as she slammed on the breaks.

The car came to an abrupt halt.

Candice sat for a while, her heart thumping, her palms moist, while she regained her equilibrium. When she finally felt calm enough to haul herself (slightly inelegantly) from the driver's seat, it was to find three salesmen staring at her through the showroom window.

Oh God, had her driving really been bad enough to draw a crowd?

One of them peeled himself away from the rest and sauntered over. She waited for him to start his sales pitch, but instead he walked around Jelly Bean, his hands in his pockets, nodding his head. He did this twice before he finally spoke to her.

'Nice car, good condition; you're wanting to part-exchange it, are you, love? For something more suitable?'

What did he mean "something more suitable"? Cheeky git.

'I'm not selling this because it isn't mine to sell. I'm just borrowing it for a couple of days,' she explained.

He nodded. 'I must admit, I was a bit surprised to see a lady such as yourself driving this.' He nodded again, this time at her car.

'Why?' she asked, wondering what he was on about? Was there some reason she shouldn't be driving it?

'Why what?' he asked her, frowning.

'Why were you surprised?' she wanted to know.

'Well, I mean, it's a bit on the sporty side, isn't it? I'd have pegged you as more of a Volvo driver myself.'

'Volvo,' she repeated woodenly.

'Very popular with older drivers,' he said, without a hint of discomfort at calling her old.

How old did he think she was, anyway? She was tempted to ask him, but she had an awful feeling she wouldn't like the answer.

'We've got a couple of models in,' he was saying. 'Do you mind me asking what your budget is?'

'Two thousand pounds,' she said.

The salesman did a sort of double-take. 'Er, I'm not sure we have anything in that price bracket at the moment,' he said. 'Are you sure that's your limit?'

She *was* quickly reaching her limit, but not over money. Her patience was nearing the end. After the day she'd had, she hadn't got a lot of it to begin with, and now here was this man, hardly older than her own sons, with his shiny shoes, flashy pink-striped tie, an earring in one ear, and no manners, firstly calling her old, then having the cheek to insinuate that she couldn't afford what he was selling.

She looked beyond his lanky frame and polished smile, to focus her attention on the shiny vehicles behind him.

He was right, she realised, her heart sinking as she squinted at the prices on the windscreens nearest to her (maybe she needed to get her eyes tested again). She didn't have that kind of money, but even if she did, she was reluctant to spend it on a hunk of metal. Were cars really so expensive these days?

Trying not to let her dismay show and, although she wanted to beat a hasty retreat, she made a show of strolling around the cars on display. Each one seemed to be a variation on a theme, with hardly any differences except size. Most were silver or black, although there were a couple of brighter coloured ones and she once thought she recognised a Beetle. All these samey vehicles reminded her of the problem she used to face every Christmas when buying the obligatory satsumas – she couldn't tell the difference between oranges, clementines, easy-peelers (what on earth were they supposed to be?), satsumas, or tangerines. They were all oranges to her, and the selection of cars splayed across the garage forecourt reminded her of those assorted orange fruits, although these gleaming vehicles were a darned sight more expensive.

'It's a long time since I bought a car,' she admitted. 'I hadn't realised prices had gone up so much.' The lie was a small one – *she'd* never actually bought a car in her life. Malcolm had bought the Focus for her when the kids were young and she needed a decent car to ferry them to rugby, or football, or whatever else they required a taxi service for.

But when she turned away from the sleek offerings, resolving to try the next garage down, she paused, as something caught her eye.

Her breath caught in her throat and a smile spread across her face. One car stood out from the rest. One car caught her gaze and held it. One car made her smile.

Jelly Bean.

She just hoped she could afford it.

CHAPTER 3

'You've bought a *what?*' her eldest son, Ivan, said loudly down the phone. Candice was tempted to simply hang up and go do something less stressful, like clean the oven, but she may as well deal with this now as later, she thought.

'A Mazda MX-5,' she replied evenly.

There was a silence, followed by a sharp intake of breath where she guessed her son was Googling it. He pretended he knew all about cars, but he didn't, not really.

'You do know it's a sports car, right?' he said, after a while.

Really, I hadn't noticed, she felt like retorting. Instead, she replied, 'I know,' in as patient a voice as she could muster.

'What on earth made you do that?' he asked.

'Because I fell in love with it.'

'What about the Focus?'

'It broke down. The garage said it would cost more to repair than it was worth. Much more.'

'How much did the Mazda set you back?' he wanted to know.

'Enough.' She wasn't prepared to enter into a discussion about the amount she'd paid for it. What she spent her money on was her own business. She knew he was only trying to look out for her and that he had her best interests at heart, but honestly! It got a bit much sometimes.

'Did the same garage that you took the Focus to, sell you the Mazda?' Ivan demanded.

Candice heard the suspicion in his voice. 'Yes,' she said, 'but it wasn't like that.'

'I bet it wasn't.' His tone was a mixture of annoyed and despairing. 'You should have waited for me to come with you.'

'I needed a car this side of the summer,' she replied, without any hint of censure or recrimination. She was simply stating a fact. Her eldest wasn't the most dependable person in the world. She knew he meant well, but he did have a tendency to say he'd do something, then make her wait months for it to be done. Take the shed door, for instance – nine weeks she'd waited for Ivan to sort it out after he'd talked her out of getting a man in. And what did she have to do in the end? She'd had to get a man in. It had taken the bloke ten minutes to remove the padlock and retrieve the keys she'd left inside. Ten minutes. Luckily, it had been winter so she hadn't needed either the lawn mower or the secateurs.

She understood that it wasn't Ivan's fault. He was so busy with his business, and she knew he worked all hours of the day and night. It was simply better not to ask him in the first place – she would only be adding one more thing to his long and never-ending list of things to do.

She heard Ivan bristling down the phone and guessed he might be getting ready to argue with her, so she jumped in with, 'It's done now. I'm very pleased with it.'

Peering through the nets, she watched the woman opposite hauling her bins down the drive and onto the pavement. She wondered if she should put hers out this week or could they wait until next week? Seven ready-meals plus the odd milk carton didn't make for much in the way of rubbish. Thinking of food reminded her...

'Are you coming to lunch on Sunday?' she asked, as she did every week, hoping to change the subject. When she heard his hesitation, she added, 'I need to know because if you're not I'll go to Birmingham and do a spot of shopping.'

She had no intention of going anywhere, but it gave her son a get-out-of-jail-free card. She could tell he was going to say he couldn't, and she didn't want him to think she had nothing better to do than wait for his visit, because it simply wasn't fair to lay a guilt trip on him. She actually *didn't* have anything better to do, but she didn't want *him* to know that, and she certainly didn't want to come across as the sort of mother who only lived for her children's visits.

'You go shopping,' he said, the relief in his voice so clear it made her want to cry. 'Enjoy yourself, have lunch out, buy yourself something nice.' He sounded as though he was giving her permission, and a little bubble of resentment rose up through her chest to burst at the back of her throat. She ended the call with a slight feeling of resentment towards her eldest child.

She couldn't put her finger on exactly when she had gone from being the mother who sorted out all her children's little problems – the person they ran to when they scraped a knee, or when they were struggling with their homework, or the woman who dropped whatever she was doing to fetch a forgotten rugby kit, or the thousands of other things they'd turned to her for – to someone who they thought needed looking after by them. The gradual untying of the apron strings had been as imperceptible as continental drift, but just as inexorable. She supposed all teenagers did it, it was part of growing up, but she couldn't remember if she'd been as reluctant to share her life with her own parents as her sons appeared to be in sharing theirs with her. She guessed she must have been, but it didn't alleviate the pain she felt at the knowledge that her boys no longer needed her.

And when had this role reversal taken place, she wondered, ending the call with her usual urging for Ivan to take care of himself, and to make sure he ate properly. Not that he took any notice of her – these days her son treated her like he was the parent and she was the child. Suddenly she found herself resenting it. As if she wasn't capable of making the decision of what car she should buy!

Thinking of Ivan eating properly made her consider her own evening meal, so she wandered into the kitchen, opened the freezer, and peered inside. She gave a desultory sigh, unable to face yet another ready-meal. She could always have soup, she thought, and opened a cupboard. Another disappointed sigh. The only soup to be found, hidden behind a tin of mushrooms, was oxtail, which was (she checked the expiry date) several months out of date. She didn't even *like* oxtail soup.

Things hadn't always been this way. When the boys were younger she used to cook a hearty meal every evening. She hadn't had any choice, not with their voracious appetites. The cupboards had been stocked full and the fridge had usually been bursting at the seams.

Abruptly, she found she couldn't face another thirty or forty years of frozen meals. It was feasible she might live to eighty or ninety, but she wouldn't if she didn't start taking proper care of herself. When had she stopped cooking anyway? She used to enjoy it, to take pride in presenting a delicious meal and watching her sons devour it with enthusiasm.

Thinking back, it had started when Preston went to university. With both her sons out of the house, she'd become lazy when it came to cooking, only making an effort in the kitchen during the holidays when the boys were home, asking herself what was the point of going to all that trouble just for herself. When the pair of them had finally fledged and left home for good, Candice had taken culinary laziness to a whole new level, she now realised on looking back, hardly bothering to cook at all.

Making a decision, she grabbed her keys.

The garage was warm, sucking in the last of the evening sun through its blue-shuttered metal door, and dust motes drifted in the air. Flapping a hand in front of her face, she walked around Jelly Bean, plucking up the courage to remove the hardtop.

Mike had shown her how to do it (several times), then had stood back to watch while he made her do it on her own. This was her first time attempting a solo, unsupervised removal of the hardtop. She'd had no choice but to drive her new car home with the top on, because there was no other way of transporting it. Now, however, she wanted it off because she intended to go topless for the whole summer if she could, otherwise what was the point of owning a convertible? Besides, if it did rain, there was always the soft top she could pull up. She already knew from what Mike had shown her, that the soft top was a doddle to lift up and down.

She grabbed one of the old dust sheets which she used for decorating, and folded it over the car's boot. She'd made sure to wash the sheets thoroughly before she'd put them away after the last time they were used, so she knew this one was clean. She wasn't prepared to take any chances with the car's paintwork. Then she folded another sheet and placed it on the ground directly behind Jelly Bean.

Finally, she set about releasing the two forward catches and sliding the hardtop towards the back of the vehicle.

'I can do this,' she muttered. 'I can.'

Slowly, carefully, after a bit of wiggling and jiggling to ease it free from the metal clasps at the back which helped hold the whole thing in place, she slid the heavy piece of metal down the length of the boot and lowered it gently to the floor.

Then she took a minute to get her breath back (bloody hell – she hadn't realised she was so unfit) before walking it gingerly across the floor, still on its sheet, to cautiously prop it up against the wall of the garage.

Worried that it might slip, Candice dashed back into the house, and whipped the duvet and pillows off the bed in Preston's old room, to use them to form a nest for the car's precious roof, padding them around the edge where it rested against the wall, and stuffing them underneath to protect the hard top from the concrete garage floor.

She was all hot and sweaty by the time she'd finished and she was tempted to go back inside to ding something in the microwave instead, but the thought of the wind blowing through her hair as the pair of them hurtled down the bypass made her smile. Besides, the car could do with a run out before bedtime.

Realising what she'd been inferring, she let out a self-conscious laugh. Anyone would think Jelly Bean was a dog, not a car! *It* certainly didn't need a walk before bed, but *she* did. A drive, that is, not a walk. The fridge wasn't going to stock itself, was it?

Candice couldn't remember the last time she'd had so much fun in a vehicle. And yes, she was including all those sessions in the back seat of Malcolm's old Rover when they were going out together. Dating they called it now, but whatever name you gave it, it was still a fumble and some making out in a very confined space, with a gear stick poking you in the bum and the worry that someone might be watching. Not that the fear of being spied on had ever worried Malcolm – looking back, Candice suspected he had actually revelled in the excitement.

She preferred a bed, thank you very much, although she hastily turned away from the knowledge that it had been a very long time since anyone had shared one with her. Not since Malcolm in fact and, as she reversed the car out of the garage, she wondered if she'd still remember what it was for – and she wasn't referring to the car!

The village of Little Duckton was tiny, just a church with a graveyard to the side of it, a green in front, a small pub which was heaving when it had any more than ten people in it, and an even smaller shop which doubled as a hairdresser on Tuesdays and every other Thursday evenings, plus a handful of houses.

It was the sort of place where everyone knew your

business whether you wanted them to or not, so it was with resignation that Candice drove slowly out of the village. By this time tomorrow, all her neighbours would know that Candice Summerville had bought herself a flashy new car (new to her, that is) and was parading around in it like a twenty-year-old. Which was exactly how Jelly Bean made her feel, she realised. Young. Carefree. Sexy. OK, not sexy; not with her middle-age spread and her sensible shoes. But it sure did feel good to have the wind ruffling her hair, the scent of freshly mown grass in her nose, and power in the pedal under her foot.

As she negotiated her way out of the village and onto the first of several narrow, twisting country lanes, she realised for the first time in a long while just how much of this countryside she'd been missing. Bed, work, and the telly was the routine for most days. Her days off were spent doing the cleaning, the laundry, and seeing to her large garden in the summer.

She couldn't remember the last time she'd been for a walk. Maybe not since the kids had stopped being entertained by tadpoles, birds' nests, and the lure of wearing Wellington boots on muddy paths through the fields. Almost as soon as they'd hit their teens, they'd lost interest in the delights of the great outdoors and had become entranced by the bright lights of the town and their computer games.

Candice realised that she'd been so busy ferrying her boys here, there, and everywhere, that she'd forgotten what it was like to slow down and smell the bluebells. In fact, she couldn't remember the last time she had actually seen a bluebell. Or when she had seen a lamb up close and not just through the car window as she sped past.

Talking of lambs, there was a field full of them to her left.

On a whim, she pulled up beside the gated entrance to the paddock and peered through the bars. A group of the little woolly animals were jockeying for position on top of a small mound, pushing each other off, and generally bouncing around. What was the collective name for a group of lambs, she wondered? A bounce, a skip, a naughtiness? All of those words were apt. She couldn't remember the last time she'd seen such unbridled joy, and some of the lambs' zest for life seeped into her own soul. The tiny creatures, with their endearing antics, lifted her heart, making her realise what she'd been missing. She vowed to get out and about a bit more.

Feeling happier than she had felt in a long time, she watched them for a while, before hunger made itself known by way of a rumbling tummy, so she got back in the driver's seat, restarted Jelly Bean, and made her way towards the outskirts of town.

The soft top was so much easier to pop on and off than the hardtop, she discovered, finding a space in the supermarket's carpark, and pulling the shell over her head to click it into place. She only intended to be a few minutes, but she wasn't taking any chances, so she locked the car carefully, pulling on the door handle to check Jelly Bean was secure.

It was a long time since she'd browsed the supermarket shelves. Her shopping trips were normally a quick in and out, like a guerrilla mission, or else she'd order online if she was prepared to wait for the delivery. Her mouth watered as she picked up a punnet of strawberries, an item she wouldn't normally consider buying. Oh, look at those blueberries! She could make a fresh fruit salad, she decided – the last piece of fruit to pass her lips had been a slightly wrinkled apple bought from the café in work one day last week. It was lucky the library had a café, otherwise she probably wouldn't bother to eat anything for lunch except for the biscuits she kept in her desk drawer for emergencies. The trouble was, she often had an emergency biscuit, usually several, so it was no wonder she was getting plump.

Finally, with her shopping done, she headed back to

the car, the trolley nearly full.

It was at this point that Candice discovered just how little one can actually get into the boot of a Mazda MX-5.

'I used to have a BMW Series 3,' a voice behind her said. The owner sounded wistful, and when she turned to look at the bloke speaking to her, she noticed his gaze was fixed longingly on Jelly Bean.

'The wife let me keep it for a couple of years,' he added. 'But when the grandkids came along, she made me sell it. I've got a blasted people carrier now.' He didn't sound very happy about it. 'I miss my BMW.' He stepped closer and jerked his head at the open boot and the overflowing shopping bags. 'Not exactly a family car, is it? Well, gotta get on. I've been sent out for nappies.' He held up a pack to show her. 'The wife thinks our daughter-in-law uses the wrong size.' He tutted and rolled his eyes before wandering dejectedly over to a monster of a vehicle. As he went, he kept throwing glances at Jelly Bean over his shoulder.

The next person to speak to her as she tried to close the boot, was quite a bit younger than the last man. 'Nice car, missus. Give us a go in it?'

Candice looked up to see a couple of youths slouching up to the car, nodding sagely at it as they approached.

'No chance!' She closed the boot carefully, not wanting to squash any of the bags. She'd been forced to put two of them on the passenger seat because the boot was so small. The gentleman was right – the Mazda wasn't a family car.

'Go on, don't be mean. Bet it goes like stink,' the youth who had spoken, added.

'No, and yes it does,' she replied.

The boy wasn't old enough to drive and neither was his spotty mate, standing behind him with his hands stuffed into the pockets of his low-slung jeans and shuffling from side to side, a mix of embarrassment, boredom, and envy on his face.

'Mean cow,' the first boy muttered, throwing her a dirty

look and walking away, his friend shambling after him. When they got to a safe distance, he called over his shoulder, 'What's an old biddy like you doing driving a car like that? Effing criminal that is, wasting it on an old-age-pensioner.'

Cheeky little sod! She wasn't *that* old, and certainly not old enough to draw a pension. Although, to a kid barely out of short trousers, she probably did appear ancient.

As she drove back home, she mused over the reason why some random strangers had stopped to talk to her. Usually, unless she was in work and someone needed her help, she was invisible. Then she realised that it wasn't her that had caught their attention but the car. Jelly Bean was making her visible again. She was being noticed, spoken to, smiled at, waved to… She wasn't used to it.

It was a long time since anyone had noticed her, and she wasn't sure how she felt about it.

CHAPTER 4

Candice reversed out from underneath the desk, backside first, hoping she wouldn't get stuck, while clutching a length of cable in one hand, and muttering about dust bunnies and cobwebs. She might have a fancy title, but her job of keeping the IT equipment with its various components and software running, was far from glamorous.

'Beep, beep, beep,' Dermott said, with a chuckle. 'Watch out, wide load coming through.'

'Oh, piss off,' she grunted, easing her head and shoulders out, her knees aching from kneeling on the wooden floor. If she carried on like this she'd be lucky if she didn't develop arthritis in a few years' time.

Clambering awkwardly to her feet and dusting her hands off, she glared at her colleague. 'Are you calling me fat?'

Dermott held up both hands. 'No, certainly not, not me. I'd never... er… just having a laugh.'

'Yes, well, I didn't find it very funny.' Actually, she had to admit that Dermott had a point – her rear end was growing. Not at an alarming rate, but steadily at the rate of about an inch or so a year, she reckoned. An inch wasn't so bad until you counted up the years, then the inches amounted to quite a few indeed. Her clothes were starting to feel decidedly tight and if she had to crawl under any more desks, she was in danger of not being able to get back out again.

She straightened up, her hands pressed into the small of her back to ease out the kinks, realising she was stiffening up with every year that passed. She even had to heave herself out of her favourite armchair at home, and had been known to make a weird grunting noise as she did so. She was getting too old for scrabbling about on all-fours, but if the council wasn't so stingy about replacing knackered hardware, then she wouldn't have to risk knackering *herself* on such a regular basis.

'Have you thought about yoga?' a voice said.

'Eh?' Candice looked around. She was so used to crawling about on the floor among customers' legs to fix various leads, that she tended to forget the library was open for business, so the library-users often became part of the fixtures and fittings.

A young girl, in her late teens maybe, stared back at her, all fresh-faced and dewy-skinned, and wearing an expectant expression.

Candice narrowed her eyes.

'I noticed you on your hands and knees. It can't be easy,' the girl added.

Candice filled in the "for a woman of your age" bit for herself, and bristled slightly at the insinuation. She'd been crawling under desks and fiddling with wires and connections since before this kid was born – she didn't need a girl young enough to be her daughter telling her that she was getting past it.

The teenager appeared not to notice Candice's less-than-welcoming attitude, because she carried on with, 'My granny has been doing yoga for years – she's bendier than I am!' Her expression was half awe and half disgust. 'She can do the splits and everything,' she added.

Candice wasn't sure she wanted to know what the "and everything" was, but she couldn't stop herself from asking, 'How old is your granny?'

'Sixty-nine.' This time the teenager's tone held a hint of

pride. 'You wouldn't think it to look at her. She keeps saying that if you don't use it, you lose it.' The girl smiled up at her and Candice smiled back; after all the youngster hadn't meant any harm. Besides, the girl had put an idea into her head.

It made sense to try to retain one's flexibility as one grew older. Although Candice wasn't that old in years, sometimes she felt ancient in both body and mind. It wouldn't hurt to have a quick check on the Internet to see if there were any local classes she could have a look at. She fancied getting a bit "bendier" – it would help when she had to squeeze into a tiny space to replace a loose connection, like she'd had to do just now.

She could also do with shedding a pound or two, preferably off her bum. Returning to her little office just off the main fiction floor, Candice typed her password into the computer and clicked on a search engine.

There were three council-run leisure centres within easy driving distance as well as a couple of private gyms. Mindful of the pennies, especially since she'd blown most of her rainy-day money on a pretty, purple sports car, she decided to try the cheaper version first. Severn Valley Leisure Centre was on the outskirts of town, and only a small detour on her way home. It wouldn't hurt to call in. Their website said they ran yoga classes on Tuesdays, and the fee per session was £4.50. That wasn't going to break the bank. Anyway, what she was saving by bringing her own lunch into work would more than pay for it.

She smiled to herself, thinking about the cooking spree she went on last night. Two kinds of soups, which she had separated into portion sizes and stored neatly in containers in the freezer, a batch of sauce which could be used for spaghetti bolognese and lasagne, a broccoli and cauliflower curry, and enough fruit salad to keep the Queen's garden party going for a month.

She'd brought some vegetable soup in with her today, and a pot of fruit with Greek yogurt spooned over the top.

Tackling the food with enthusiasm, she ate her lunch quickly, grabbed her bag, and trotted out of the door. She used to find that working in the middle of town was both a pleasure and a pain. A pleasure, because she didn't have to go very far if she wanted to buy something, and a pain for the exact same reason – it was hard not to go shopping when temptation was right on her doorstep. But today she was relieved to be able to dash into Sport Science during the second half of her lunch break.

Once inside the shop, she stopped to get her bearings. What on earth did one wear for yoga? Was there such a thing as a yoga outfit? Was she expected to wear shorts? The last time she'd done any kind of exercise, apart from walking or taking the kids swimming, had been in school. In her day, the pupils had been made to wear horrid, navy, nylon shorts, which had been more akin to oversized knickers. No way was she wearing anything like that ever again.

She scanned the racks but everything looked far too samey. She even had difficulty differentiating between men's and women's stuff. After several minutes of fruitless wandering, she caught the attention of a sales assistant. 'Excuse me, I'm looking for something to do yoga in?'

The child (for he was little older than a school kid), bit his lip as he looked at her doubtfully, before leading her over to a rail of children's clothes. Or what she had assumed to be children's clothes, until she saw the sizes on the hangers.

Candice picked up a pair of skin-tight lycra leggings. The top it was teamed with on the display was, to all intents and purposes, a bra. She stared at it in dismay. If she wore that (assuming she could actually get one in her size), her boobs would bounce all over the place, and her flabby upper arms would be exposed. Also, she had a feeling that the elastic underneath the bra-thing would compete with the elastic on the waistband of the leggings to see which could squash her in the most. She'd be left with a bulge of flabby stomach oozing out between the two like some kind of disgusting sandwich filling.

'Have you got anything that isn't so tight? Or as skimpy?' she asked.

With all his (probably) ten minutes of product training, the boy shook his head. 'You need the lycra to hold you in,' he said. 'And you need it skimpy to stop anything flapping about when you do the downward dog.'

She had no idea what the downward dog was, but she knew exactly what *would* be flapping about if she wore anything like that, and it wouldn't be pretty.

'No, thanks, this isn't for me,' she said firmly and went in search of something more there.

After another wander around the shop and frequent checking of her watch to make sure she wasn't going to be late back from lunch, she settled on a T-shirt (men's) and a pair of jogging bottoms (also men's). She was about to pay for the items when something else occurred to her – trainers.

It would look a bit daft if she wore her yoga outfit with a pair of court shoes. She wasn't so silly that she didn't know that yoga was performed bare-footed, but she still had to walk from the car to the leisure centre (she had a warm, fuzzy feeling when she remembered that the Focus had gone to the great big car park in the sky, and that she'd be driving to her class in Jelly Bean), and she didn't fancy getting odd looks.

She actually did own a pair of trainers, but they were old and tatty, and she only ever wore them for gardening, so she treated herself to a turquoise and pink pair. It was only later, when she took them out of the box, did she wonder what on earth had possessed her to buy such garish ones. She needed sunglasses just to look at them! She should have gone for a nice black pair. Black went with everything and didn't show the dirt. The trainers were really pretty though, and for the rest of the afternoon she found herself taking the odd peek at them. It had been a long time since she'd owned something so girly.

On the way home later that day, Candice dropped into the leisure centre to enquire about the yoga class and was relieved to be told there were spaces.

She was about to thank the woman behind the counter and leave, when the receptionist asked, 'Would you like to take out a membership, because it will save you money in the long run?'

'Oh?' Candice was always happy to save money and, as the woman talked her through the various options, she noticed a "corporate" price on the leaflet. 'What's this?' she asked.

'You get a discount if you work for the council,' the woman explained.

Candice's ears pricked up. Discount? Wonderful! 'I work for the council,' she said.

'If you can let me have something like a wage slip, I can set you up straight away.' She was so keen that Candice wondered if she was on commission.

'I've got an electronic pay slip,' Candice said. 'Will that do?'

The woman shook her head. 'I need to take a photocopy.'

'I can email it to you, and you can print it off from there. It's password protected, but if you give me a minute I can get round that.'

'You can?'

Candice nodded. 'My job is mainly IT, so I've learned a few tricks in my time.' She got her phone out, scrolling and clicking as she spoke. 'There, that should do it. All you need to do is print it off. You'd better do it now though, because the email will self-destruct in five minutes.'

The woman's eyes widened. 'Wow!'

Candice didn't have the heart to tell her that she was joking. Although she did intend to urge the receptionist to delete the email once the wage slip was in hard copy, because she had no intention of leaving such personal details on any old computer, council-owned or not.

She filled in the necessary form while the woman downloaded the attachment and printed it off.

'Can you delete the email now, please?' Candice said. 'It may cause a problem for your server if it self-destructs. It could take days to get back online.'

With her mouth open (was it shock, disbelief, or awe?) the receptionist hastily deleted it. 'I wish I knew how to do that,' she said wistfully. 'Think of all the bitchy emails I could send to my ex-husband, then deny I'd ever sent them. He'd start thinking he was going mad.'

The slightly manic chuckle made Candice feel glad that the receptionist didn't know. Imagine all the trouble she could land herself in. Candice didn't know how to do anything like that either, although she was pretty sure the facility existed. If she *did* have the ability, the only emails she'd send to Malcolm would probably be of the please-come-back variety.

Not that she really would beg him to come back. After all, he was the one who'd left her, but in the lonely wee hours her thoughts sometimes turned to him and the life they'd shared.

They'd been happy once, hadn't they?

CHAPTER 5

Candice unlocked the shed door and lifted the secateurs down from their peg, remembering when Malcolm had screwed the board onto the wall, populated it with various sized hooks then carefully hung each implement and tool in order. The shed and the garage had been his domain, his pride and joy. She often used to wonder how he managed to spend so much time in them and what he found to do in there. In hindsight, she understood that he'd probably been on the phone to his mistress. Now, however, Malcolm had another pride and joy in the form of a six-year-old son, Felix. Candice hoped her ex was paying this new child of his more attention than he'd paid Ivan and Preston, and that he wasn't cheating on the new woman in his life.

Still, he'd had the decency to let Candice have the house, signing everything over to her as soon as the divorce had come through, so he hadn't been all bad, had he? If he'd have insisted they sell the house, she didn't know what she would have done. She wouldn't have been able to afford anything in Little Duckton, that's for certain. The village commanded high prices, and she wouldn't have been able to buy a shoe box here on her salary.

With a sigh, Candice turned to the task in hand. The daffodils were well past their prime, but some of the tulips were still good, and the hyacinths were just coming into bloom. With an added bit of greenery, they'd make a nice display for the altar.

It was Candice's job to provide the flowers for the church service every Sunday. Not that she got paid for it and neither did she expect to be, but somewhere along the way and in the depths of time, she'd found herself roped into the role of chief-flower-provider. She had no idea how it had happened, either. One day she'd been minding her own business, walking past the church with a little boy's hand clutched firmly in each of hers; the next had seen her agreeing to man the cake stall at the annual church fete and offering to cut half the flowers in Malcolm's rose beds to grace the altar the following Sunday. After that, it was simply expected of her, although she never attended a service and made no secret of the fact that she wasn't at all religious.

She angled the secateurs to make the first cut, then paused, a thought occurring to her.

There used to be a lilac tree just along the path behind the church. The path was part of the Wychavon Way, a long-distance walking trail which started in Droitwich and ended in Broadway. Along its route was some of the most beautiful countryside in England: spanning meadows and farmland, rivers, woods, calm canals and pretty villages. Little Duckton was lucky enough to have the path skirt the edge of the village. When the children were little, she had taken the boys several miles in both directions, armed with nothing but a picnic and a sense of adventure. Candice wondered what had happened to it – the sense of adventure that is, not the picnic. She knew exactly what had happened to that – each one having been quickly scoffed by a pair of hungry children!

A wave of loneliness crashed over her with a suddenness that had her reeling. It had been a while since she'd felt this way; the day-to-day monotony of simply existing usually numbed her mind to such a degree that she normally didn't feel very much at all.

Shaking her head at herself and wondering where this

feeling had come from but determined to send it back where it belonged, she marched into the house, swapped her gardening trainers for an old pair of Wellington boots, grabbed her keys, and was out of the door faster than she'd moved in a while.

A walk would do her good. Some fresh air would blow this silliness right out of her head and hopefully, at this time of year, she'd find the lilac tree in full bloom.

Breathing deeply, she strode purposefully out of her front gate towards the church, not stopping but only smiling and waving when Mr Davenport, the churchwarden, sent her a questioning look as she walked through the graveyard towards the path.

Little Duckton was hardly a bustling metropolis, but Candice's shoulders felt less tense as her feet hit the dirt track and she inhaled the fresh scent of growing things carried on the breeze which blew gently from the distant Malvern Hills. Bushes and trees lined the path on one side, open fields on the other, the vista stretching out to reveal the purple ridges of the Malvern Hills and the tiny tower of Worcester Cathedral in the distance, which she could only just make out with her naked eye.

Why had she left it so long to do this? She'd forgotten how much she'd once loved this landscape, with the boys charging ahead of her and the sun on her face, feeling the pleasant sensation of muscle riding easily against bone. The muscles weren't quite so obliging today she discovered, a stiffness in her legs making her stride slightly less smooth than normal. Thank God she had joined a yoga class – she hadn't realised just how unfit she really was until now.

But the walk was doing her good and it was wonderful to be out in the fresh air for once (the garden didn't really count). Birds sang in the hedgerows and she made out the voices of several blackbirds, each telling the other to steer clear, this was their territory. She spotted one of them balancing high up on the tip of the tallest tree, singing its little heart out and fluffing up its glossy black feathers. She looked around for Mrs Blackbird, but the lady in question clearly had more important things to do, like sitting on some eggs, or hunting for grubs.

Sparrows chased each other in and out of the foliage, chirping their alarm at the intrusion, and the demanding bleats of lambs from nearby fields were better than the finest choir. The faint barking of a dog and a cow lowing some distance away, added to the symphony.

She stopped for a moment, turned her face up to the sun and closed her eyes, feeling the warm rays on her winter-pale skin, seeing the pinks and oranges swirl behind her closed lids. Although she sometimes sat out in the garden on a sleepy Sunday afternoon, she realised she missed the feeling of getting away from it all. There was always something she could be doing at home, always something calling her – mow me, prune me, water me, sweep up the leaves, trim the lawn where it met the path and tended to overgrow... Out here, she wasn't required to do anything. Mother Nature managed it all by herself, thank you very much, and didn't need any help whatsoever from Candice Summerville.

With the secateurs still clutched firmly in her hand, she walked at a steady pace for about half a mile, feeling rather hot in her wellies (the path was far less muddy than she'd anticipated), then stopped. The lilac tree was somewhere around here, she was sure of it. Things couldn't have changed that much since the last time she had come this way, could they?

There was a big horse chestnut tree, she recalled, just before the Wychavon Way dropped down towards the wide valley floor formed by the River Severn. She remembered bringing the boys here to collect conkers, and she smiled at the memory. They'd had so much fun grubbing about in the leaves hunting for the fallen conkers, all three of them trying to outdo each other in finding the biggest one (of course, she'd let the boys win).

Then they'd spend the rest of the day baking their prizes in the oven and piercing holes in them, before threading the conkers with string. The looks on the children's faces when they trotted out to play, the conkers dangling from their little hands, would stay with her forever.

How she missed those carefree days.

There it was, the lilac tree. She smelled the heavenly perfume before she actually saw it, then as she rounded a corner and passed the old horse chestnut tree, a mass of blooms came into view.

Every branch sported purply-pink blossoms. Candice almost squealed with delight. It seemed such a shame to cut them, but when she imagined how they would look in the silver vase on the altar, she couldn't resist.

With great delicacy, she gathered an armful of stems and when her arms couldn't hold any more, she took a step back to make sure the tree didn't look like it had been savaged by an over-enthusiastic Rottweiler.

It looked OK, maybe a bit lopsided, but that was the great thing about plants – they mostly grew back.

The walk back to the village was just as pleasant, and when she stepped through the lychgate onto the little cobbled path leading to the church's porch, she found she was humming, which was as much a surprise to her as it was to Mr Davenport.

'What have you got there?' the elderly gentleman asked.

'Lilac,' she said proudly, holding the blooms up for him to see. 'For the altar.'

She took them out to the sacristy and laid them on a table, then busied herself fetching the vase and removing last Sunday's drooping flowers. After washing the huge vase and refilling it with fresh water, she carefully arranged the stems, making sure each one was placed for best effect.

Finally satisfied, she carried the new display into the nave, walked up to the altar, and placed the vase on its marble surface. There, that was pretty. It had been a good idea to bring the countryside into the church, she decided.

The less-cultivated blooms were more in keeping with the age of the church. It had been built over eight hundred years ago, shortly after the Norman Conquest, and the church was typical of its period. As churches went, it was a small one, constructed of blocks of smooth, buttery sandstone quarried from Highley in Shropshire, and was made of the same stone which comprised the bulk of the impressive Worcester Cathedral. Mr Davenport was a bit of a history buff, and over the years Candice had absorbed a great deal of interesting information about their little church.

Her favourite part of the ancient building was the huge stained-glass window behind the altar (a later addition, she'd been told), and she loved it when the morning sun poured through the window, sending rainbows of light over the pews and the flagstone floor. On the opposite end of the nave, another huge window allowed the setting sun to enter, so at each end of the day the church was flooded with glorious light. Even when the weather was dull and overcast, the light inside was uplifting.

Although not religious, she enjoyed being there, soaking up the serene atmosphere. Somehow the place grounded her. When she imagined all the thousands of people who had worshipped here over the centuries, and the thousands that were yet to come long after she had gone, it gave her perspective, made her see that she was part of history herself, even if she didn't achieve great things, or if she didn't change even one small iota of it.

'Will you stay for the service?' Mr Davenport asked, as he did every Sunday morning, and Candice replied, as she always did, 'Maybe some other time,' then she followed it up with a cheery, 'See you next week.'

Once outside, she breathed in the fresh air, feeling at peace. There was another feeling too, one she had to cast around in her mind for a moment to find the right word for – she felt contented.

CHAPTER 6

Oh dear, she really was feeling very uncomfortable indeed. The soup she'd eaten for lunch (home-made lentil and vegetable) was making its presence felt and there was absolutely nothing she could do about it. It was probably the very worst possible time for something like this to happen.

Her stomach rumbled again, low down in the region of her bowels, and she winced. Maybe it was a good idea to knock the yoga class on the head. Why was she torturing herself with exercise anyway?

Oh, yes, because the pounds were creeping on and she was beginning to stiffen up like a geriatric, that was why.

Just get on with it, she told herself, but even driving Jelly Bean didn't make her feel any better, like it normally did, and she pulled into the car park wondering how she was going to get through the next hour or so.

Entering the leisure centre, she changed quickly, not meeting anyone else's eye, then made her way to one of the side rooms off the main hall. A handful of people were already there, sitting cross-legged on mats, chatting. Feeling out of place and out of her comfort zone, Candice stood by the door to watch.

A few more people came in, most of them women, she noticed, with only one man, who had hidden himself away in a far corner. One of the ladies grabbed a mat off the pile next to the long mirror at the front of the room, so

Candice decided to get one for herself, then she picked a spot towards the back and sat down.

She tried to cross her legs in the easy manner she had seen the others doing, but one knee refused to behave itself, so she ended up sitting with her legs stretched out in front of her, trying not to appear as awkward as she felt.

A tap on the back made her turn around and look up.

'If you're going to sit like that, keep your spine straight,' someone who Candice thought must be the instructor, said to her.

'Um… okay.' Candice sat up straight, but as she did so, her knees lifted up off the mat. She pushed them back down with her hands.

'First time?' the woman asked.

Candice nodded.

'Don't worry, you'll grow more flexible with every session. You'll be surprised how quickly the suppleness returns to your muscles and joints. Now, for this session, do only what you feel comfortable doing and no more. A little bit of a stretch is good but if it starts to hurt, ease off. Don't be discouraged by what some of these show-offs can do. A few of them have been coming to this class for years.' The woman smiled around the room to show she was teasing, and Candice realised that while she and the instructor had been talking, the rest of the class had stopped chatting to listen.

Candice dropped her gaze to her legs and wished she hadn't come. She was too old for this. Most of the others were far younger than her, except for a couple of women who appeared to be of a similar age but who were considerably slimmer than she was. As was the sole man. She couldn't see his face, only the back of his head and a tiny bit of his profile, but his body looked fit and toned.

Wondering whether anyone would notice if she left, she was about to do just that when the woman who had spoken to her a few minutes ago sank gracefully onto a mat at the front. Sitting cross-legged facing the room, she put her hands together in a praying position, bowed from the waist and said, 'Namaste.'

Everyone mirrored her, muttering, "Namaste, Moon," then a deathly silence fell.

It was too late to make an escape now, Candice realised, resigning herself to an hour of embarrassment.

'Let's start with gentle head and neck exercises to loosen you up and get the blood flowing,' Moon said, and proceeded to do them herself to show what she meant. Dear God, Candice thought, she really should have scarpered when she had the chance.

Resignedly, she followed suit, stretching her head from one side to the other, aiming to get her ears down to her shoulders. She couldn't, but the stretch in her neck felt good all the same. For the first few moves, she actually thought, this isn't too bad, she could do this.

Yeah, right.

That was only the warming up part. The rest of the session consisted of her trying not to fall over as she perched on one leg (tree); continually losing her balance while trying to keep her shoulders back and her hips level with her knees (triangle); and feeling more like roadkill than a pooch when she attempted the downward dog. With hands struggling to bear her not-inconsiderable weight (which was odd when she considered that most of her bulk was on the bottom half of her) and her legs at full stretch (which wasn't much, and she couldn't for the life of her straighten them out, so they remained bent at the knees), she felt the blood rushing to her head and wondered if her skull was about to explode. Her eyeballs were just beginning to feel as though they were about to pop out of her head, when a familiar, terrible feeling swept over her.

Her stomach rumbled again, and Candice clenched her bum cheeks together, hard.

She knew that if she moved an inch, the unthinkable would happen, and she'd be forced to look for another yoga class. *If* she ever found the courage to attend another one.

Please, please, please, she chanted in her head, her teeth clenched as hard as she could while holding her breath at the same time, until she saw her already bright red face begin to turn an unusual shade of puce in the reflection of the floor-to-ceiling mirror. She wasn't sure whether the lack of air would kill her first, or the embarrassment, should the worst happen. Surely she could hold it in for a few more minutes – the class was bound to be drawing to a close and she could safely escape to the loo.

But the pain and the effort was so uncomfortable, she thought she might pass out. Besides, if she didn't take a breath soon, passing out was beginning to feel like a very real possibility.

Just at the right time, a group of kids clattered down the corridor outside, banging on each door as they went and shouting. The class rustled and stirred, concentrations were broken. A few people actually jumped when the kids reached the door to the yoga class.

Seizing the God-sent opportunity with both hands (or should she say, bum cheeks?) Candice relaxed at the exact same moment the door thundered, and her humiliation was lost in the commotion.

She let out a long sigh of relief and eased herself out of the position by walking her hands down the mat and going into a pose called the plank. Except, for her, it wasn't so much of a plank, rather it was more of a scrappy length of chipboard. She collapsed after three seconds, her arms and shoulders trembling with the strain, and not to mention the abominable ache in her stomach muscles which had absolutely nothing to do with the recent unfortunate incident.

She lay on her front, breathing hard, feeling as weak as when she'd had the flu and it had taken every ounce of energy left in her body to drag herself off to the bathroom once in a while. Did people really do this yoga stuff for fun? It was more like being in a torture chamber with lycra and faint music.

Finally, it was time for the relaxation bit.

Candice, along with the rest of the group, was instructed to lie on her back with her knees raised to take the strain off her lower spine, and her arms lying loosely by her sides. She closed her eyes.

Moon turned the barely-there background music up a fraction and dimmed the lights. Candice let the calm wash over her, concentrating on her breathing. In, out; in, out. This part was nice, she thought; she could do this all day, so she was quite disappointed when the music ceased and the lights were turned back on.

'Come back into your body, feel the energy of the universe flowing through you, feel at one with the world, feel at one with yourself,' Moon chanted in a soft sing-song. 'Sit up, taking your time, and shake out your hands.'

Candice did as she was told, sitting up in a rather less graceful fashion than her mat-mates, shaking her hands in the air, wondering what that was supposed to achieve. She then got into a semi-cross-legged position, copying the others as they placed their palms together in front of their chests, bowed their heads and repeated, "Namaste" after Moon.

'Thank you, friends. See you next week,' the instructor said.

Candice picked up her mat and placed it on top of the others. She noticed that several yogaists (was that even a word?) had brought their own, and she made a note to buy one before the next class. You never know whose sweaty body had been reclining on the one she'd just used, she thought, with a shudder. When she got home, she intended to have a nice, hot soak in a bath full of bubbles.

'Did you enjoy it?' Moon asked her. The instructor had walked around the room a few times during the session, quietly and gently correcting postures, and murmuring words of advice and encouragement. She had given

Candice more than her fair share of her attention. Moon was nodding and smiling to the others as they left, but her focus was on Candice.

'I think so,' Candice said. 'I'll let you know tomorrow,' she added, with a wry laugh. She had a feeling she was going to ache like the devil in the morning – she was already beginning to stiffen up, although she felt weirdly relaxed yet slightly wired at the same time.

'Thanks for that. See you next week,' the only man in the class said as he strolled past, rolling his shoulders and smiling at both Candice and Moon.

Candice smiled back at him. He had been one of the people she'd focused on during the sequences, admiring his ability to segue effortlessly and gracefully from one pose to the next.

He was older than she'd first thought, she noticed, now that she could get a good look at his face, and she decided that if a man in his fifties could be so flexible, there must be hope for her yet.

'Bye Paul, you did good today,' Moon said, with her attention still on Candice. 'You did well too,' she said to her. 'Don't be too hard on yourself. It takes time for your muscles to remember how they should perform. I hope you'll come back next week.'

'Oh, definitely,' Candice said. She grabbed the fat around her stomach and squeezed. 'I've got to get rid of this middle-age flab.'

'You will,' Moon promised. 'The benefits of yoga can't be overemphasised. I'm glad you enjoyed it. Oh, and—' She paused, a twinkle in her eye. 'Don't feel embarrassed; it happens to all of us. You ought to hear me trumpet after I've eaten mung beans.'

Candice watched the instructor return to her mat to roll it up, heat surging up her cheeks.

Had the whole class heard her loss of control?

Wonderful!

CHAPTER 7

'What would you get, if you were going to have one?' Dermott wanted to know. For some inexplicable reason, they'd got onto the subject of tattoos. They often talked about some quite random things when the library was quiet, Candice mused, and today was no exception.
'I've got one. Well, more than one, actually; I've got six.' Keisha smirked at the expression on Dermott's face.
'A young girl like you with six tattoos!' he exclaimed.
'I'll show them to you, if you like, although technically two of them are really one.'

Candice thought Dermott was about to faint. She'd never met a man so out-of-touch with the real world. He probably thought a tattoo was decadent or exotic. Even Candice knew that these days getting a tattoo was as run-of-the-mill as having your nails done. Not that she'd ever done either. The nearest she'd got to a manicure was swiping some clear varnish over her nails once in a while.

Keisha pulled her T-shirt down, exposing the top of her chest and a bit of lacy bra. Dermott didn't know where to look. Actually, he did know, Candice gathered, as his eyes practically jumped out of their sockets to focus on the expanse of exposed flesh Keisha was showing. The poor man was blushing to the roots of his receding hairline.

Candice leaned in for a better look.

On both sides of Keisha's chest, centred between her

collar bone and the swell of her breasts (which were small and pert, Candice saw with envy), were a pair of matching claw marks. The girl looked as though she'd been gouged by a big cat.

'Lovely,' Candice said, for something to say, because Dermott clearly wasn't going to comment. He simply stood there with his mouth open and his eyes out on stalks. The tattoos weren't lovely though; Candice thought they were hideous, and she wondered if the girl would come to regret them in later life.

'I've got another on the back of my head, see?' Keisha said, swivelling around and lifting her hair up off her neck.

Not only were there a pair of bright red lips tattooed high up on her neck where the slender column joined her skull, but the girl had had half of her hair shaved off underneath those deceptively thick, long tresses, with a swirling pattern cut into the resulting stubble. 'It's called an undercut,' she said. 'Do you like it?'

Actually, Candice did. 'I do,' she said. 'It's unexpected, different.' She wasn't too keen on the lip tattoo though, but at least it was easily hidden under the girl's hair.

Keisha looked quite respectable on the outside, although she did wear slightly too revealing clothes for a librarian, and Candice wasn't all that keen on the amount of make-up she plastered on, either. But that was the way young women dressed these days, so Candice tried not to be too disapproving. In fact, Candice was quite envious that she had never found the courage to dress a little less conservatively herself, when she was younger. It was clearly too late now; she was comfortable in her jumpers and skirts. Occasionally, she wondered what it might feel like to wear a pair of those skinny jeans the youngsters (and the not-so-youngsters) wore, but her monthly look in the full-length mirror soon rid her of that silly idea. She'd look like a brick with two lengths of string dangling underneath it.

Her legs weren't too bad, which was why she liked

wearing skirts. Malcolm used to say he liked her in a skirt because it made her look feminine (although Candice had only ever seen the woman he'd left her for wearing jeans, so maybe his opinion was to be taken with a pinch of salt), which was why she had worn them to work, and whenever she went out somewhere nice ever since. Not that she went anywhere nice any more, and the only time she'd bought any new clothes over the past couple of years had been a suit from Marks & Spencer for Preston's graduation ceremony, and the yoga stuff she'd recently treated herself to.

Her face flamed at the thought of the yoga class. Five days later, and neither the memory nor the humiliation had yet faded.

'You're getting our Candice all hot and bothered,' Dermott said, as Keisha pulled her already low-slung trousers down over one of her prominent hip bones (Candice wondered if she still had any hip bones, because she hadn't seen or felt hers in years) to expose a black skull with a red rose coming out of the eye socket.

It wasn't Candice's cup of tea, but she had to admit it was beautifully done and it suited Keisha's personality perfectly.

She smiled at the girl, thinking that if anyone was getting hot and bothered it was Dermott. If his eyes protruded any further, he'd have to pick them up off the floor, and if he wasn't careful he'd have a heart attack, judging by his extremely high colour. Anyone would think he hadn't seen female flesh before. Come to think of it, he possibly hadn't, if what Candice had gleaned about his home-life was true. The man still lived with his eighty-year-old mother, for goodness' sake, and he spoke about the old lady more as if she was his partner than his mum.

Keisha was saying to her, 'Have you got any tattoos you admit to having? A bird on your arse? Flames coming up from your what-not?'

Candice spluttered. 'My *what?*'

'What-not, you know, your *va-va-voom.*'

Dermott made a kind of choking, strangled sound and Candice bit back a giggle. 'No, no tattoos,' she admitted.

'Have you ever thought of getting one?' Keisha asked.

'Me? Good lord, no!'

'Why not?'

'For one thing, I can't think of anything I'd want on my skin permanently.'

'What about the names of your children?' Keisha suggested.

Candice laughed. 'Is that in case I won't be able to remember who they are when I get old and decrepit?'

From the look Keisha gave her, the girl clearly thought Candice was already halfway to being old. Which wasn't great, considering she felt younger today than she had in years, despite the ache in her legs. She obviously didn't look it!

Brought back down to earth with a bump, Candice suppressed a huff and went off to fix a printer. But as she walked away, an insidious thought kept prodding at her. Would it hurt to get a tattoo? After all, hundreds of thousands of people had them. They were hardly the risqué things they once were. If anything, they were hip and in, if either of those words was still used – or should she say *cool*? She saw more and more women her age sporting the odd motif painted on their skin. Of course, if she ever did decide to get one, the question was, what would it be?

Certainly not the names of her children (for the exact same reason she'd told Keisha) and she couldn't think of anything else. A flower? A bird? Neither of those meant anything. If she was going to have something tattooed on her skin from now until she breathed her last, she wanted it to *mean* something, to have some significance.

Frowning, she put the idea to one side. There was no point in thinking about it now. She had to lose some weight first, otherwise the tattoo might look like nothing more than a baggy, distorted picture on her loose arm or ankle, or – heaven forbid – on her rear end. It didn't bear thinking about.

Now, back to the important stuff, she told herself – which printer was it that needed fixing?

With her usual calm, Candice took the machine apart, cleared out the scrap of paper which had caused it to have a hissy fit, then put it back together again.

'Send something to it,' she said to Carol, one of her colleagues.

'What should I send?'

'Anything. Something. It doesn't matter what.'

'How about the staff rota for next week? Or the overdue list?' The woman dithered. 'But I normally send those by email. I don't normally print them.'

Candice gritted her teeth. Carol couldn't help it, she was always indecisive, but the woman tried Candice's patience to the limit some days. 'What were you trying to print when it broke down?' she asked, and was astonished when Carol turned bright red.

'Er, nothing. I'll print the rota, shall I?'

'Good idea,' Candice agreed, wondering what it was that made the woman so embarrassed.

She was about to ask, when Dermott appeared at her side, out of breath and bursting with news. 'We've got the WI in,' he announced, grandly.

Dermott loved the ladies of the Women's Institute because they made such a fuss of him during their fortnightly meetings in the conference room. He adored those Saturdays and would happily swap shifts with anyone who wanted that day off, but there wasn't any point in asking him to swap when it was a non-WI Saturday, because the answer would be an indignant "no".

'I've made them some cakes,' he said, rubbing his hands together.

Candice did think that making cakes for the WI was a bit like taking coals to Newcastle, but Dermott enjoyed it and the ladies didn't seem to mind, judging by the empty plates and scattered crumbs.

'I'll just go and fetch them,' he said. 'Can you hold the fort for a bit?'

Candice didn't mind holding the fort at all, considering Dermott had been cataloguing the new fiction intake before giving them dust jackets to wear. It gave her a chance to check the books out – literally – if something caught her eye. She had a soft spot for psychological thrillers, the more twisted the better. One of the main perks of working in a library was being able to get her hands on the new publications as soon as they came in.

She was on the front desk with her nose buried in C.L. Taylor's latest in between scanning books in and out, and answering queries, when some sixth sense caused her to look up.

She met her ex-husband's gaze with a jolt. A flash of discomfort crossed his face before he gave her a polite smile. He clearly hadn't expected to see her manning the desk, and it was sheer bad luck that she was – she didn't often do it these days.

He had his son with him. His other son. The one who carried none of her genes, but who she felt a connection to, nonetheless. It was probably because the boy looked so much like her own children when they had been his age.

She tried not to stare. She also tried to keep her resentment under control, and she succeeded for now; although it would undoubtedly surface later as she lay sleepless in her lonely bed, hating her ex-husband for... well, everything, really. Where should she start? At the point when he walked out of her life and into another woman's? At the point when Candice discovered he was going to be a father again, after emphatically denying her a third baby?

Or should she go further back, much further, to when their marriage still appeared solid on the surface but she had already felt the tremors under her feet, and knew deep down that sooner or later the earthquake would strike and tear their lives apart. It was just a pity it had taken fifteen years and two children before it had happened.

Oh God, if anyone heard her thoughts at this moment, they'd think she wished she'd never had her boys, but nothing could be further from the truth. She loved her children with every breath in her body. It was just a shame that she feared she might still feel the same way about their father.

Making sure the shutters were firmly down on her heart (she'd die before she'd let Malcolm see she still had feelings for him) she returned his polite smile. 'Hello, Malcolm, hello, Felix.' She nodded at them. 'What brings you here?' As far as she knew, no one in that little family ever visited the place where the discarded wife worked.

'Shoes. He needs new ones.' Malcolm pointed at the boy's feet, shuffling his own, and looking everywhere but at Candice.

'You've come to the wrong place,' she quipped, trying to keep things light-hearted, and feeling anything but. 'This is a library.'

'I know.' Malcolm was serious.

'Oh.'

'Felix, my son,' he added, as if Candice wasn't aware of the boy's lineage, 'needs to join. It's for the Ladybird Project. He has to join the library,' Malcolm repeated.

Candice got the subtext immediately. Primary schools in the area were doing a literacy drive, and part of that was introducing pupils to their local libraries. There had been a considerable number of small people joining in the past week or so. If she had thought about it, she would have realised it was only a matter of time until Felix appeared. Malcolm was telling her that he was only here because Felix had to be. Candice guessed his mother had probably refused to set foot in the building where the woman whose husband she had stolen worked, so it was down to the cheating ex himself to accompany their child.

'Keisha, would you mind enrolling this young man,' she called, not wanting any more contact with Malcolm than she'd already had.

Keisha glanced at her, then at Malcolm, then back to Candice again, but thankfully she didn't say anything, just nodded and retrieved the necessary forms from a drawer. Candice pretended to look something up on the computer, but her gaze kept straying to her ex-husband, and she couldn't help scrutinising him out of the corner of her eye.

It was a while since she'd seen him – a couple of years at least, unlike those several months (longer, if she was honest) just after he'd left, when she used to find herself driving past his house, the one he shared with *That Woman*, trying to catch a glimpse of him. Or, and she blushed at the memory, she used to find excuses to hang around outside the bank where he worked, hoping to bump into him, to start up a conversation, anything to make him realise what he'd been missing.

Thankfully, neither he nor his new wife had been on social media at the time, or her stalking would have escalated to new heights.

Eventually she'd stopped, but it had been hard; for a long time after he'd said his vows to another woman, Candice had still considered him as belonging to her.

He looked good, she thought, trying not to let him see her interest. A few more lines around his eyes, a bit more grey in his hair than she remembered, a slight rounding of the belly which he'd not had before, but essentially he was still the same.

She guessed she was too, and that was probably the problem. It had always been the problem. How was she to know he'd craved a bit of glamour? More than a bit, if *That Woman* was anything to go by – shoulder-length hair, more make-up than you could shake a stick at, too-short skirts, too-tight tops, and those skinny jeans. Years ago, during the one and only time Candice had tried to grow her hair out of its customary bob, he'd wrinkled his nose when her locks reached the slope of her shoulders and had told her she'd needed a trim. It appeared that he did like longer hair after all – just not on her.

Talking about a trim, a visit to the hairdresser was still somewhat overdue, and Candice self-consciously tucked a wayward strand behind her ear and gave a rueful glare at her ink-stained fingers (damned printer), wishing she'd made more of an effort. If only she'd known she was going to see Malcolm today, she'd have—

What? What would she have done? Nothing if she was honest, except maybe she would have gone for that haircut beforehand, and scrubbed the ink powder off her hands.

That was all she ever did.

The realisation filled her with sadness.

CHAPTER 8

Candice often felt quite ambivalent about days off, Sundays especially. She never really knew what to do with them. This particular Sunday had started off like most (make that all) of them did, with her sitting on the sofa chewing on a piece of toast while watching the news. After that, she stripped the sheets off her barely-rumpled bed (it had been a very long time since her bed had been rumpled and today the sight of those still-pristine bed-covers made her feel very out-of-sorts indeed), raided the laundry basket for its meagre offerings (she barely had enough for one full load and that was only if she mixed lights and darks together), then got her vacuum cleaner out.

By the time the washing machine had come to the end of its cycle, she'd also done some dusting, cleaned the inside of the kitchen window because it was forever getting droplets of water on it from the sink below, scrubbed the more-or-less already clean bathroom, and reorganised the fridge.

When she stepped out into the garden carrying her laundry basket, she briefly considered getting the lawn mower out later and whizzing it over the grass, but as it was a job she hated and one which Malcolm had always done, she decided she wouldn't bother. There was always Tuesday, her next day off; she needed to keep something back to fill that day.

Much as she looked forward to not being in work, Candice also looked forward to going back to it. The idea of a day off was appealing, but the reality was not so much fun. The day-off days had a tendency to seem longer than her working days, as if someone always added a few extra hours to them when she wasn't looking.

After pegging the washing out, she grabbed her secateurs and set to work choosing some flowers for the church. The first service was due to start in an hour and she wanted to be gone before the reverend began the sermon. Although, while she was standing in front of the altar arranging her new display, she actually did consider staying. Not because she wanted to hear what he had to say, but because it was something to do.

She didn't need to check her watch to know that it was only half-past ten or so, because she did the same thing at the same time every Sunday. Suddenly, the hours stretched out before her, interminably long and rather daunting.

As she made her way back to her house, she wondered what Malcolm was doing now. Taking Felix to swimming lessons, maybe? He had often done that with his older sons, leaving her at home to wash dirty school uniforms, clean the mud off school shoes, dig out the remains of half-eaten lunches from the depths of school bags, tackle the eye-sore that was each child's bedroom, and do the millions of other things a busy mum with a family had to do. She would also remain behind to ensure that the Sunday roast was cooked to perfection. Her boys and their father would tumble through the front door in a cacophony of shouts and squabbles, dumping wet swimming kits in the hall, and thundering into the kitchen demanding to know when lunch would be ready, because they were starving.

By contrast, Felix had seemed a well-behaved, quiet boy yesterday, and although she knew looks could be deceiving, she didn't think he was the thundering type. Maybe he wasn't the sporty type, but he had piano lessons instead, or made model aircraft. Candice could just picture him and Malcolm sitting together at a table, their heads bent over a tiny plane, paintbrushes in their hands, Malcolm with his tongue protruding ever so slightly, which he often did when he was concentrating hard.

Candice loved her sons fiercely and unconditionally, but every now and then as they were growing up, she had wished they were a little less boisterous, had wished for a child more like Felix. The only time they were quiet was when they were asleep, but even then, Preston had a habit of yelling out in the middle of whatever weird and fantastical dream he was having. He used to wake up and insist on telling her all about it in great detail, which she wouldn't have minded had the hour been a more reasonable one, but two o'clock in the morning hadn't been the best time for Preston to expect her to share his enthusiasm for giant tigers chasing him on strange planets.

She wandered back into the kitchen and stood staring out of the window. It was a lovely day, the sun was already hot, and the air was filled with the sounds of insects and birds. Years ago, she would have suggested they pack a picnic and head off to the seaside. It was a bit of a trek, but ultimately worth it. The boys would usually fall asleep on the return journey, worn out from digging holes and building sand castles, dashing in and out of the waves, and rooting around in rock pools. Then there were the games of football, tag, who could run the fastest on the wide beach, Frisbee-throwing, and anything else her children could think of which involved non-stop physical activity and lots of noise.

She'd like to do that now, she thought. Go to the seaside, she meant, not play games on the sand, although if she could return to those wonderful days when the kids were small and Malcolm was still her husband, she would do so in a heartbeat.

The beach was a decent drive away, and she wasn't sure she felt confident enough to go on her own, but as soon as she'd had the idea, she realised with dismay just how much her life had shrunk. These four walls and those of the library, had become her everything. Her world had closed in on itself without her noticing, until it consisted of nothing but home and work, with the occasional trip to the supermarket. Her recent adventure into yoga had been the highlight of the week. No, make it the highlight of the month.

How sad.

I know, she thought, her gaze roaming over the distant Malvern Hills, she could visit those. The purple ridges rose hundreds of feet above the surrounding landscape, and the drive to and from them would kill a couple of hours. More, if she stopped off somewhere for a bite to eat.

Feeling unusually excited, Candice ran upstairs to run a comb through her hair, wash her face, and change into something a little more summery. Remembering she had a lovely pair of sandals that she'd bought a couple of years ago and had hardly ever worn, she dug them out of the wardrobe and buckled them onto her feet.

There, she was ready.

She made sure she had enough money in her purse, then went to let Jelly Bean out of the garage. The top was already down, having been left that way after she had driven home from work yesterday, and she had parked the car in the garage without putting the top back up, secure in the knowledge that nothing untoward could happen to Jelly Bean overnight.

'We're going on a nice, little drive,' she told the car. 'It'll be fun, you'll see, all those twisty roads and a good view.'

Oh. She was talking to her car. But it wasn't in the usual way a person would speak to a car, like "Start, you bugger!" She was having a full-on, one-sided conversation with it, as if it could actually understand her.

Feeling a bit of an idiot, she turned the stereo on, found Radio 2 and cranked up the volume, lest she was tempted to tell Jelly Bean anything else. Maybe it was about time she got a pet. Ideally, she'd love a dog. Maybe not a puppy, but an older animal, from a rescue centre. She could just imagine a pair of ears flapping in the breeze and an excitable nose sticking out of the window, as a canine companion sat in the passenger seat, glancing over at her now and again with a grin on its happy little face. A dog would certainly be a valid reason to talk out loud. Many people held quite meaningful conversations with their pets, and at least there was a good chance of some kind of a response.

But it wasn't fair to a dog to be left on its own all day when she was out at work, and she could hardly take it to the library, could she? If she was going to get a pet, it would have to be a cat, although she couldn't imagine a cat sitting in the passenger seat with its nose lifted to the window to sniff the breeze. A cat was for the house, not for taking to the beach or for a long walk in the hills. So, she still might end up talking to her car anyway, she decided. Candice shrugged; did it really matter if she spoke to her car? After all, there was no one around to hear her.

The drive to the Malvern Hills was delightful. Avoiding the main roads, Candice wove through small villages, along narrow lanes (not too narrow of course, because she didn't fancy having to reverse for a couple of miles with a tractor bearing down on her), with the sun on her face and the wind ruffling her hair. She kept having to tuck one side behind her ear, the side nearest the window, because it tended to blow in her face, and she made a mental note to keep a hat in the glove compartment in case she needed it.

Strange smells wafted over her every so often, smells which she was convinced would have gone undetected in a car with its lid on. Farm smells (not so nice), smoke from a wood fire (lovely), the aroma of baking bread when she slowed right down on a hairpin bend in the middle of a little village whose name she didn't know (her stomach growled as she sniffed appreciatively) and flowers, lots and lots of flowers.

She seemed more aware of her surroundings in this car, as if having the roof off had taken the lid off the little box she had been living in for the past few years. She was noticing things she hadn't noticed in a long time, like the hover of a kite overhead and its haunting cry as it surfed the thermals, or the dapple play of light and dark as she passed under an arc of trees, and the sun shining through the leaves to pattern her hands as she gripped the steering wheel.

Today, she felt more alive than she had felt in a long time, and she revelled in the unfamiliar feeling. She wasn't happy exactly, but she was content, as though being out in the sun, driving this glorious little car, had made her forget her loneliness and sense of dissatisfaction with her life for a while.

'I love you, Jelly Bean!' she shouted at the top of her voice, waving madly as another open-top car sped past her in the opposite direction.

The flat, river-valley land gradually gave way to the pull of the series of interconnected mounds called the Malvern Hills, which rose like a West Midlands version of Ayers Rock out of the wide valley floor. The little mountain range could be seen from miles around. Candice remembered the excitement she had always felt on returning from holiday with her parents and seeing those hills in the distance, signifying she wasn't far from home.

The gradient was hardly noticeable at first, growing steadily steeper until she was forced to change down the gears to cope with the sharper corners. She knew from numerous visits to the area, that if she were to look over her shoulder she would see half of Worcestershire laid out behind her. To her left, through the gaps between the houses as she drove through the town of Great Malvern, she could see Gloucestershire lying to the south and east.

Her stomach rumbled, and she realised it was lunchtime. She'd not eaten anything since the slice of toast at breakfast. The main road winding through Great Malvern and out the other side towards Malvern Wells (of the Holy Well and bottled spring water fame) sported a number of pubs and restaurants. Candice didn't want to eat in those kinds of places. She didn't feel that she had enough confidence to walk into a pub or a restaurant by herself and order a meal, but a café was an altogether different prospect. She could manage a café, and she even had a book in her handbag, in case she needed to hide behind its cover and lose herself in its depths.

She chose a café with pretty planters and a jaunty chalkboard outside, which advertised sandwiches, jacket potatoes, and other light snacks. There was a moment of panic when she pulled into the little carpark, wondering if she should put Jelly Bean's top up. She decided against it when she noticed a free table by the window. She could happily sit there, eating her lunch and keeping an eye on the topless car at the same time. Not that she expected anyone to hop in and run off with it, but she didn't want to risk it. With that in mind, she locked the doors and popped the keys in her bag as she headed inside.

The warm, inviting smell of coffee greeted her, and she placed an order for a cappuccino and a ham salad sandwich, then sat down facing the window, thinking how cute Jelly Bean looked. A couple of passers-by gave the car an admiring glance, and Candice swelled with pride. She almost felt like a parent whose child had been complimented, and she decided to call into Halfords on the way home to buy some shampoo and wax to treat the Mazda to a wash afterwards.

Washing cars had always been Malcolm's job, and therefore her old estate car hadn't had so much as a hosepipe aimed in its general direction since he'd left, but he wasn't here now, was he? Jelly Bean deserved a good clean after traversing across half of Worcestershire, so she'd have to do the honours herself. Anyway, it was about time she stopped thinking about "his" jobs and "her" jobs, and she learnt to do what her ex-husband used to do. She'd start with washing the car and see how she got on.

'Thank you,' she said when her coffee and sandwich were placed in front of her by the smiling waitress.

Taking a large bite, Candice debated whether to get her novel out. She did feel a little self-conscious sitting there on her own, especially since no one else appeared to be by themselves. In fact, everyone else seemed to be part of a couple, she noticed, watching two quite elderly people holding hands across the table. Aww, they really did look very sweet, and the gentleman was gazing into his companion's eyes as if she were the most beautiful woman he had ever seen.

Candice found herself wishing she had someone who looked at her in the same way. She didn't think Malcolm had ever looked at her like that, not even when he had asked her to marry him, or when they were on their honeymoon.

And there was another pair, younger, but just as much in love, if their moon-eyes were anything to go by. The woman had a flirty, coy expression on her face, and every so often, one or the other of them would lean forward and whisper something, causing the recipient to blush and giggle.

Envy jabbed at her; she wanted some of the closeness she was seeing all around her. She wanted someone to share days like this with; someone who she could come home to at the end of a long day at work and share her woes and frustrations with; someone who would bring her a cup of tea when she felt poorly and give her a kiss when she felt well; someone who she could make a cake for just because she knew he would like it; someone to look after; someone…

Maybe it was time she turned her life around and started living again? How long was it going to be before she finally extinguished the torch she held for Malcolm and lit it for someone else, a person who'd be more deserving of the love she had to give?

But who? She couldn't think of anyone. Candice took a drink of her coffee and she thought about the people she worked with. The only man there was Dermott, but she wasn't remotely attracted to him. She wasn't at that stage in her life yet where she would settle for companionship or simply rubbing along together. She wanted to be swept off her feet, to feel passion and love at first sight; all of the things she now realised she hadn't felt with her ex-husband.

She also realised something else – men weren't simply going to drop in her lap. They weren't going to appear on her doorstep to ask her out. She would have to make some kind of an effort to meet them, which meant she would have to get out more, go to pubs, or clubs, or join a group or two.

Her mind inevitably returned to Malcolm and how he had made her feel yesterday, when a thought struck her. Men used libraries too! There was every chance she could meet the love of her life in work, if only she gave herself permission to do so. She wasn't going to pounce on the first man who wanted to know where the books on travel were kept, or who needed help logging onto a computer, but there was nothing stopping her from making friendly conversation with a person of the opposite sex who happened to have walked into the place where she worked, was there? Surely there were no library rules about dating people one met through work, like there were for doctors and patients.

Sandwich eaten, she wiped her lips on a serviette, and glanced around for the waitress. Candice was in the mood for cake, a jolly large slice, and another coffee to wash it down, when she caught a glimpse of yet another blissfully happy couple canoodling as they walked in through the door.

With a sigh, she grubbed around in her bag for her book. Until she found her own man, she really wasn't too keen on watching other women with theirs, so she opened the paperback and buried her nose between the pages. For the time being, a fictional romance would have to do.

CHAPTER 9

Ding, ding, round two. Candice hoped today's yoga class would be a bit less embarrassing this time. So, clutching the brand-new mat to her chest, she stared around for somewhere to put it. Not too near the front, but not too far back either, because she needed to concentrate on what Moon was doing. Last time Candice had been too far away to see clearly (obviously a visit to the optician was needed soon). She'd been forced to watch the one and only man in the class (actually, he really did seem to know what he was doing) and the weedy women in the front row. Maybe slim was a better word to describe them, but today Candice wasn't feeling very charitable. She was still reeling from unexpectedly seeing Malcolm with his little boy on the weekend, despite her new resolution yesterday.

Her ex had kept popping into her head all last night, disturbing her hard-won peace and recently-found contentment. In fact, she would go as far as to say that she was almost back to square one when it came to self-esteem.

It was seeing Felix that did it. By rights, he should be hers, and Malcolm should still be her husband. But he'd had his head turned by a bit of fluff and had thrown Candice aside like a soiled tissue. The only thing that had prevented her from going totally off the rails at the time, had been her children, and the fact their father still had contact with them, which meant Malcolm saw them every other weekend and sometimes during the holidays too. If they saw their father, then she did too, for a while; until they grew old enough to make their own way to Malcolm's new house, or were able to meet their father in town. Seeing him during hand-over had been what she lived for.

Thank God that had finally worn off.

Until now.

It hadn't helped seeing all those loved-up couples yesterday either, or reading that daft book. Happy ever after? Huh! That was for fairy tales, not for the likes of her. Who had she been kidding, thinking she could meet all kinds of eligible men at work (most of them were pensioners or students), or that she would get out more, to pubs and things? The only places she was likely to go after work were the supermarket or the leisure centre.

She plonked her mat on the floor, then cringed when it made a loud slapping noise. Several people glanced around, but none of them acknowledged her. You wouldn't come to a class like this in order to make friends, she thought. Plus, the other women all seemed rather cliquey, and a bit stuffy.

Well, sod them. She was only here to lose a pound or two, and to stop herself from falling over if she attempted to put a shoe on without sitting down first. Her aim was to be able to touch her toes, and she probably hadn't done that since she was in her teens. Once she had achieved what she'd come here to achieve, then she needn't come every week; just now and again to make sure she didn't slide back down the slippery slope again.

'Hi,' a voice said.

Candice turned her head to her right, awkwardly because it refused to turn as easily or as far as it once did, to find that Paul, the guy from last week, had set his mat down next to hers.

Great. This meant that whenever the class was instructed to stand sideways on their mats, Paul would have a front-seat view of her bottom. Depending on the position and the stretch, he would get to see other parts of her, too. She wouldn't wish that on her worst enemy. Poor bloke.

She smiled back at him, sympathetically. He had no idea what he was letting himself in for.

'It's not that bad, is it?' he enquired, and she realised her expression must have come across as apprehension, or worry, or… Oh, no, had he heard her breaking wind last week, and thought she was concerned it would happen again?

She closed her eyes, counted to ten, then opened them again.

'Oh, sorry, I didn't realise you were meditating. I'll shut up, shall I?' he said.

'No, that is… I mean…' She took a breath. If he wanted to think she was meditating, she wasn't going to disillusion him. Besides, he might not think she was such a newbie if she was meditating before a session.

Hang on – she was stiffer than an old broom handle and kept losing her balance, even with both feet planted firmly on the floor and standing upright, so of course he knew she was a total novice.

'Hello,' she said to him, realising he was still watching her. Then, as her innate manners and the typically British inclination to fill any gaps in the conversation reared their twin heads, she said, 'Have you been coming here long?'

'A couple of years. It does wonders for your health.'

'Have you been poorly? I'm sorry to hear that.'

'I've not been ill,' he said, puzzled. 'Why do you think that?'

'Haven't you?' She felt like an idiot. 'Oh,' she repeated. 'Er… you said yoga does wonders for your health, and I thought…'

'I see!' He laughed and his face, which had been quite solemn, lit up. His eyes creased and a dimple appeared in each cheek, just above his closely-trimmed beard. His slightly curling, thick, brown hair, which was shot through with silver-grey strands, was cut short at the back and sides, slightly longer on the top.

He had nice arms too, with a decent bit of muscle. Not so much that he looked like he was trying too hard, but just enough (just enough for what, Candice had no idea). He was flat-stomached too, unlike Malcolm's newly-formed paunch. Paul was quite fit when she came to think of it, and rather nice looking, with his facial features in all the right places and in the correct proportions. He clearly looked after himself too, else why would he come to this torture chamber for two whole years? Candice sincerely thought that she, herself, might not last the month.

'Namaste,' Moon chanted.

'Ah, our leader is here,' Paul whispered.

'Is that what she's called, our leader?'

'No, it's just an expression.'

'Oh.' Candice forced her reluctant legs into a semblance of the lotus position.

For the next sixty minutes she had little chance to think of anything else, except her breathing ("Breathe out on the release, and in on the stretch"), the pull and cramp of muscles protesting at being forced into new and unusual positions, or trying to hold any pose for more than three seconds. When she copied Moon's child pose, Candice thought she had it nailed. She did too, for the first few breaths, until her boobs began to feel alarmingly squashed against her thighs, her knees howled in protest, and she couldn't breathe. Even her forehead was sore where it rested on the mat – she never realised heads could weigh so much. But the stretch in her spine was nice. Maybe she could do this when her back ached next time she was in work. Or maybe not – Dermott would probably have a fit.

Relaxation time was swiftly becoming Candice's favourite part and the only bit she seemed to be any good at. In fact, she was so good at it that she had a sneaking suspicion she'd fallen asleep, as a tiny snore in the back of her throat jerked her awake again.

She opened one eye a fraction and glanced to her right. Phew, neither Paul nor the woman next to him had noticed. They were both too busy concentrating on their breathing and she watched their chests rise and fall in deep steady rhythms.

Closing her eyes again, she tried to concentrate on hers, but the moment was gone and her brain decided that right now was a perfectly good time to show her images of Malcolm. With her brief hard-won tranquillity lost, she lay there, cross with herself, for the next few minutes until Moon's voice brought her back to the present, and the class came to an end.

She was convinced that wrestling with her socks and trainers wasn't quite as hard as it had been last time. Or was it her imagination? Her stomach didn't appear as roly-poly, either. One less roll perhaps? Come to think of it, the skirt she'd worn to work today had been of the non-elasticated-waist variety. She'd taken to wearing clothing with expandable waists a couple of years ago, but with a wardrobe full to bursting, she hadn't been thinking all that clearly this morning when she had simply grabbed the first item she put her hand on. The skirt had a zip and buttons, and absolutely no give whatsoever, and it had been a while since she'd worn it because it tended to cut her in half. But not today. Maybe healthy eating and yoga were doing the trick. She must weigh herself when she got in – or better still, first thing in the morning, after she'd had a wee and before she'd eaten breakfast.

'Did you enjoy that?'

Candice looked into Paul's grey eyes. 'Erm… yes, I did actually.' She was only telling a little fib – she'd enjoyed bits of it.

He seemed to be able to read her mind (or her face) because he said, 'It does get easier, honest.'

'It does? When?' she demanded, only half joking.

'It'll take a few weeks, but if you practice at home that

will help,' he suggested. 'Try some of the simpler poses, for a few minutes each evening and you'll be surprised how much of a difference it makes.'

'Thanks, I will.' She decided she'd take his advice; after all, she didn't exactly have anything else to do in the evenings.

'Fancy going for a drink?' he asked, unexpectedly.

Eh? A drink? *With him?* 'Um…'

'Just a quick one?' he added.

Candice was flabbergasted. Was this a date? Or was he just being polite? She hadn't been out for a drink with a man for… well, not since Malcolm. I bet Malcolm wouldn't say no, she thought. I bet Malcolm wouldn't dither around, questioning people's motives, or whether he should go, and if he did go, what it might mean. Malcolm would say "yes", have a pint, then toddle off home without a second thought. It was only a drink, it wasn't as though the bloke was suggesting a weekend away, or asking her to go back to his place. A drink. Surely she could manage a swift half with a nice man, without making such a song and dance about it?

She'd left it too late to answer him now, because he had bent down to pick up his mat, before rolling it up and shoving it under his arm.

'No worries, if you can't. Maybe another time?' he said, casually. It was clearly no big deal to him, so why should it be to her? He wasn't to know that she was a total introvert and hadn't been alone with a man since Malcolm (the dentist or the doctor didn't count).

'I'd love to,' she blurted, then blushed furiously, heat flooding her cheeks.

'Great. I'll just pop this in the van.' He nodded towards at the mat tucked under his arm. 'The pub is only around the corner. We don't have to stay long, just long enough to wet our whistles. I don't know about you, but I get thirsty after all that stretching.'

Candice glanced at the water bottle he was holding in

his other hand. She hadn't thought about bringing a drink last week, and this week she'd completely forgotten, having had too many other things on her mind.

She could do with a lemonade, and one friendly drink with a friendly bloke wasn't going to hurt. 'I'll take my stuff out to the car, too,' she said, and they strolled out into the fresh air.

'That's me,' Paul said, jerking his head towards a big white van taking up two parking spaces.

A Man Who Can was emblazoned down the side. Underneath was the caption, *'If you can't or don't want to, I can and I will. Call me for all your DIY and handyman needs'* followed by his name and phone number.

'Do you break into sheds?' she asked with a smile.

'It depends on who the shed belongs to,' he replied with a twinkle, as he aimed a fob at the van. 'Why? Do you need me to break into one?'

'I did, but not anymore.'

'Well, if you need anything else broken into, keep me in mind,' he joked, opening the door and shoving the mat onto the passenger seat. 'Where do you live?'

'Little Duckton.'

'Nice place.'

'It is. How about you?' she asked, as she led him to the opposite side of the car park, where she'd left Jelly Bean in a corner, out of harm's way.

'Lime Orchard.'

She knew of it, and had been there once or twice when she was married. It was a pretty village on the east of the city, surrounded by fields and farmland, much like her own village was. The place had a quaint old pub, and she and Malcolm had eaten a decent meal there not long before he'd left her. She guessed he used to take *That Woman* there too, she thought sourly. Malcolm tended to be a creature of habit – except when it came to her. She was a habit he'd been only too eager to break.

'There used to a nice pub there, the... um...' She

searched for the name but it eluded her.

'The Crow's Nest,' he said. 'It's still there. Does a bloody good Sunday lunch.' He halted and gave a low whistle. 'Woohoo. I like the car. Yours?'

'It is.' She unlocked the boot and placed her mat inside, as Paul walked around Jelly Bean.

'How many miles does she have on the clock?' he asked.

'Just over sixty thousand.'

He whistled again. 'That's not bad for a car of her age. She's in good nick too. I bet she's fun to drive. Right, the pub's not far, just around the corner, so how do you fancy walking?'

'A walk will do me good,' she said, and they set off, chatting all the while.

By the time they'd settled at a table by the window, drinks in hand, a lemonade for her, a half of Snotty Mule for him (why did these speciality ales have such weird names, she mused), she was beginning to feel really comfortable in his company. He was easy to talk to, laid back, and relaxed. Over the course of another round of drinks (lemonade for him too, because he was driving and a half was his limit), he regaled her with funny stories of some of the jobs he'd been called to.

'Being asked to bury an Alsatian was odd and a bit sad to be honest, but having to cut fluffy pink handcuffs off some naked fella in Droitwich took the biscuit.'

'You didn't!' she exclaimed, giggling.

'I couldn't leave him there, could I?'

'Why was he in handcuffs in the first place?'

'Apparently, his mistress found out she wasn't the only one. Apart from the wife, who the mistress *did* know about, there were another two women he was also seeing. This particular mistress decided to take her revenge by waiting until his wife was away for the weekend, persuading the guy that his place would make a change from hers, then cuffing him to the brass bedstead. She planned on him still being there when the wife came home. It was lucky he had the strength to drag himself and the bed halfway across the room to reach the chest of drawers.'

'Why was that?' Candice was captivated.

'That was where the mistress had left his phone – in full view, but just out of reach. Anyway, enough of me. You must think I'm a right plonker, talking about myself all night. How about you? What do you do?'

'I work in a library. I started off as a librarian, but now I'm in charge of IT.'

'Sounds interesting,' he said, and she looked at him closely to see if he was joking. He didn't appear to be.

'I think it is,' she replied, neutrally.

He caught on straight away. 'No seriously, I'm not too good with computers. My grandson has to show me everything, and he's only seven.'

'You have a grandson?' she asked. Did that mean he had a wife too?

'Yep, he's a great kid.' His face shone with love and pride.

Candice felt a slight ache in her chest. It was about time she had a grandchild to moon over, but since Preston was too busy throwing himself off mountains and she had yet to even meet Ivan's girlfriend, she suspected she might have to wait a while.

Picking up her almost empty glass, she finished her drink. 'Right, I must get on. Things to do.'

She stood up, and Paul got to his feet, too. 'Of course. I'll walk you back to the car, shall I?'

The walk back was nice but when Paul said casually, 'See you next week,' Candice replied, 'See you next week,' and she got in Jelly Bean, feeling a little deflated. What had she been expecting? This was only meant to be a friendly drink between two yoga-mates. He was hardly likely to ask her out to dinner, was he?

She sat for a moment, watching him stroll across the

car park (nice bum, not a hint of builder's butt about it) and gave herself a good talking to. Get over it, she said. It was a drink, not a love affair. At least she'd broken the ice in terms of going out with the opposite sex. Now that she'd done it once, what was to stop her from doing it again? Not with Paul, obviously, because he hadn't asked (she shied away from worrying about the answer she'd give him if he did, because it was a moot point) but there was nothing stopping her from going out with someone else, was there?

Oh, actually there *was* something stopping her – no one ever asked her out.

Maybe she should be the one to do the asking, she thought. These days, women didn't sit around waiting to be asked, they took the bull by the horns and went out and got what they wanted.

The only problem was, there was no one she remotely wanted to ask.

CHAPTER 10

'Avoid,' Keisha muttered, scowling and putting a mark on a sheet of paper.

Candice stared at it. 'What are you doing?' It clearly wasn't work.

Keisha let out a yelp before quickly hushing herself, and Candice bit back a giggle. Although libraries were far from the silent oases they had once been, she also found it hard to break the habit of trying to be quiet when she was in one.

'You scared me to death,' Keisha said, then she smirked at Candice, chewing on her gum like a cow with a blade of grass stuck between its teeth.

Not that cows had teeth, Candice mused, or at least, not on the top jaw. They had a pad instead, apparently, or so she'd read; Candice did a lot of reading, some of it quite odd stuff; it sort of went with the job.

Keisha shoved the piece of paper at Candice, who glanced at the headings on the three columns.

'Kiss, marry, avoid?' she asked the girl. 'Is that what you're playing?'

Keisha giggled. 'We used to call it fu—'

'Yes, no need to say any more,' Candice interjected, swiftly, cutting her off before she said anything more.

'But I thought it better to write "kiss" instead,' Keisha added.

'I'm glad you did,' Candice retorted primly. Swear

words had no place in a library.

'Bored, see,' the girl offered by way of an explanation.

Candice knew the library was quiet (it often was on Wednesday afternoons for some reason) but surely Keisha could find something more constructive to do? 'Have you entered those new books on the system?' she asked.

'Yep, and I've put dust jackets on them, and they are out on the shelves.'

'What about the pulled ones?'

Periodically, the library was sent a list of books to remove from loan, and sometimes these were sold off.

'All done.' Keisha jerked her head towards a small stand-alone bookcase near the entrance.

'OK, how about reading a book?' Candice suggested. 'We've got one or two to choose from.'

'Had enough of reading, haven't I?' Keisha said.

Candice gasped in mock horror. 'Had enough of reading? Go and wash your mouth out!'

'I'd prefer to do something else with my mouth,' Keisha said, her eyes wide, and Candice followed her gaze.

The man was twenty-something, good-looking, and tall – no wonder her colleague was drooling. If Candice had been thirty years younger, she'd have been drooling as well. She caught him checking Keisha out and she smiled ruefully.

Keisha was pretending to ignore him, half-turned away, but she frantically signalled Candice with her eyes. 'Is he coming over?' she hissed.

'No, he's typing something into the search computer.'

'Should I ask him if I can help?' Keisha wanted to know.

'You've got nothing to lose,' Candice said, and grimaced when Keisha shot her an incredulous look.

'You haven't,' Candice persisted. 'What's the worst that can happen?'

Keisha gave her another disbelieving stare.

'You're only doing your job,' Candice continued. 'Do

you want me to go over to him?'

'What? *No!*

'I can tell him that my mate fancies him,' she teased, and Keisha growled.

'Don't you dare. Oh…' Keisha's face fell.

The "oh" was a slender girl with long, silky hair who had walked up to the young man and was busy wrapping her arms around him.

'See,' Keisha said. 'All the good ones are taken.'

Wait until you get to my age, Candice wanted to say, but she held her tongue. What did she know about dating anyway? She'd only ever dated Malcolm and he most definitely was taken. He'd clearly been well and truly taken when another woman had come along and decided she wanted what Candice had. So, no, Candice was the least expert person on the planet when it came to dating.

'Avoid,' Candice muttered under her breath an hour or so later, having been persuaded by a still-bored Keisha to join in her game. Definitely avoid. The man was seventy if he was a day and appeared to be ill. He might be a lovely man and she felt a little sorry for him, but for the purposes of this game she had to be ruthless, so she put a mark underneath the "avoid" column.

She stared at the sheet of paper, frowning. So far, out of the fifty or so unaccompanied men who had walked in through the library's door, most of them had been in the "avoid" category, and she didn't even think she was being particularly picky.

'It's more fun when you play it with someone else,' Keisha had said, and Candice found she was having fun; grim, determined fun, which grew grimmer each time she made a mark under "avoid".

'Ooh, I'd fu— kiss that one there,' Keisha said, having recovered from the setback of earlier and pointing to a youth who Candice was positive wasn't old enough to drink.

Candice had to admit he was rather good-looking, but

she had kids older than him for goodness' sake. He was still a child. So was Keisha, she conceded, who was only twenty-one. Candice gave him a long stare – he and Keisha would make a lovely looking couple. He had a tattoo on his exposed arm, running from his shoulder to his wrist, and Candice wondered if youngsters today spent their time comparing their "ink". See, she smiled to herself, she could do young-speak too, if she wanted.

'What about him?' Keisha nudged Candice with her elbow and Candice looked away from the lad with the tattoo, to the gentleman who Keisha was referring to.

'Avoid,' Candice said instantly.

'Why? He looks OK.'

'He's about ninety. And he's got a Zimmer frame.'

The girl paused for a moment. 'Too old, then?' she said, eventually.

'Keisha,' Candice grumbled, 'just how old do you think I am?'

'Er… dunno.' Keisha was blushing, two spots of colour on her cheeks. It made her look quite pretty, a change from the gothy look she'd been sporting over the past few days. The blush made her look as though she was actually still alive.

'Not that old,' Candice said.

Keisha shrugged. 'Old people all tend to look the same – old.'

'By old, I take it you mean anyone over thirty?'

'Thirty is ancient,' Keisha stated with a shudder. 'I never want to be that old.'

Candice smiled wryly. Let's hear her say that in another few years, she mused. She'll soon change her tune when she gets to that age – she'll be claiming thirty is the new twenty, and will still believe that she'll live forever, that her looks won't fade and her body will stay strong. Yeah, youth is definitely wasted on the young, Candice concluded; they waste it, take it for granted and don't have a clue what to do with it. Then all of a sudden, they'll wake up one day to the realisation that it's gone, and middle-age is staring them in the face. Just like Candice had done; except Candice wasn't sure she'd actually had a youth in the first place — she suspected she'd gone straight from child to wife and mother, completely bypassing the youth bit entirely because she'd always felt middle-aged inside, no matter what the age on her significant birthday cards said.

It was truly terrifying how quickly the years sped by. Candice was becoming very aware she had wasted rather a lot of them in loving a man who had dumped her for another woman.

When the next bloke came through the door, Candice was determined to say "marry" regardless of what he looked like or his age!

'What you need is to join a dating site,' the girl announced, peering at the nearest computer. 'This one here looks good.'

'I don't think so,' Candice said.

'Why not? Lots of people do. It's nothing to be ashamed of. Even Carol does internet dating.'

'Carol? You mean, Carol who works upstairs?'

'Yeah. Look, he's nice.'

Candice looked. The man Keisha had selected for her was at least ten years too young. If she went on a date with him (which, let's face it, was highly unlikely) she'd feel like she was taking one of her kids out for a meal.

'He might fancy a cougar,' Keisha said.

Candice rolled her eyes. 'Well, I don't fancy being one,' she retorted. 'I'd like a man my own age, thanks very much.'

'There are plenty more on here, but you've got to sign up to see them. Ask Carol to show you which site she uses; maybe she'll give you a guided tour, and if you like the look of someone, you can join up. Try before you buy, like.'

'I don't think so,' Candice replied. She might be a whizz with computers, but some things — like finding a soul mate – shouldn't be digitalised. How could you tell from a photo (which had probably been taken ten years ago, or photoshopped to within an inch of its life) if you were going to gel with someone? Or tell from his description of himself, whether he was as funny as he claimed to be, or as caring. You couldn't.

'I'll think about it,' Candice said, knowing full well that she wouldn't.

But at least that explained why Carol had been so embarrassed when Candice had sorted her printer problem out for her!

CHAPTER 11

Paul had been right – the yoga sessions were getting easier. Only a little, but Candice could see the difference in herself when doing the stretches. She seemed to have gotten the hang of her breathing, too.

She caught his eye now and again during the class, and tried not to blush because she always seemed to be in a less-than-flattering position when she did so. For his part, he sent her a couple of reassuring smiles. Once he even winked at her when she had her backside up in the air and her nose practically buried in the mat. Not her best angle, by any means, but it did bring a smile to her rather heated face.

'How did it go tonight?' he asked when the session ended.

'Good, I think. It isn't quite as hard as it was the first couple of times. I think I'm becoming a bit more flexible, which was the whole point of joining the class in the first place. I can touch my toes now, almost, and I feel better for toning up, plus the wobbly bits aren't quite so wobbly.'

Oops. She hadn't meant to say that, and she had no idea why she had. Was she flirting with him?

'I like your wobbly bits,' Paul replied, then blushed. 'I… er… I didn't mean that you have wobbly bits,' he stammered.

Candice had to smile. He really was quite sweet, especially when he was embarrassed.

'Never mind my wobbly bits, how do you fancy a drink?' The words were out of her mouth before she had a chance to think about them. Now it was her turn to blush. Never in her life had she asked a man out. Not that this was "out" exactly; more in the way of a quick refuelling with a friend after a good workout. At least, that's what she told herself, while she waited for what seemed like an excruciatingly long time for his answer.

Paul gave her a measured look, then said, 'That's a great idea. Same place as before?'

Once again, they left their respective vehicles in the leisure centre car park and strolled towards the pub, chatting away about nothing in particular, although the weather featured fairly heavily. When they arrived at their destination, Paul held the door open for her, the smell of beer and food wafting out.

He was so sweet and was a gentleman too, Candice realised, as he pulled a chair out for her to sit on, before he went to the bar to get their drinks.

He came back with a half of bitter for himself and an orange juice for her. 'They do food here,' he said. 'Fancy a bite to eat? I'm famished.'

Candice was hungry, too. She'd only had a hastily-eaten sandwich when she'd got home from work, realising she didn't have enough time to prepare and eat a proper meal before the yoga class started. As soon as Paul mentioned food, her stomach growled.

'That would be lovely,' she said.

They ordered, and while they waited for their food to arrive, they chatted about their respective families. Or rather, Candice chatted, and Paul listened.

'Ivan is twenty-five and runs his own business,' she told him proudly, 'and he's got a steady girlfriend. I've yet to meet her, but I'm sure she's nice. He's so busy, poor thing. I wish I could do something to help, but although I'm OK with computers, I don't know the first thing about marketing.'

'You've got two boys?'

'Yes, my youngest, Preston, is… well… I'm not sure exactly what he does, apart from travelling the world and doing crazy things which I'd rather not know about.'

'Like what?' Paul picked up his drink and took a good swallow.

'Rock climbing, bungee jumping, base jumping…' Candice shuddered. 'Half the time I'm glad I don't know what he's up to, and the other half I'm worried sick.'

'You never stop worrying about your kids, do you?' Paul commiserated. 'I still worry about my daughter, Rowena, and she's got a decent bloke and a good job which fits in around Barny. He's my grandson. I can't imagine how you must be feeling, but I'm sure Preston is a sensible lad and wouldn't take unnecessary risks.'

Candice wasn't so sure – since when did rock climbing become so run-of-the-mill that it wasn't regarded as a risk? 'I just wish he was still at home, where I can keep an eye on him,' she said.

'It's hard, but you have to take a step back and let them get on with it, let them make their own way in the world, but be there in case it goes wrong. Take Rowena, for instance. She went off the rails a bit when her mother passed away and my grandson is the result.'

'Oh, I'm sorry about your wife.' Her heart went out to him, the poor man.

'Twenty-three years. We'd been together since school, though, so it seemed a lot longer.'

'It must have been hard for you, and for Rowena, too.'

He smiled sadly. 'It was. It still is, if I'm honest, although I have my grandson to keep me busy. Barny is a good lad.'

Paul took another sip of his beer, and Candice was about to ask him more about his wife when their food arrived, and the moment passed in a flurry of salt, pepper, requesting tartar sauce (to go with her fish) and vinegar for his chips.

When they had both eaten a few mouthfuls the conversation turned back to Candice as Paul asked, 'I don't mean to be insensitive, but what about the boys' father? I notice you don't wear a ring…' He trailed off.

'Malcolm and I divorced about ten years ago, when he decided to exchange me for a younger model.'

'Oh, I'm sorry—' Paul began, but Candice waved his sympathy away.

'It was a long time ago,' she said, although sometimes the distance between then and now was too close for comfort. It still hurt, even after all this time; talking about it just made it worse.

After that, the conversation turned to lighter things, both of them discovering they had a mutual love of *Strictly*, and both hated cabbage but loved broccoli.

It was odd the things that strangers talk about, Candice mused, as she drove home, but it was only when she was safely tucking Jelly Bean up in bed for the night (aka putting the car in the garage) that she realised Paul was no longer a stranger – he was starting to become a friend – and a little surge of contentment went through her.

CHAPTER 12

'New car?'

Candice looked up from her enthusiastic washing of Jelly Bean, and nodded at her neighbour. 'Sort of. New to me, anyway. I've had her a few weeks now.'

'I thought I saw you driving it. Nice.' Mr Harris crossed over the expanse of grass separating their two houses and circled the car, nodding to himself. 'Bet she's got a bit of oomph.'

What was this fascination for speed, Candice wondered, but all she did was smile knowingly, as if she'd taken the car to its limit but wasn't prepared to admit it. Actually, she was tempted, just a little bit, to do exactly that...

It was a beautiful evening, and Candice had decided it was about time she washed Jelly Bean again. She was even going to vacuum the inside, too. She'd picked up some more wash and wax stuff from the garage on her way home, had grabbed some rubber gloves from under the sink, a bucket from the shed, and had set to with a sponge and a chamois cloth until Jelly Bean gleamed and sparkled in the late evening sun. At this rate, Candice was washing the car almost as much as she washed herself.

Proud of her accomplishment, she stepped back to admire her work. The car looked like new; although it almost hadn't, because she'd only just remembered to put the soft top up at the last minute. That would have been a disaster, she thought, as she put it back down again ready for the morning, and reversed the car into the garage. She liked to keep it in there, because it saved the nonsense of top-on-top-off every time she got in it. At least, that's what she told herself – the real reason, if she was forced to admit it, was because it felt safer having it in the garage than leaving it on the small drive. The thought of anything happening to Jelly Bean made her cringe.

Car-washing task completed, Candice put the sponge and bucket away, and wondered what to do with herself next.

The summer months had always made her a little restless, she noticed. Not so much when the boys were still at home, but since they'd left she had felt at a bit of a loose end when it was still relatively light at 9:30 in the evening. During the winter, she had no urge to leave the comfort of her central heating and her sofa once she got in from work, only wanting to snuggle up with a hot cup of tea and something dramatic on the telly. Summer was different – it was made for long evenings chatting in the garden, and sipping a G&T with ice, while wondering how safe it was to eat chicken which had been cooked on the barbecue.

Not that she or Malcolm had ever drunk gin, or had a barbecue for that matter, although they had been known to sit in the garden for a couple of hours until it was time to call the boys in for supper and a bath.

She had usually read a book, while Malcolm had buried his nose in the Guardian newspaper and made cross comments every now and again. Not much in the way of chatting had taken place, she recalled. He'd never really been interested in her day, although he did make the appropriate noises when she talked about the boys. He'd happily talk for hours about his day, although for the last year or so of their marriage, he'd been reluctant to discuss his job. Which was no wonder, considering *That Woman* had worked in the same branch as Malcolm. He'd obviously been scared he might slip up.

She eyed the phone, thoughtfully. She had friends she could call, but she was reluctant to disturb them at this time on a Thursday evening. She'd kind of lost touch with some of their joint friends after Malcolm left, when she had realised they had been more his friends than hers. The friends who had stuck by her through the divorce were less than a handful, and all of them had husbands and families. She'd felt like a spare wheel, and tended to make excuses when they asked her out for a meal. She only ever accepted invites when it was girls only.

Bored, she called Ivan, but the call went straight to voicemail, then she tried Preston, hoping she could catch him, but without any idea where in the world he was, she had no clue about any time difference.

The phone rang and rang; in the end she gave up.

She could always do some cooking or there was a bit of ironing to be done, or… Maybe another walk was in order, she decided. It wouldn't be dark for an hour and it would give her some exercise while getting her out of the house. Anything was better than watching the rubbish on the telly and the book she was reading wasn't holding her attention, so she put on her trainers and marched out of the door. If she walked as fast as she could for half an hour, then turned around and came back, she should have managed a couple of miles at least. Enough for her to earn a chocolate muffin and a cup of tea before bed.

Candice only got as far as Mr Davenport's little house, tucked away down a lane which led to a farm track and the fields beyond.

He was in his pretty front garden, dead-heading some dahlias and looking as though he meant business. 'It's getting a bit too much for me,' he informed her, flagging her down for a chat. 'The garden, I mean. Everything takes three times as long as it used to, and I'm exhausted at the end of it. One of your lads wouldn't like to earn themselves a spot of pocket money, would they?'

Bless him, she thought. 'They're a bit old for that, Mr Davenport. The one is twenty-five and running his own marketing business, and the other is twenty-three and travelling the world. Isn't there anyone who could do it for you?'

Mr Davenport sighed and put his bag down. There were very few dahlia heads in there, Candice saw. She also noticed the elderly man was rubbing the knuckles on his right hand and wincing in pain.

'Not really,' he said. 'No one seems to want to do the little jobs any more. I've got some window frames that need painting, but the only thing that builders are interested in these days is putting up extensions or knocking down walls. I only want a bit of painting doing. It's not as though I haven't got any money to pay someone, either. I don't expect people to do it for free. I'd have a go myself, but I'm a bit wobbly on a ladder these days.'

For some reason, Candice had never really thought of Mr Davenport as old, but he had to be in his seventies, she realised. He'd been such a fixture in the village with his unrelenting enthusiasm for church fetes, bingo for the pensioners, cream tea afternoons, making paper lanterns with the children at Christmas (not that there were all that many kiddies in the village), that she'd not really noticed him slowing down and growing older.

'I might know someone,' Candice said hesitantly. She wasn't sure if she should go around recommending Paul to people, especially since he hadn't done any work for her, but Mr Davenport didn't have to give him the work if he felt Paul wouldn't do a good job or charged too much, did he? From what the old gentleman said, there was clearly the need for the kind of service Paul offered.

She fished her phone out of her pocket and did an online search for *A Man Who Can*. He didn't have a website or anything, but he was listed, so she followed Mr Davenport into his neat, snug cottage as he went inside to find some paper and a pen to write the number down.

'I don't know if he's any good,' she advised the elderly man, 'but I've met him a couple of times and he seems really nice. I don't think he's the type to rip you off.'

'I'll give him a call,' Mr Davenport promised. 'Now then, how about a nice cup of tea?'

So Candice found herself eating a slice of lemon drizzle cake, drinking tea and listening to some fascinating stories about the history of Little Duckton, then helping an old gentleman take the heads off some flowers. Which was far more preferable than stomping around the countryside by herself.

CHAPTER 13

Candice surveyed her trolley with a sad smile. Although it was no longer quite so obvious that she was buying just for one (no telltale assortment of ready-meals), it was still only half full and many of the items in it were of the smallest pack-size available.

She was proud of herself, though, for sticking to her healthy eating and she already felt better because of it – her skin seemed brighter and had more of a glow to it, although that could be attributed to the gradual tanning of her face over the course of the previous few weeks; even the short journeys to and from work exposed her to more sunlight than she'd seen for years.

Actually, thinking about it, it might be a good idea to pop some moisturiser with an inbuilt sunscreen into her trolley, otherwise, by the end of the summer, her skin may well resemble one of the raisins in the packet of mixed nuts and fruit she had bought.

'Hello, you,' a voice said from behind, and she turned to see who had spoken.

'Paul?' The pleasure she felt at seeing him was quite out of proportion to the circumstances. 'And this must be your grandson,' she said, spying a small boy standing next to him.

The child had brown hair, a little round face, glasses, and an earnest expression. He was so cute, she wanted to pinch his cheeks.

'Say hello to Mrs Summerville,' Paul said to him.

'Call me Candice', she suggested. 'What's your name?' she asked him, although she already knew it.

'Barny?' He said it as a question, almost as if he wasn't entirely sure.

'Your grandad tells me you are seven. That must mean you're in Year Two?' she guessed.

He nodded solemnly.

'Do you like school?' she asked.

Another nod.

'What's your favourite part?'

'Experiments and animals.' He had the slightest of lisps and her heart melted.

'Oh?' She gave Barny an encouraging smile.

'Barny is a bit of a science buff,' Paul explained, the pride on his face plain to see. 'And on the animal front, the school has fish, a hamster, and they're busy incubating chicks at the moment.' He leaned close to her and said in a loud whisper, 'Although what they intend to do with them once the school breaks up for the summer, I simply don't know.' He winked at Candice.

Barny tugged on his grandad's sleeve, his expression having become worried. 'You said they could stay at your house until they're big enough to join the others.'

'And they shall,' Paul reassured him. 'The school has some chickens,' he told Candice. 'They keep them in a run at the rear of the playground. The parents have a rota for seeing to them during the holidays and on the weekends. During the week, each class has a set day to look after them and as a reward, that class can have the eggs for lunch. You'd never believe how popular cheese and tomato omelettes have become.'

'I think it's a wonderful idea, helping the children understand where their food comes from,' Candice said. 'There's a farm park out near Evesham that welcomes school children. They run educational days,' she continued, trying to recall the details of one of the many leaflets on display in a stand near the main library doors.

'I think I've heard of it. I'll tell Mrs Leffe, Barny's teacher. I know the kids adore going to the West Midland Safari Park and seeing the petting zoo there. Barny likes that more than the lions and the monkeys, don't you?' Paul ruffled the boy's hair.

'It's years since I've been there,' Candice said, images of her own boys when they were the same age popping into her head. She recalled Preston's fascination with the insect house. Ivan had tended to prefer the larger animals, like the elephants and the rhinos.

'You ought to go,' Paul suggested.

Candice giggled. 'I'm not sure if they'd let me into the park proper with Jelly Bean,' she said.

'Jelly Bean?' Paul's expression was puzzled, and Candice blushed.

'Er… that's… um… what I call my car,' she stammered, highly embarrassed.

'Jelly Bean.' Paul's voice was full of amusement and his eyes twinkled with humour.

'It reminds me of one,' she declared, in pretend indignation. 'Don't tell me you've never named any of your cars?'

Paul stared over her shoulder, focusing on a shelf of eggs. 'The van is called Agnes,' he admitted sheepishly, not looking her in the eye.

'See! I'm not the only one!'

'Yeah, but *Jelly Bean*?' He sniggered.

'Go on, admit it,' Candice urged. 'You think she looks like a purple jelly bean, too.'

'OK, you win, she does kind of look like one, if you aren't wearing your glasses and if you squint a bit.'

Candice gave him a playful nudge. Playful? Her? That was a first.

'Grandad, what are you talking about?' Barny wanted to know.

'Candice has a little sports car, one where you can take

the top off. The official colour is called "Strata Blue", but I suppose it is more of a purple. Candice thinks the colour is like a purple jelly bean.'

She cocked her head in surprise that Paul should actually know what the colour was. A warm fuzziness settled in her stomach as she realised he must have looked it up. But, was it the car he was interested in, or her? That was the question.

'Don't forget the shape,' she said. 'It's all curves and rounded corners. It even looks as if it's smiling from the front. It's a happy car,' she declared.

Another solemn nod from Barny. 'Some cars do look happy, don't they, Grandad? And some look cross.'

Barny was referring to the shape of a car's grill, and Jelly Bean's upturned smile had been one of the things about the car that had drawn her to it.

'Grandad called the van Agnes because he said it looks like Granny Fraser. He says she's really grumpy but she always gives me a sweet. Are sweets supposed to be furry, Grandad?' Barny peered up at Paul, inquisitively.

'Oh dear…' Paul looked sheepish again. 'I really must be more careful what I say, because little pitchers have big ears.' He took a deep breath. 'Granny Fraser is my mother-in-law, and she never did like me much. She's a hundred and two, and still going strong, and no, Barny, sweets aren't meant to have fuzz on them.' He shuddered. 'She keeps a supply of boiled sweets in her pocket and hands them out to her favourites. Unfortunately, they are loose, and any bits of fluff and lint tends to stick to them. I've never had the pleasure of being on the receiving end, thank goodness, although poor Barny is handed a couple every time he visits her.'

Candice couldn't help but laugh; the old lady sounded a right madam.

'I can't say anything,' Paul added. 'I was the same with Rowena. I still am – no one will ever be good enough for her, as far as I'm concerned.'

'Aren't I good enough?' Barny asked, and Paul chuckled.

'You are more than good enough,' he said. 'I was talking about your mum and boys.'

'Ew, kissing?'

'Yep.'

'That's nasty,' he lisped.

'Yep.' Paul smiled at Candice.

The little boy was so adorable, she wanted to scoop him up and smother him in kisses herself.

'Do you and Candice kiss?' the child asked, and Candice let out a squeak.

'No, Barny.' Paul was biting his lip to keep from laughing.

Candice fought the urge to jab an elbow into his side.

'Do you *want* to kiss Candice?' Barny persisted.

Candice glared at his childish innocence; she wondered just how innocent the boy was actually being or was he deliberately winding his grandfather up.

'Not in the middle of the supermarket, lad,' Paul said, tears of mirth gathering in the corner of his eyes, his face going an alarming shade of pink. 'Right, we must be off.' He held up a bag of kale. 'Rowena is waiting for this. She can't make her vegetable lasagne without it apparently. Considering I've been invited for tea, I'd like my daughter to make a good job of it, otherwise it'll be fish fingers again.' He sighed dramatically and rolled his eyes.

Barny giggled. 'I *like* fish fingers.'

'But not for every meal, son,' Paul objected. 'You'll end up looking like a fish finger!'

'You're so silly, Grandad,' the boy said, and Candice wanted to pinch his cute little cheeks and make gooey noises at him. He really was totally adorable.

Come to think of it, so was his grandfather.

'Why don't you let me take you out in Jelly Bean for a spin?' she blurted, the words escaping from her mouth before she had a chance to rein them in. 'If you want to, that is…um…'

'I'd love to!' Paul cried. 'I've been wanting to sit in that little beauty ever since I set eyes on her.'

'How about Sunday?'

Paul thought for a moment. 'Sunday sounds good.'

'Great.'

'Lovely.'

With sudden, inexplicable awkwardness, Candice couldn't find anything else to say, and she stood there in embarrassed silence. Had she really just asked a man out on a date?

'Shall I come to your house?' Paul asked her.

'Yes, good idea.' She gave him her address.

'Ah yes, Little Duckton.' He narrowed his eyes at her. 'I had a call the other night from an old gentleman regarding some windows which need painting and a spot of gardening that needs doing. You don't know anything about that do you, considering you live in the same village.'

'Me? No?' she squeaked.

'I'm going over there tomorrow morning, to have a look and price it up for him.'

'Good. I mean, that's nice. I'll be in work.'

'Pity…'

Candice cleared her throat. 'Sunday?' she reminded him. 'Would ten o'clock suit you? It's only just over an hour's drive – we could spend the day there?'

'Ten is fine,' he replied, and they said their goodbyes.

Candice paid for her shopping absently, thinking about what she'd just done. She had, hadn't she; she had actually asked Paul out on a date.

Oh. A thought occurred to her, making her come back to earth with a bump.

Had she asked him on a date? Going for a spin was hardly the same as dinner, was it? Anyway, was it her he liked the look of, or the Mazda?

She couldn't help smiling all the way home, though; she had a day out on Sunday to look forward to with an attractive, friendly man by her side. No matter whether it could be regarded as a date or not, she was going out for the day, and she could hardly wait!

CHAPTER 14

Sunday dawned bright and glorious, birdsong waking Candice long before she needed to get up. Unable to stay in bed any longer and with excitement bubbling in her chest, she wandered downstairs, and made herself a cup of tea, taking it outside to drink on the patio.

As she sipped her drink, her gaze drifted over the too-long grass and the on-the-verge-of-becoming-unruly bushes. The flower beds, once Malcolm's domain, were filled with an equal number of weeds as there were proper flowers. For once Candice didn't feel guilty about not taking as much pride in the garden as she thought she should. If the truth be told, she actually wasn't all that bothered. Gardens were a bit like housework – as soon as you'd done it, it needed doing again, except that the carpet didn't insist on continually growing and there were no ornaments to deadhead. Unless she counted the awful figurine Malcolm's mother had given them one year for their anniversary and which, she'd noticed sourly, Malcolm had failed to take with him when he'd left for pastures younger and slimmer.

To be fair, with the boys no longer living at home, the house rarely got dirty and was never, ever messy. But the large garden was getting to be a bit of a burden. She might enjoy sitting in it and looking at it, but she certainly didn't enjoy dragging a mower over it every other week.

She took another sip of her tea and wondered if it was

time to think about moving to something smaller. Why did she need a three-bedroomed semi, anyway, when there was only her to rattle around in it?

It would be a wrench to leave the home where she had raised her children, she had to admit. All those memories: like the marks on the inside of the pantry door, recording the height of each child at six monthly intervals, were still there. Sometimes, if she listened hard enough, she was convinced she could hear the sounds of their boyish laughter echoing down the stairs, or the thud of their feet as they plodded around overhead.

Tea finished, Candice took her mug inside, then set about searching the attic for the ancient cool box which she knew was up there somewhere.

Thankfully, at some point not long after she and Malcolm had bought the house, Malcolm had installed an extendable loft ladder. Although the mechanism was a bit tricky to operate, it did mean that Candice could get up there without having to resort to wobbling precariously on a ladder.

Deliberately ignoring the vast assortment of boxes, which held everything from Christmas baubles to Ivan's first dinky pair of shoes, she aimed for where she had last seen the cool box.

And there it was, dusty and slightly grubby, but with its lid still firmly in place. A tartan travel rug sat in a plastic bag next to it – a duo of memories and almost-forgotten days out. The rug had belonged to her parents, and Candice recalled her father bringing it out every time the family went for a drive, along with a tiny folding table, a pair of canvas chairs and a supply of cucumber sandwiches with their crusts cut off. In the vain hope the weather would hold out and it wouldn't rain, her father would park the car in a layby and they'd have a picnic, usually by the side of a busy main road, the sandwiches being given added flavour from the smell of petrol, diesel, and acrid exhaust fumes. There had always been a flask of tea (a small bottle of squash for her) and slices of Battenberg cake to go with it.

Having a car had been quite a novelty for her parents, her father especially. They'd had Candice when they were in their forties, long after giving up on having children. They'd become settled in their ways, used to the quiet and order of their lives, only to have their very existence rudely interrupted by a demanding infant. But her arrival hadn't stopped them from "taking a run out" on a Sunday afternoon, and having a "bite to eat" on the side of the road. Candice wouldn't have minded so much if they'd actually gone somewhere, like down to the canal or the river – anywhere would have been more fun than watching the traffic speed by on the A38.

Her dad had been dead a while now, and then her mum a couple of years ago, but as the years went by Candice realised that her mother hadn't truly left her; she was still there in the way Candice inclined her head, in the things she herself sometimes said, and the way she tutted when she was cross. Whoever said fifty was the new thirty hadn't met Candice's mum, or Candice herself for that matter, because the older Candice became the more like Belinda she found she was becoming, and very often Candice felt every one of her forty-eight years.

But not today. Today she felt like a girl going to the seaside with her young man, so she left the travel rug where it was. She and Paul would find a bench to sit on, or failing that, a rock or some grass. If she released the rug from its dusty attic prison, she might as well change her name to Belinda and be done with it.

Idly, as she buttered some bread to make sandwiches (and deciding to leave the crusts well and truly on, for the same reason the travel rug was staying in the attic), she wondered what her father would have made of Jelly Bean. A load of old nonsense he'd have probably called it, having always favoured sensible saloons with plenty of boot room. Candice giggled softly as she packed the cool box, trying to imagine wedging two folding chairs into the Mazda's tiny boot. As it was, it would be touch-and-go whether the cool box would fit.

With the picnic lunch made, the flowers in the church taken care of, and with half an hour to go before Paul was due to arrive, Candice had a shower before quickly drying her hair. Then she put on a skirt, a blouse, and a pair of sandals, swiped pale pink gloss across her lips and declared herself ready.

She was having a quick final check of her appearance in the hall mirror when the doorbell rang. Her heart gave a little skip of anticipation. Even if this wasn't a date (and it probably almost certainly wasn't) and Paul only thought of her as a friend (which he almost certainly did), Candice didn't care. Or, if she did, she was going to do her best to pretend she didn't. She was going out for the day for the first time in ages, with a lovely man, the sun was shining, and she had a trip to the seaside to look forward to.

'What's in here, then?' Paul asked, after she'd opened the door and gave him the cool box to hold.

'A picnic.'

'Ooh, lovely. Where are you planning on us eating it?'

'Weston,' Candice told him, smiling from ear to ear as she locked the front door behind her.

'I haven't been to Weston for years,' Paul declared with a wide smile of his own. 'I wonder if they still have donkey rides on the beach?'

'I hope so! I love donkeys; they've got such gentle faces and their long ears are really cute and strokable.'

Paul leaned in as she unlocked Jelly Bean's boot. 'I dare you to ride one,' he said in her ear.

Candice blinked. She'd never ridden a donkey in her life and wasn't sure she wanted to start now, not at her age. 'Only if you ride one too,' she replied. There, that would teach him to dare her!

'You're on,' he said, hefting the cool box into the boot before slinging his jacket in for good measure. Candice placed her cardi in there too, along with a lightweight rain mac. Even if rain wasn't forecast and the sun was shining out of a clear azure sky, it was always best to be prepared. This was England, after all; the weather could turn on a sixpence as her mother used to say.

'We'll see,' she said, wishing she hadn't counter-dared him. She wasn't exactly dressed for riding donkeys; perhaps she should change into a pair of trousers? But she only owned a couple of pairs and both of those were old and scruffy, solely used for gardening purposes.

Paul opened the driver's door and held it for her, waiting for her to get in. Oh, well, it was too late now; she could always use the excuse that she couldn't possibly climb onto the back of a donkey while wearing a pleated, chiffony number from Marks & Spencer.

She got in, started the engine and they were off, the wind in their hair and the sun on their faces.

'I must say, this is a real treat,' Paul announced, one arm draped casually on the windowsill. 'It makes a nice change from being in a van.'

'I'm sure Agnes is just as lovely,' Candice said.

'She is, if you like the sound of a dozen tools clanking in the back and the smell of diesel up your nose,' he joked. 'This is much more fun.'

It was, wasn't it, Candice agreed silently, exchanging a cheery wave with another MX-5 driver as they headed towards the motorway.

Candice had always been a careful, slightly on the slow-side driver, but the temptation to put her foot down, to see what the car was capable of on the open road proved irresistible, and she sped up once they were on the M5.

The car, being so low to the ground, felt like a rather nippy dodgem car as she pulled out into the outside lane with a squeal of excitement.

Risking a swift glance at Paul to make sure he was OK, she saw him grinning from ear to ear, his eyes alight with laughter. Candice joined in with the merry atmosphere by turning on the radio. Sunday Love Songs was playing on Radio 2 and they both sang along to the songs with total abandon, Candice relieved to hear Paul's singing voice was almost as bad as hers. She didn't care. She was enjoying herself immensely. It made such a difference having someone to share things with, that even a simple drive in a car took on a whole new meaning with Paul by her side.

She also had a sneaking suspicion that she wouldn't be having quite as much fun if, say, Ivan or Preston had been in the passenger seat. They would have rolled their eyes and tutted at Radio 2 for a start, wanting to listen to the more modern rubbish that was played on Radio 1. She didn't mind the odd tune there, but the better, nicer songs always made their way onto Radio 2 eventually anyway.

Candice had never driven to Weston before and she had to admit she was feeling a bit nervous about navigation, even though she'd checked out the whole route online last night; but as they left the motorway behind them, Paul was calm and confident, and guided her towards the town centre. They only had to follow the signs, but Candice was scared she might miss one so was grateful for his clear instructions.

'There's a carpark ahead,' he warned. 'Turn right here.'

She did as he said, and soon they were parked up, surveying their surroundings, and deciding which way to go. Electing to leave the cool box in the car for the time being (they could always pop back for it when they were ready for lunch) they headed off.

'This way,' Paul said, pointing to a sign which directed them to the beach and the pier. When they made their way through the town and came out by the pier itself, Candice took a deep breath of sea air, intermingled with traffic fumes.

'It's not quite as I remember it,' she stated. 'When I was a child, it was a little more...' She struggled to find the right word. 'Magical?'

'I know what you mean,' Paul agreed. 'But hey, they've

still got donkeys on the beach.' He pointed.

Candice followed the direction of his finger.

So, there were. Three groups of them to be exact, dotted at intervals along the massive stretch of sand.

Candice didn't know whether to laugh or cry.

CHAPTER 15

'I fancy taking my shoes and socks off and going for a paddle, before the tide goes so far out that we'll need binoculars to see it,' Paul suggested.

Candice thought it was a wonderful idea. She couldn't remember the last time she'd felt warm sand between her toes, so she undid her sandals and slid them off with alacrity.

'My parents used to bring me here when I was little,' she said, squishing her toes into the fine grains and wriggling them around. Ooh, that felt so good! 'They used to buy me a bucket and spade, unroll the travel rug, and let me get on with it. You wouldn't believe how many holes I dug!'

'Yes, I would, because I used to do exactly the same thing myself. I was convinced I'd hit Australia if the hole was deep enough.'

'And remember the disappointment when you got to a certain depth and it just kept filling up with sea water?' Candice added, giggling. 'I loved building sand castles, too. I used to nag my mum to buy me a pack of those little flags you can stick on top of your sandcastle, but she never did.'

'I've got an idea,' Paul said, glancing around. 'Wait here.'

Wondering what on earth he was up to and hoping it didn't involve donkeys, Candice sank down onto the sand to wait, with her head tipped back, the sun on her face. She wished she could do this every day, she thought contentedly. They'd only been here five minutes, but she was already happier and more relaxed than she'd been for ages. She put it down to being out in the warm, fresh air. So far, this summer was proving to be a lovely one indeed, with a distinct lack of the usual rain. Mind you, she concluded, the kids hadn't broken up from school yet, which was usually when the weather decided not to play ball and it normally bucketed down every other day.

A gentle tap on the shoulder brought her out of her reverie. She opened her eyes to see Paul brandishing two buckets, a couple of spades, and a packet of those flags she'd coveted so long ago.

This time she almost did cry. It was as if he was trying to recreate her childhood for her, with the addition of brightly coloured flags.

'We need to get a bit closer to the water,' he said. 'This sand is lovely but it's too dry and fine to build a decent sand castle.' He wiggled his own toes to demonstrate.

He had nice feet, Candice noticed, as feet went. Clipped nails and not too Hobbity, with only a sprinkling of fine hairs.

He handed her a pink bucket and a matching spade, and they sauntered down the beach towards the sea, weaving their way past people sprawled out on towels or slumped in deckchairs, children digging or playing ball, and everyone determined to have fun in this unexpected and very welcome run of wonderful weather.

'There's nothing quite like the good old British seaside on a nice day, is there?' she said, the waves growing a little closer with each step. The tide was gradually going out, but they were making steady progress towards the sea. Paul suggested that they had a paddle first and Candice agreed; she couldn't wait to feel the water lapping at her toes.

Gazing into the distance, across the Bristol Channel, she was startled to see the dark smudge of the Welsh coastline in the distance, and the rounded hump of one of the little islands in the middle of the expanse of water, and wondered what it would be like to live there or if, in fact, anyone actually did.

The slope on the beach was very gradual and she recalled how she used to be amazed at how far she could wade into the sea, and for the water to still only be up to her knees.

'I've lost count of the number of times I went in the sea when I was a girl, only coming out when I was blue with cold, then forgetting where my parents had been sitting because the beach was so crowded,' she said. 'It used to scare me half to death, but it didn't stop me from warming up then going straight back in the water again.'

Paul glanced back the way they'd come. 'It looks like it's going to be another busy day,' he pointed out. 'There'll be a load of lost kids, I bet. Barny would love it here.'

Candice bit her lip. Maybe she should have suggested bringing Paul's grandson, but... 'I wish Jelly Bean was a four-seater,' she said. 'You could have brought Barny. You're right, this place is for kids, not for oldies like us.'

'Who said?' he objected, waving his blue bucket in the air. 'Kids can't have all the fun. We deserve some too.' With that, he popped his bucket and spade down on the sand and cried, 'Race you!', before taking off down the beach like a rat down a drainpipe, as her mum used to say.

'That's not fair,' she called, dropping her own things and chasing after him, giggling like mad. 'You've got a head start.'

Paul just laughed and carried on running, although he did slow down a bit she noticed, allowing her to catch up so they were trotting side by side for a few moments.

'Stop, I've got to stop,' she panted as they reached the first little wavelets, coming to rest with her hands on her knees, breathing heavily. 'I can't believe how unfit I am,' she declared when she'd got her breath back, although she was secretly pleased to see Paul was equally as winded.

'I keep forgetting I'm not twenty any more,' he said, blowing hard. 'But it's no excuse. There's a fella up the road from me who is seventy if he's a day, and he runs marathons. Puts me to shame, he does.'

Candice grimaced. 'I'm not built for running, however I can paddle,' she said, and she dipped one toe in delicately, squealing at the cold water on her hot skin.

Paul, not so reserved, rolled up his jeans to the knee and waded right in. 'It's not so bad,' he declared. 'It's actually quite warm when you get used to it.'

She decided to find out for herself; holding her calf-length skirt over her knees, she tiptoed in. The water was deliciously cool and she splashed around for a while, kicking through the waves, thoroughly enjoying herself.

When she'd had enough, they walked back up the beach to where they had abandoned their digging equipment, knelt on the sand, and began to put their spades to good use. Candice was all for digging as deeply as she could, but when Paul suggested they build a fortress with turrets, walls, and a moat, she was gripped with enthusiasm for the task.

Nearly an hour later, the pair of them sat back to admire their work.

'I think that's the finest sandcastle ever built,' Paul said, although the moat didn't work as well as they'd hoped because with the tide still going out any water that they poured into it simply drained away.

'Hungry?' Candice asked.

'Not just yet, there's something else we've got to do first.' He was staring along the beach and Candice followed his gaze.

Oh, no, donkeys. 'Er… I don't think so,' she said.

'You don't have to get on one. We can just stroke their noses, although I might have a ride if you don't mind?'

Candice didn't mind at all, as long as she wasn't expected to join in. 'Oh, look, there are babies!' she cried as they got closer.

The donkeys stood in a line, in front of a piece of rope but not tethered to it, and she marvelled that they were so well-behaved. She noticed there were several large buckets of water dotted around and a few bales of hay, some of which had been broken open. Clumps of the dried grass had been placed on the sand along the length of the rope. Partly hidden among the larger bodies of the adults, were two small babies.

They were the cutest things she had seen in a long time. Long, fluffy ears twitched and soft little noses wrinkled as they approached. One of the foals got up to stand on knobbly-kneed legs. She felt quite sorry for disturbing it and, although she was desperate to stroke the little creature, she stayed back. The mum didn't seem in the least bit bothered by the presence of these two strange humans, but the baby was clearly a little nervous.

A wooden sign in the sand told her it was £3 a ride.

Paul sidled up to her. 'I don't think I can go through with it,' he whispered. 'They're much smaller than I remembered.'

'That's because you're bigger now,' she pointed out.

'I know they can carry a considerable amount of weight compared to their body size, but look at me.' He gestured to himself. 'I'll be too heavy, and even if the owner actually lets me get on one, I wouldn't feel right about it.'

'It's nice seeing them again, though,' she said. 'I haven't seen a donkey up close for a long time.' She walked over to the nearest one and stroked its warm, soft nose. The donkey blinked but otherwise ignored her. They must be so used to being fussed over, she thought, that it was all in a day's work for them. She wished she'd thought to bring one of the sweet, red apples which she'd stashed in the cool box this morning, to give to it. But there were only two apples, not nearly enough to go around, and she knew she'd feel guilty because not all the donkeys would have one.

They petted a few more of the gentle animals,

breathing in the scent of them and admiring the babies, until Candice's stomach rumbled loudly.

'Lunch now?' she asked.

Paul nodded, so they retraced their steps up the beach and back to the promenade.

'If you give me your car keys, I'll nip back and fetch the cool box,' he offered, after washing the sand off his feet using one of the taps on the edge of the promenade, before wrestling his socks and trainers onto damp feet. 'There's no point in both of us going. You find a nice bench and I'll go and fetch it.'

He really was a lovely man, Candice thought, watching him walk briskly across the road and disappear down a side street in the direction of the car park. He was thoughtful, too; the idea of building a sandcastle had simply been genius. It had brought her childhood back to her in a way she never would have imagined.

Paul was gone less than fifteen minutes. When he returned, she opened the cool box and showed him the contents. Chilled lemonade, assorted neatly foil-wrapped sandwiches, mini pork pies, cheese and crackers, some fruit, and a little bag of cookies.

'Oh my, this is nice,' he said, taking the sandwich she offered (ham and salad) and biting into it. 'The sea air really makes me hungry.'

Candice was starving, too. She polished off a sandwich, some cheese and crackers, a pork pie, and the apple, all in the space of a few minutes, saving her cookies for later.

Once they'd finished their picnic Paul took everything back to the car, then they decided to go for a stroll along the promenade. It felt so natural, so right, to be walking along Weston's front with Paul, and for one silly, heady moment she almost felt as though she was one half of a couple again. It gave her a warm feeling in her tummy.

Don't be so silly, she kept telling herself, coming back to her senses, but the feeling would creep up on her again, until once more she was imagining things she definitely shouldn't be imagining. It wasn't as though Paul had given any indication that he thought of her that way, or that he was the slightest bit attracted to her. But a little part of her was beginning to feel more than friendship for this lovely man with the twinkling eyes and the ready smile. She knew she had to take care, or else she might be in danger of getting hurt.

Suddenly, the day lost some of its shine for her and she was about to suggest they made their way back to the car to head for home, when Paul grabbed her by the hand, whirled her around so they faced the other way, then pulled her back towards the pier and the direction of the car park.

OK, so it looked like he'd had enough too, she thought sadly. After all, she'd only suggested going for a drive in the car. Instead, she'd dragged him all the way to Weston for a full day out. No doubt he had other things to do with his Sunday, than to entertain a lonely, middle-aged woman.

She expected to turn away from the sea and dive back into the streets towards where they'd parked Jelly Bean, but instead, Paul, who was still clutching her hand, guided her in the opposite direction. When she saw where they were headed, she smiled.

'The pier?' she asked.

'Of course,' Paul said. 'You can't come to the seaside and not visit the pier. I used to save my pocket money for months just for this,' he admitted, 'and blow it all on the penny arcade in the first five minutes.'

'Is that your only vice?' she joked. 'Gambling?'

'Nah, just one of them.' He grinned impishly at her. 'Come on, I feel the urge to win you a cuddly toy. And they've got rides!'

Oh, why not? she thought and, giggling like a giddy schoolgirl, she ran past him, her skirt flapping around her knees, feeling like a teenager again.

This was turning out to be a day she would remember for a very long time!

CHAPTER 16

Candice had forgotten the fear she had felt when, as a child, she had walked along the wooden boards of a pier and had looked down between the cracks at the heaving grey sea below. Rationally, she knew she couldn't slip through them, and neither was any of those boards suddenly going to split in half to cast her into the ocean. Even as a child, she understood that, but it didn't prevent her from nervously feeling for Paul's hand and gripping onto it for dear life.

He sent her a curious look but didn't comment, as she tried to walk along the pier normally and not show that she was concentrating hard on not placing her feet on any of those inch-wide spaces between the weathered planks of wood. Thank goodness she never wore anything with a thin heel, she thought, imagining getting a stiletto caught in one of those cracks and not being able to wrench it free.

She shuddered. Paul, sensing her unease, squeezed her hand.

To her consternation, she found she was enjoying the sensation of her hand nestled in his, far more than any unease she was feeling on seeing those gaps between the boards warranted. She toyed with the idea of pretending to be more concerned than she really was so she'd have an excuse to continue to hold on to him.

Don't be so silly, she told herself. But the warmth of his hand on hers was sending little tremors up her arm and into her chest. She didn't want him to let go of her. Ever.

It was an alarming and quite worrying thought.

Because it was such a nice day, they elected to walk down the outside of the pier instead of aiming for the covered walkway which ran down the full length of it.

'Imagine what this must be like when the tide is right in and it's blowing a gale,' Paul said. 'I bet it's really wild. I'd love to see that, wouldn't you?'

Candice wasn't so sure she would, but if this lovely man ever suggested it, she would accompany him without a second thought. Anyway, with him by her side, she suspected she might enjoy herself regardless of the weather. With the option of being under cover if it was needed, she should feel safe enough. Besides, she had a feeling she was safe in Paul's hands; he wouldn't let any harm come to her.

They paused for a moment to turn around and gaze back towards the shore. Because the tide was so far out, the land didn't seem all that far away. They had a great view of the big wheel, the beach huts, and the headland to the south. Weston really was a very pretty bay, she saw, immensely glad she had suggested coming here.

Not that Paul had actually managed to have any say in the matter; she'd simply told him where she was taking him, and he'd fallen in with her plans with enthusiasm.

She saw where he was looking. 'No, nope, not on your life,' she said, shaking her head. 'I don't do heights.'

'It's perfectly safe,' he said, eyeing the big wheel wistfully.

'I've no doubt it is,' she retorted. 'But you're not getting me on that thing.'

She grimaced. Being God knows how many feet in the air, sitting in what was little more than a scanty metal seat held no appeal, whatsoever.

This far away from the shore, the smell of the sea was stronger. It mingled deliciously with the scent of fish and chips (not that she was hungry – far from it – but the aroma made her mouth water all the same), doughnuts, frying onions, and candyfloss. The sounds of the waves slapping against the massive pylons which held the pier up, seagulls wheeling and calling overhead, arcade games, the laughter of children, all brought back lovely memories of days out as a child. She'd been here on a school trip once while in primary school, in the days when trips were more about fun than education.

Sunlight glittered on the sea, and the sky overhead was a brilliant blue. Candice had a feeling of joy, contentment, and utter freedom. She really didn't want this magical day to end.

It looked like it wasn't about to draw to a close any time soon, Candice realised, when she saw Paul's face light up as they reached the building at the end of the pier and he spotted a sign for the world's smallest roller-coaster.

'You really are just a big kid, aren't you?' she said to him fondly, as he ushered her inside.

The building was nothing like she remembered (not that she could actually recall a great deal about it, except for the slot machines). It was light, airy, modern, constructed over two floors, and crammed with activities. The most amazing thing of all, was that it really did have a small but perfectly formed roller-coaster inside it, plus a go-kart circuit, dodgems, and a hideous contraption with a long arm which threw people around; no way was she ever going to be persuaded to have a go on that! However, Paul did manage to talk her into going on the roller-coaster, although Candice suspected her motives weren't so much that she wanted to experience the thrill and excitement of the ride itself, but the fact that even when they were queueing to get on, Paul had his arm around her shoulders and was holding her close to him.

Of course, he had to let go once they were seated because of the restraints which came down over their heads, pinning the victims (as she thought of them) in place. But he did hold her hand all the way around, giving it an encouraging squeeze when she screamed and shrieked as she sat there terrified, her eyes firmly closed, a thrilling sense of danger making her heart pound.

Neither the ride nor the feel of Paul's thigh next to hers had done her blood pressure any favours, she thought, as they were finally released. She staggered off on shaky legs, giggling with relief and pride that she'd actually found the courage to get on the darned thing in the first place.

Paul wasn't finished yet. He persuaded her to have a go on the helter-skelter (she laughed hysterically all the way down, trying to stop her skirt from ending up around her waist), the dodgems (although Paul complained that he thought he had whiplash and his neck would never be the same again), and the Formula 1 simulator (where Candice drove it like she stole it and simply had a blast).

Breathless with excitement, they agreed to have a pot of tea and a cake, then move on to slightly more sedate activities before it all became too much for them.

Candice couldn't believe just how large the inside was. The building at the end of the pier hadn't looked that big on the outside, but it was a veritable Tardis on the inside. They were spoilt for choice for somewhere to have their tea.

'I've not had so much fun since… ever,' she announced, surprised to discover it was true. 'Of course, I've taken the boys to places like this, but when you're supervising two kids, you can't really let your hair down and relax, can you?'

'I know what you mean.' Paul poured her a cup of tea and offered her a cake. Greedily, they'd decided on the mini-selection, which meant they had tiny slices of several different cakes to try. 'You're always on duty, he added. 'Even when they're happily playing they're usually making some kind of demand, like they are hungry, or they need the loo, or they want this, that, or the other. You can't just be you.'

'When Preston finally left home, I was at a bit of a

loose end. I still am, if I'm honest. But today has shown me how much fun it can be without having children with you.'

'Yeah, I love Barny to pieces and I thoroughly enjoy spending time with him, but this is a different kind of fun.' He reached out to stroke the back of her hand. The contact didn't last long, but it was enough to make her insides fizz.

She really, really wanted him to kiss her.

Once again, she told herself she was being silly and reading too much into a friendly gesture from a thoroughly nice man, and when he suggested trying the mirror maze next, she was relieved the subject had moved on and his fingers were now wrapped around his teacup instead of making her skin tingle.

'Oh boy, that was fun,' Candice gasped when the pair of them emerged from the maze. They were falling about laughing, but both of them were happy to slow down for a bit in order to visit the Museum of Memories. The attraction started with the Victorian era. Candice found herself mesmerised and fascinated at the way people used to live. But as the displays moved into the twentieth century, growing closer and closer to the decade of her birth, she began to recognise and remember things she had totally and utterly forgotten about.

'Look, look!' She tugged on Paul's sleeve and pointed to a packet of sweets. 'Spangles! Do you remember those? I hated them. And those multi-coloured polos. Can you still get them?' she wondered.

Candice and Paul spent far longer in the Museum of Memories than they had anticipated and when they emerged, they had an ice-cream each and sat on one of the benches outside to eat it.

'Before we go, I simply have to win you a cuddly toy,' Paul insisted, so when they had eaten the last mouthful of the crispy cone, (which was Candice's favourite part as it had a chewy piece of chocolate in the bottom) they made their way to the arcade section. Once there, they discussed his strategy at the grab machines with as much seriousness as if they were planning global domination. It paid off, as Paul, with a triumphant yell, guided a precariously and far-too-loosely-held pink rabbit to the hole. When it fell in, he reached inside and handed it to Candice with a flourish.

'Now, all that's left is to buy a stick of rock for Barny, because I did promise him that I'd bring him one back, then we can move onto the next thing,' Paul said.

'What next thing?' Candice wanted to know.

'SeaQuarium,' he announced, handing over some money in exchange for a paper plate filled with candy versions of egg, bacon, and beans. 'Barny will love this,' he said, as she offered to pop it into her handbag to save him from having to carry it.

'How come you know so much about Weston when you didn't even know we were coming here until this morning?' she asked.

He held up his phone. 'Google is a wonderful thing,' he said. 'You, of all people, should know that.'

She gave him a nudge with her elbow at his teasing. 'When did you research that?' She hadn't noticed him using his phone much, although both of them had taken a few photos on their mobiles.

'When I took the cool box back to the car.' He turned to look at her. 'I didn't want to go home just yet, so I thought if I found things to do…?'

'I didn't want to go home either,' she said.

For a second or two they stared at each other, until Candice looked away because she was scared he might kiss her. Or, was it that she was scared he might not?

'SeaQuarium it is then,' Paul said, after clearing his throat.

Once again he caught hold of her hand, and once again Candice felt a little shiver of pleasure at his touch, but this time it felt natural as if her hand had been made to fit into his. He continued to hold it until they reached SeaQuarium and went inside.

'This is nicely done,' Candice said as they strolled around looking at the various displays filled with a huge variety of assorted water creatures. Her particular favourite was the tunnel, where sharks swam on three sides and she felt as though she was underwater herself.

There was so much to see, from the Freshwater Zone to the Tropical Reef, and so many other things that it was nearly closing time when they'd had enough.

'I don't know about you, but I'm hungry again,' Paul said. 'It must be all this sea air. How about getting some fish and chips?'

'Lovely,' Candice agreed happily.

Could this day get any better?

CHAPTER 17

Candice licked the salty vinegar off her fingers, gathered up the remains of her paper-wrapped meal, got up off the bench and walked the short distance to the nearest bin. Paul was still eating, devouring his fish and chips with enthusiasm. She waited for him to finish, disposed of his rubbish for him, then unscrewed the top off a bottle of pop and took a long drink.

Paul leaned back, his hands resting on his stomach, a gentle smile on his lips. 'That was lovely,' he announced. 'The whole day has been lovely.'

'It has, hasn't it? I suppose we'd better make a move in a minute.'

Neither of them did anything of the kind.

A half an hour later they were still sitting there in companionable silence, enjoying the late evening sunshine. It was odd, Candice mused, that she didn't feel she needed to make conversation. She was totally comfortable in his company, only making the occasional comment or responding to something he said. There was no frantic scrabbling through her brain to find something to fill in the gaps, and no awkward silences. Paul seemed just as content as she was to sit quietly together and watch the world go by.

Eventually, he stood and gave her his hand to help her to her feet. Not that she needed helping, but she appreciated the gesture, nevertheless. She took it and, without letting go of each other, they strolled slowly back to the car.

Candice, with Paul's help, negotiated Jelly Bean through the town onto the main road which would take them to the motorway, but when she saw the sign for the M5 she pulled over and switched the engine off.

'What's wrong?' he asked worriedly.

'Nothing.' She swivelled slightly in her seat, an impish smile on her face. 'Would you like to drive Jelly Bean?'

'Now?'

'Why not?'

The way his face lit up made her giggle. 'I *am* insured,' he said. 'And I've been dying to get my hands on this little beauty from the minute I set eyes on her.' He frowned. 'Are you sure? I mean, you're not asking me because you're feeling ill, or something?'

She laughed. 'No, I'm not ill. I just thought you might like to have a go.'

He was out of the passenger side in a flash, opening her door before she'd finished speaking.

'That's a "yes", I take it?' she said.

He nodded eagerly.

She got out and sat in the passenger seat, watching while he familiarised himself with the controls. When he was happy he knew where the indicator was and which knob turned the lights on, he carefully pulled off.

For a few minutes, Candice had her heart in her mouth, praying he wouldn't bump her precious car, but after a while she relaxed a little and began to enjoy being chauffeured for a change.

It was strange to be sitting in the passenger seat. Although she had confidence in Paul's driving, she occasionally found herself reaching for the brake pedal with her foot from time to time, or checking the side mirror on a regular basis to see what was behind them. Not being the driver did have a couple of advantages though, and one of them was being able to enjoy the scenery. The other was *also* being able to enjoy the scenery, but the view she was referring to was inside the car and not outside. She just hoped Paul wasn't aware that she couldn't seem to stop staring at him.

Every time she saw him, she became more and more attracted to him. Not just his looks either. He was simply gorgeous inside and out, and she studied him as surreptitiously as she could during the whole journey home.

Far too soon for Candice's liking, they were back at her house and Paul was switching off the engine and handing her the keys.

'Thank you for a perfect day,' he said. 'I really enjoyed myself.'

'So did I.' Candice was exhausted. She'd only planned a drive to the coast and a spot of lunch, but they'd been out for hours, and had crammed so much into their day.

It had been fun, though…

He got out and she followed him to his van. For a moment she wondered if she should invite him in for coffee, but even as the thought crossed her mind, she discarded it. They might have had a fantastic day together and they might be getting on like a house on fire, but apart from some quite exciting (on her part) hand-holding, he'd made no move to suggest he was interested in her in *that* way. Plus, she didn't want to give him the wrong impression or spoil their burgeoning friendship.

Anyway, it was his turn now. She'd already "asked him out" once. If he wanted to see her again it was up to him to do the asking.

To her disappointment, he aimed his keys at the van and opened the door. She stood on the drive, feeling awkward, wondering if she should just give him a little wave and go into the house, or should she stay where she was until he drove off.

This non-dating, friends-thing wasn't straight-forward, was it? she thought.

Paul threw his jacket on the passenger seat and stood there. Candice thought he looked as awkward and as uncertain as she felt.

He cleared his throat. 'We should do this again sometime.'

'Yes,' she agreed, 'we should.'

He shuffled his feet and looked at the ground. The silence that stretched between them now was a far cry from the easy silences of earlier. Candice worried at her bottom lip, trying frantically to think of something to say.

Paul beat her to it.

'Would you like to have dinner with me on Thursday?' he stammered, the words tumbling out of his mouth in a rush. 'No obligation, of course. Don't feel you have to, but it would be nice to see you again. If you want to see me again, of course—'

'I'd love to,' she interrupted, her heart going out to him and his obvious embarrassment.

'Good. Great.' More shuffling of feet. 'We'll… um… we'll firm up the details at yoga, yeah?'

She nodded and was about to take a step back, thinking he was going to climb into his van and drive off, when he lunged forward to give her a one-armed hug and a kiss on the cheek, then darted back to the van again.

'See you Tuesday,' he called, and this time he did get in and drive off.

Candice watched him go with a bemused smile. She had sort of been hoping for a bit more than an awkward hug and a brotherly kiss on the cheek (a proper kiss would have been nice), but at least he wanted to see her again, and she did have Tuesday's yoga session to look forward to.

CHAPTER 18

Candice arrived at yoga, clutching her mat firmly under her arm, her hair brushed, a smidge of lip gloss on her lips, and a soft bubbling excitement in her heart, to discover Paul wasn't there yet.

She was early so she chose her place with care, knowing he liked to be near the front and to the left (most people seemed to have their favourites spots) but not wanting to be too close to him in case it cramped his style. Actually, it was more likely to cramp hers, as she suspected she might not be able to concentrate if she was right next to him.

The room gradually began to fill up. Each time the door opened she glanced around expectantly, a ready smile on her lips, only for it to fade slightly when she saw it wasn't him.

Even when Moon sank gracefully to the floor and brought the quietly chattering class to order with a simple "Namaste", he still hadn't arrived, Candice clung to the hope that he'd appear shortly.

A late entrant briefly raised her hopes, which swiftly subsided again as the newcomer mouthed "sorry" at the rest of the class and unfurled her mat in a corner at the back of the room.

All through the session, Candice fretted over the reason for him not showing up. Was it something she'd said? Or not said? Or had she done something he hadn't liked? Was it because she hadn't invited him in for coffee (with coffee being a euphemism for something else entirely)? Had he changed his mind about liking her (although he hadn't actually said as much, she'd got the impression that he did quite like her) so had decided to avoid any embarrassment by not coming to the class?

All these worries, and more, scuttled through her mind, over and over, spoiling her concentration, affecting her breathing, and generally making her performance less-than-satisfactory. So it was with some disgruntlement and more than a little concern that she sidled out of the leisure centre door and made for her car as fast as her legs would carry her without breaking into an all-out run.

She couldn't wait to get out of there, certain her humiliation at being stood up was clear for all to see. To think she had been so looking forward to their drink together afterwards, too.

She unlocked Jelly Bean, slung her mat and water bottle onto the passenger seat with unnecessary force, got in, then slumped back as gloom enveloped her. She'd thought their day out on Sunday had gone so well, and now here she was, all alone and wondering where it had all gone wrong. He'd not even had the decency to phone her to tell her he wasn't coming. It would certainly make bumping into him in the future somewhat on the awkward side, she decided, wondering whether she should find another class, or just not bother at all. She'd gleaned enough to be able to carry on with the positions at home. If she felt she needed new ones then she could always buy a DVD or download a video off the internet. She didn't need to take part in a class, at all.

Candice was about to start the car when an odd buzzing noise caught her attention.

It sounded like her phone, but that was safely tucked away in the pocket of her fleece, which was resting against her hip. If it *was* her phone, she would have felt the vibration through the fabric, because she'd turned it onto vibrate only before the class started.

She put her hand in her pocket.

No phone.

She checked her other pocket.

Still no phone.

Shit! It must have dropped out. She'd placed her fleece on a table at the back of the room before the class had started, with her trainers neatly underneath. The phone must have fallen out of her pocket when she'd picked it up.

Hoping to God that it would still be there or that some kind soul had found it and handed it into reception, she opened the car door.

The buzzing noise came again. This time she was sure it came from down to her left, between the seats maybe, or on the floor?

Stuffing her hand down between the seat and the central console, Candice felt around until she touched smooth plastic.

The buzzing sounded once more, and the tips of her fingers vibrated gently.

She'd found her phone.

The relief was enormous – she really hadn't wanted to face the nuisance of having to report it lost and all the ensuing hassle afterwards.

Holding it firmly in her grip, she thumbed the screen and took a look at who'd been calling her.

The air whooshed out of her lungs in a rush, when she saw the name.

It was Paul.

He'd phoned a couple of times, then had sent her a text.

She read it and a smile spread across her face. He'd not stood her up, after all (well, he couldn't have, considering tonight hadn't been a proper date) but had been delayed on a job and probably wouldn't make yoga in time. Was she still on for Thursday?

With her index finger poking at the keyboard, she

texted that she was. They agreed to meet at The Crow's Nest in Lime Orchard, not far from where Paul lived. It seemed silly for him to come all the way over to hers to pick her up, then have to go all the way back to where he started.

Besides, she hoped she'd get a sneak peek at Paul's home.

If he invited her back to his house that is. And *if* she decided to accept the invitation.

CHAPTER 19

The Crow's Nest hadn't changed a bit, Candice thought, looking around. It still had that olde worlde charm and a slight air of neglect. But if the food was half as good as she remembered, she didn't care that the wallpaper was from the eighties or that horse brasses went out of fashion in the previous century. Or that there was still a tiny barrel of sherry behind the bar. She hoped it wasn't the same one that had been there during her last visit, which had been at least fifteen or twenty years ago.

Paul had thoughtfully reserved a table. 'It might only be Thursday, but it does tend to get busy,' he told her, 'so I thought it was better to be safe than sorry.'

They were shown to a table near a window overlooking a pretty garden at the rear of the pub, ordered their drinks, then settled down to peruse the menu. Candice hadn't eaten much lunch in anticipation of this meal. She was now starving. Everything sounded delicious and the smell of cooking was mouth-watering.

'I think I'll have… um… one of everything? I can't decide,' she admitted.

'How about you order one dish we both fancy, I'll order another, and we can go halves?'

'Good idea!'

They took a while to whittle it down, but eventually the task was done, and Paul settled back in his chair.

'I'm really sorry about Tuesday,' he said. 'But this old

dear up the road had a leak from her bathroom and water was dripping through the ceiling and onto the kitchen light downstairs. It's lucky she didn't get electrocuted. I turned the water and the electric off, dried everything as best I could, then I had to switch everything back on, find where the leak was coming from in order to isolate it, because I couldn't leave her without water or power overnight.'

'Of course, you couldn't. Did you get it fixed?'

'Eventually. I think the bath and the plumbing were at least fifty years old! Mind you, ours was older than that when we first moved in. We had a bath in the middle of a bedroom, no central heating, and there was even an ancient mangle in the downstairs loo.'

'Is that the house you live in now?'

He nodded.

'How long have you lived there?' Candice wanted to know.

'Ellen and I bought the place thirty years ago.'

Ellen, so that was his wife's name. He'd not mentioned it before. In fact, he'd hardly talked about her at all.

'I thought about selling up after she died,' he said. 'But it didn't seem right, somehow. It felt like I'd be trying to move on from everything we'd built together, as if I was trying to pretend she'd never existed.'

This is getting a bit deep, Candice thought, but in a way she was glad he was talking to her about it because if, as she was hoping, their relationship was to progress from the hand-holding stage, then she wanted to know everything there was to know about him. And like Malcolm, Ellen had been a massive part of Paul's life, a part he still mourned. Candice needed to know if he was ready to start a new chapter.

'You have to do what feels right for you,' she said. 'How old was Rowena when it happened?'

'Twenty-one. She wasn't a kid, but it still hit her hard to lose her mum.'

'I expect it did,' Candice murmured, her heart going out

to this young woman who she had yet to meet. She felt sorry for Barny, too, for never really knowing his grandma. He could only have been a baby when Ellen passed away.

'At least she was there for Rowena when she got pregnant,' he said. 'Rowena had Barny when she was twenty. I gave her a bit of a hard time about it.' He shrugged. 'You know the sort of thing – "how could you have been so stupid", "you've thrown your life away", and so on. But not Ellen, she just rolled up her sleeves and got on with it, no criticism, no reproach, only support and love.'

He had been fiddling with a beer mat as he spoke. Candice noticed how he had shredded it bit by bit, peeling the papery layers away.

'Looking back, I think she knew right from the start that there was something wrong. Even before she'd seen the doctor, I reckon she knew.'

Candice worried at her bottom lip. 'What was it?'

'Cancer.' His tone was matter-of-fact but the pain was etched across his face. 'There was nothing they could do.' He looked up and away, lost in grief. 'At least she lived long enough to get to meet her grandson. I think that's what kept her going in the end – she wanted to make sure Rowena and the baby were OK.' He laughed softly. 'Barny is the spitting image of her. He has her ways, too. It was having to look after him that kept me and Rowena going. How can you give up when there's a baby crying to be fed, or have his nappy changed? You can't, can you? You just get on with it. For the first couple of years, Rowena and Barny lived at home with me. It was a bit of a wrench when she got her own place, I can tell you.'

'I bet it was,' Candice murmured.

'I've got used to it now,' he said. 'I had to.' He stopped destroying the beer mat and put it down. 'Rowena has got a boyfriend and a job, and although she hasn't forgotten her mum, she is making a life for herself.' He hesitated, then said, 'I think it's about time I did the same.'

'Do you think you're ready?'

'Yes. Can I tell you something, and please don't take this the wrong way, but I have been on a few dates since Ellen died. None of them worked out. I thought it was because I wasn't ready, but that's not the reason. It was the person I was dating who wasn't right, not the timing.' His smile was small and uncertain. 'I believe I've now met the right person.'

Candice blinked. She hadn't been expecting that.

'Too soon?' he asked. 'I know we've not known each other long, but I hoped there was a connection. God, I sound like a counsellor or an agony aunt.' He grabbed for his drink and took a long swallow.

'I feel the same way,' Candice said, slowly and quietly.

'You do?'

She nodded.

'Ah, here's our dinner,' he announced, as a young woman appeared at their table bearing a couple of plates. After that, the conversation moved on to less emotional subjects, and it was only when they had settled the bill and were outside in the car park, standing by Jelly Bean (Paul had walked the relatively short distance from his house) that Candice felt a little awkward again.

This dating business wasn't easy, was it, she thought, having absolutely no idea what she was supposed to say or do now.

Paul made the decision for her.

He closed the small gap between them, standing so close that she had to tilt her head back slightly to look at his face. His lips were inches away from hers and she stared into his eyes, knowing what he was about to do and welcoming it.

Without touching any other part of her, his head bent towards hers, his mouth coming closer, his breath warm on her cheek. Then he kissed her.

His lips were warm and soft, the kiss hesitant, almost chaste, and she understood that this was as scary for him as it was for her.

Emboldened by the knowledge, she slid one arm around his waist, her other hand reaching for his shoulder.

It was all the confirmation he needed. He wrapped his arms around her, drawing her into his chest, holding her so tightly she could feel his heartbeat through his shirt.

She wanted to stay in his embrace forever, with his lips on hers, feeling the strength in his arms and the solidity of his chest. It was such a long time since she had been held like this and, as she was swept away, she was pretty certain she had never been kissed like this before.

All too soon it was over.

When they broke apart, Paul looked as stunned as she felt.

'Oh, my,' he said, his pupils huge, his breathing a little ragged.

'Oh, my,' she agreed, her heart thumping like mad, every part of her tingling. If it wasn't for the fact that he was still holding her, she thought she might float away.

He cleared his throat. 'What are you doing on Sunday?' His voice was hoarse and ragged around the edges.

'Nothing.'

'Fancy a day out? My treat?'

Candice most certainly did. 'Where are we going?'

'It's a surprise, but we have to go in Jelly Bean.'

'Why?'

'You'll see,' he chuckled, sounding more like his usual self.

'It's because you want to drive her again, isn't it?' she teased, then caught her breath at the darkening of his eyes.

'The only woman I'm interested in is you,' he muttered and kissed her so soundly he stole her breath.

When he finally released her, she suspected he had stolen her heart too.

CHAPTER 20

Sunday certainly was a surprise! The last place Candice had expected to be taken to was to an MX-5 rally. Held across several fields in Warwickshire, the event was simply enormous.

'Park over there, love,' an official said to her, pointing to line after line of Mazdas in several different shades of blue.

'They're colour coordinating the parking area!' Candice exclaimed in delight, as she pulled up alongside a newer model.

'We don't have to stay long, if you don't want to,' Paul said. 'I just thought Jelly Bean might like an hour or two with some friends.'

'Oh, you!' Candice nudged. 'You're teasing me.'

'Only a little bit,' he replied, nudging her back, and she smiled up at him.

What a thoughtful man Paul was. She would never have thought of coming to a Mazda MX-5 owner's rally. Heck, she didn't even know such a thing existed, until now.

'You must admit, MX-5 owners are a friendly bunch,' she said. 'When I'm out in Jelly Bean, everyone waves at everyone else, especially if I've got her top down.'

'I had noticed,' he said.

They wandered around the huge field, ogling the pristine models on display (Candice much preferred the curvier, more retro lines of an older model, like hers), marvelling at the trade stands with their parts and gadgets, and trying to avoid people selling them stuff. And who knew there were so many future events? The MX-5 Owners' Club had organised loads of things, from meals out to treasure hunts. It seemed that any old excuse for a get-together and a drive around in their Mazdas was welcome. Candice lost count of the number of times she was asked what she drove. Actually, it wasn't really her who was asked, it was Paul. After a while, she grew a little cross with everyone's assumption that he must be the car owner and not her.

Paul realised her increasing ire and tactfully suggested they visit one of the food stands for some lunch.

'What do you fancy?' he asked. 'I've seen a stand selling paella, another with some kind of stir-fry, one with Thai curry and noodles. Or would you prefer a good old British hot dog?'

In the end, they settled for a burger each and shared a portion of chips, washing their food down with a cup of tea.

'I wouldn't have thought there were so many MX-5s in existence,' Candice mused.

'Mazda is still producing them,' Paul pointed out.

Candice let out a rather unladylike snort. 'Why do these car manufacturers have to mess with things? The newer design isn't a patch on the old one. Mazda isn't on its own, either, in this regard. There was a time when you could tell a Land Rover from any other four-by-four, and a Mini looked exactly that – a mini. Now it looks almost as big as your van.'

'I didn't realise you were so passionate about cars,' Paul said.

'Neither did I, until just now,' Candice replied with a self-conscious laugh. 'But it's true, though – newer isn't always better. At least Beetles have the same shape. I know one of those when I see it.'

'Remember Cortinas and Capris?' Paul asked. 'When I was a kid, all I wanted was a Capri. That long bonnet was to die for. They don't make cars like they used to,' he sighed.

'See, that's my point.'

Paul had to agree with her.

'Do you think cars have personalities?' she asked him suddenly.

He gave her a curious look. 'I'm not sure. I think us drivers might project personalities onto our cars based on our experience of driving it, like whether it's a temperamental starter, or whether it keeps breaking down. Why do you ask?'

'I sometimes think that buying Jelly Bean has turned my life around – that she has made a difference to me.'

'In what way?'

'You're going to think I'm going mad.'

'Too late,' he teased, 'I already know you are. Tell me?'

'I was stuck in a bit of a rut before I bought her,' she admitted. 'I'm only now coming out of it.'

Paul didn't say anything but waited patiently for her to carry on. That's one of the things she loved about him – he didn't rush her, or try to talk over her, or interrupt with his own story. He simply let her get on with it in her own time.

'You know I told you that I was married before?' she said. They'd talked about their respective pasts, but only briefly and not in much detail.

He nodded.

'Malcolm and I were together for quite a long time. He could be a bit forceful—'

This time Paul did interrupt. He gave a kind of a growl, and she realised how what she had just said had sounded.

'Not in that way,' she hastened to tell him. 'He didn't hit me or anything, he was just a bit loud and opinionated. He knew what he liked and what he wanted, and I went along with it. I suppose I was a bit of a mouse, a people-pleaser.' She glanced down at her flared skirt. 'For instance, he said he preferred me in skirts, so I always wore skirts. That kind of thing. When he left, I just sort of carried on being Malcolm's version of me. I suppose I still am. But I'm coming out of it,' she added, brightly. 'Malcolm would never have bought Jelly Bean, not even if he'd seen how much I liked her. He would have talked me out of it, saying it's not practical.'

'It's not,' Paul pointed out. 'But you don't need practical, right now. You've been there, done that.'

'I have, haven't I? Anyway, I fell in love with her and I had to have her. I think it was fate.'

'It doesn't matter what it was, if you're happy with your car that's all that matters.'

'I'm happier than I've been since Malcolm left,' she confided. 'And it's all down to the car. Actually, not all of it.' She sent him a meaningful smile.

He returned it, saying, 'Good, because I can't compete with something as cute as Jelly Bean.' Then he became a little more serious. 'It's not all down to the car; it's down to you, how you feel about yourself, and how you feel inside.'

'I've realised something these past few weeks,' she said. 'I'm over my ex-husband. I never thought I would be and I'm not sure exactly when it happened, but I'm glad it has.'

Paul's heartfelt, 'So am I!' brought a wide smile to her lips.

After their lunch, they looked around the rally some more, then decided they'd had enough and headed back to the car.

But the day wasn't over yet, Candice discovered. Paul had another surprise up his sleeve.

CHAPTER 21

'I know this might be too soon,' Paul said, as they hurtled back down the M5 towards home. 'But Rowena is feeling a little left out. Barny has already met you and my daughter wants to meet you, too. Is that OK?'

'Of course, it is,' Candice told him, which was why, less than an hour later, she was nervously pulling into Paul's street for the first time, about to visit his house for the first time, and meet his daughter for the first time.

There were a lot of firsts today, including having to pull over at the motorway services to put Jelly Bean's soft top up because it had started to drizzle. She sincerely hoped her summer of driving topless wasn't coming to an end. The weather was typical, though. Britain was two weeks into the six-week school holidays and the weather was starting to deteriorate.

'I've booked a table at The Crow's Nest,' Paul told her, 'but I thought you might like to freshen up first.'

Kind-hearted and considerate were two words that came to mind when she thought about Paul (and she thought about him often). There were a few more, like attractive and gorgeous, but she wasn't sure she should allow herself to go down that route just yet. Especially since he hadn't made any move to kiss her again.

When Paul opened his front door, she stared around with interest. A woman had clearly left her mark here, but the living room wasn't overly feminine. Candice guessed Paul hadn't changed the furniture that he and his wife must have chosen together. The walls were plain white with the minimum of pictures and photos, and there was a distinct lack of the sort of knick-knacks which graced Candice's own home.

While he went to put the kettle on, Candice's eye was caught by a photo on the mantelpiece. It showed a smiling couple, their arms entwined around each other's waists and she recognised a younger version of Paul.

'That's me and Ellen on holiday in Greece the year before her diagnosis,' he said, and Candice jumped guiltily. She hadn't meant to snoop, but she hadn't been able to help herself, feeling a need to know more about the woman who Paul had fallen in love with and married. He probably did still love her. It was only right and natural that he did.

The question was, how much? Was he in any emotional state to move on, despite him telling her that he was?

'Sorry, I didn't mean to—' she began, but stopped talking when he waved a hand in the air.

'It's fine. You can't exactly not see it, can you? Not when it's in plain sight.'

'I bet you miss her,' she said, softly.

'Every day.'

There was a short silence for a while, and Candice fished around for something to say. 'It doesn't get any easier, does it,' she said eventually, remembering her own losses. She still missed her mum more than words could say.

Paul let out a long breath. 'No, but you do learn to live with it, and life does go on.' He stepped closer. Time seemed to slow down; she heard the sound of water boiling and the click of the kettle as it switched itself off; she heard the call of a wood pigeon from the garden beyond the window; she smelled the scent of Paul's aftershave as he came close enough for her to touch.

'I'm ready for life to go on,' he said quietly. 'Are you?'

She knew he was referring to Malcolm and the conversation of earlier, and she nodded, not trusting herself to speak.

When he took her in his arms, she melted into his embrace. For a while she was lost in him, only coming slowly back when his kiss returned to the fluttering of earlier as he slowly eased his mouth from hers.

'Wow,' he said. His eyes were shining, and he gazed at her with such intensity that she thought she might swoon.

Wow, indeed.

'You wanted to freshen up?' he reminded her, his voice hoarser than usual.

Candice cleared her throat. 'Yes, that would be nice.'

But as she disappeared into the downstairs cloakroom for a quick wash and to brush her hair, all she could think about was how he had held her, and how he made her feel.

Paul was bringing to life feelings and emotions she had long since thought were buried for good. He made her tingle all over, made her heart skip a beat, and her stomach turn over. She felt like a teenager all over again, and she revelled in it.

There was only one little shadow on her horizon – what if Rowena didn't like her? Paul and his daughter (and Barny, too) had been a unit for such a long time, that the girl might resent her father having another woman in his life. Not that Candice was convinced she was actually in his life yet, but the signs were promising, and they were getting along like a house on fire, as her mum used to say.

She needn't have worried. Rowena (who looked so much like her dad that it made Candice's heart ache) welcomed her with a hug. She seemed delighted that her father had finally found some female company, and gradually Candice began to relax. Barny was a poppet, too, and Candice could see herself slotting into the lives of this little family – assuming it all worked out between her and Paul.

And she really, really hoped that it would, because she was falling for him harder than she'd thought possible.

138

CHAPTER 22

How could anyone do such a thing? It was despicable! And during the day, too. Luckily, Candice had been in work, because if she had been at home when the blighters had broken in, then things could have been a whole lot worse.

With tears in her eyes, she surveyed the mess in her living room. Her chin wobbled, and she felt distinctly trembly and a bit faint. Animals, that's what some people were. It wasn't as if she had much to steal anyway, despite the house's location.

Candice phoned the police, and while she waited for them to arrive she checked what had been taken. Her computer was one of the first things that she noticed was missing, as the bareness of the little desk in the corner of the living room testified.

She made her way slowly into the kitchen, feeling as though all the stuffing had been knocked out of her. When she'd watched people who were being interviewed on the telly after a burglary, saying they felt as though they'd been violated, she'd never really understood. She did now.

Oh, bugger, they'd taken her nice kettle as well, the copper one which had sat on the Aga since she and Malcolm had bought the house. It was old and battered, and she had no idea what a thief could possibly want with it. They wouldn't exactly get anything for it.

Something crunched under her shoes and she saw that

all the glasses in the cupboard next to the fridge had landed up on the floor, in what she could only assume had been a deliberate act of vandalism.

The thieves had clearly got in through the back door. It was an old wooden one and although she had a sturdy uPVC front door with mortice locks, the door leading to the back garden had never been replaced. She and Malcolm hadn't bothered because they'd always talked about knocking part of the wall down to put in French doors, but neither the time nor their finances had ever been right, so they'd put it off. Then Malcolm had walked out, and any thoughts of replacing the back door had been driven from her mind by her grief and desolation.

When she went upstairs, she became even more upset as she saw the state of the boys' bedrooms. Once upon a time, the two rooms would have always looked as though they had been ransacked, but as the children had gotten older and took more pride in, and more care of, their things, so their rooms had gradually become tidier and less of a bomb site.

Whoever had broken in must have been desperate, because they had taken Preston's PS2 games console. It was so old, she wasn't sure it even worked, but she'd not touched either of her sons' bedrooms after they had moved out, except to dust, vacuum, and give each room a tidy.

Her own bedroom was just as bad and, although she was tempted to start picking things up off the floor, she resisted the urge, knowing that the police would need to see everything just as it was. The only thing she did was to check the contents of her jewellery box. As she suspected, all her good stuff was gone. Not that she had much, just her wedding and engagement rings, a gold and diamond necklace, and a small gold watch her grandmother had left her. It was lucky she was wearing everything else of value, like her mother's rings (on her right hand, not her left) and the little sapphire and diamond earrings her father had bought her mother for their fortieth wedding anniversary.

She went back downstairs to wait for the police, feeling too uncomfortable to remain in her bedroom for a second longer, and debated whether she should phone Ivan, but decided against it. He had enough on his plate with his business, without her adding to his worries. She was a grown woman, and people were burgled every day. She could deal with this herself; she'd dealt with everything else on her own, hadn't she?

However, she did need to get someone in to repair the door, and sharpish too. She could hardly go to bed leaving the house unsecured, although the thought of going to bed in a house which suddenly no longer felt like her home, filled her with dread.

She rang Paul. It seemed only natural; besides, he'd be able to secure the door for her until she could get it replaced.

He was quick to check that she was all right, and even quicker to come to her aid, arriving just as the police did, remaining in the background while they took a statement and looked around.

'I doubt if you'll get any of it back, my love,' one of the officers said to her, and Candice wondered when the police had begun taking twelve-year-olds into the force. The policeman who had just spoken looked younger than Preston.

'I didn't think I would,' she sighed, tears welling up as she thought of her grandmother's watch and the computer. At least she was insured, and although the watch could never, ever be replaced, she actually stored nothing on her hard drive that wasn't backed up to at least two separate clouds. So, really, the only things she had lost which meant anything to her, was the watch and that silly copper kettle.

The police officers gave her an incident number, told her they would send someone around to fingerprint the back door, the desk, and her jewellery box, as well as a few places in the boys' rooms, then they departed.

'Come here,' Paul said, opening his arms and inviting her in for a hug. She went to him without hesitation, feeling the need for some human contact and comfort.

He wrapped himself around her. It felt so good to be held, that she broke down and sobbed against his shirt.

'There, there,' he crooned into her hair, and she felt his warm breath on her ear and heard the solid rhythmic thump of his heart as he rubbed her back.

When she was all cried out and had regained some measure of control, he released her and stepped back, giving her the space and the time she needed to compose herself.

'No need to apologise,' he told her for the second time, after she said sorry yet again. 'It's bound to be a shock. Something like this is enough to upset anyone. Let's put the kettle on and make a cup of tea, then set about clearing the mess up.'

At that, she burst into fresh tears, but these were intermingled with smiles and sniffles as she explained that 'the buggers have taken my kettle.'

'Never mind, you've got a saucepan, haven't you?' he asked and when she pointed to the cupboard under the sink, he drew out a small pan and filled it with water.

While it was coming to the boil, Candice plodded slowly upstairs to splash some water on her face. Christ! They'd not even left the bathroom alone, she noticed when she saw the bathroom cabinet door ajar. There hadn't been a lot in there, and she gave a dry bark of a laugh when she saw the Canestan cream, which she'd bought when she'd had thrush a couple of years back and which was now long past its use-by date, was still on the shelf. What had they been expecting – hard drugs? The only drugs she had in the house were painkillers, and if the burglars were that desperate, they were welcome to them.

Feeling more like her old self, she went back downstairs where a cup of steaming hot tea waited for her, with a packet of digestive biscuits sitting next to it.

Paul really was a lovely man, she thought yet again, as she sipped the tea and nibbled on a biscuit. While she had been upstairs, he'd cleaned up the glass, wiped the countertops down and had put everything away.

The living room looked worse than it actually was, the damage being only minimal. The main casualty was a knocked-over ornament that Malcolm's mother had given her, which she didn't like anyway. The rest of it was simply a matter of righting one of the dining chairs and putting the cushions back on the sofa.

By the time that was done, a man had arrived to take fingerprints (she'd never had that done before), then he left to let Candice sort her back door out. Or rather, Paul did the sorting, while Candice looked on.

'I'll secure it for now, but you really need to get it replaced as soon as possible,' Paul advised. 'Preferably with a door with a mortice lock. It'll reduce your insurance too. You have got insurance, haven't you?'

Candice nodded, saying, 'I should give them a call,' and she went off to phone them while Paul finished up.

After that, it was only right and proper that she invited him to stay for a meal. If the truth be known, she really didn't want to be on her own in the house right now. The odds of the burglars (for some reason she thought of them in the plural) coming back were slim; after all, she had nothing else worth stealing. All the same, she couldn't help feeling a little vulnerable.

'What were you thinking of making for supper?' Paul asked with a twinkle in his eye. 'Because if I don't fancy it, I'm off home for some beans on toast.'

'How does spaghetti bolognese grab you?' she asked, checking inside the fridge just in case the intruders taken it upon themselves to nick the beef mince. It was still there, and she breathed a sigh of relief. No doubt, she'd be having these kinds of thoughts for a while yet.

'Lovely. I'll just go and wash my hands.'

She listened to him walk into the hall, hearing the sounds of the downstairs cloakroom door opening and closing. It was good to have someone else in the house, she thought, and she realised just how much she missed having another person around.

She put the spaghetti on to boil, then browned off the mince, onion, and garlic, while Paul washed and chopped some salad and laid the table, all with the minimum of fuss. Even after nearly twenty years of marriage, Malcolm had needed prompting and prodding every step of the way, and not only in the kitchen, either. As soon as he'd stepped through their front door, he appeared to have sloughed off his professional banker skin along with a total inability to think for himself.

Candice and Paul worked side by side in companionable silence. For her part, she was possibly still too shocked to say a great deal, and she guessed Paul was giving her some space, letting the mundane and familiar task of cooking go some way to settling her frazzled nerves.

She hadn't been sure she was all that hungry when she'd suggested food, thinking she was too upset to eat, but by the time it was ready, she found herself getting a little peckish, so she dug in with some degree of enthusiasm. Of course, it helped that she had someone to share her normally solitary evening meal with, because it was never much fun eating on her own. She was very grateful to Paul for having agreed to stay to keep her company. He probably had much better things to do this evening than babysit her, and she said as much.

'Nonsense!' he replied. 'That's what friends are for.'

Friends? Was that what they were? After the (rather passionate) kisses they had shared, Candice had begun to hope they were heading away from friendship and more towards a relationship. It seemed she was wrong.

Her heart sank to her sensible shoes, and she suppressed a sigh. Oh, well, she was grateful to have Paul as a friend, although if that's all they were to each other, then the kissing would have to stop, because she didn't want to leave herself open to being any more hurt than she already was.

'How much do I owe you?' she asked, determined to put her heart back in the little box where it had resided for the last few years, and to stop being so silly.

'Nothing,' he replied. 'Don't worry about it.'

'Oh, but I do. I feel awful dragging you out to sort out my problems.'

'It's my job,' he said around a mouthful of bolognese.

'Yes, but jobs need to be paid for,' she countered. 'I insist on it. You can't go around doing things for free.'

'OK, then I insist on paying you for this.' He waved a hand over his bowl of spaghetti.

'Excuse me?'

'How much would a meal like this cost in a restaurant?' he asked.

'That's not the same thing at all, and you know it!'

'No, it's not – it's better. I'd have been on my own tonight with a frozen ready-meal, eating it in front of a mediocre football match on the telly. Instead, I get to eat lovely home-cooked food, in the company of a wonderful lady.'

Candice's cheeks grew warm. 'It's only a bit of spaghetti,' she argued.

'And that's only a bit of wood and a few nails,' Paul countered, his eyes doing their lovely twinkling thing as he pointed to the newly-secured backdoor. 'Do you have anyone who can sort you out with a new door?' he asked.

She shook her head.

'I'll give you the number of Wychbold Windows,' he offered. 'They'll see you right and won't charge an arm and a leg, either. I've used them a few times. Tell them Paul Olsen sent you and you might get a bit of a discount.'

'Thank you,' Candice said. 'I honestly don't know what I would have done without you.'

Paul gazed at her steadily. 'You'd have coped,' he said. 'You'd have rung someone else and they'd have done exactly what I did. Minus the bolognese, I hope.'

'I don't feed just any old workmen,' she replied primly, gathering up their empty plates.

'Glad to hear it.' Paul stood to help, carrying the Parmesan cheese to the fridge before putting the salt and pepper pots on one of the countertops, then wiping the cleared table over with a dishcloth.

'I really enjoy your company,' he said softly, coming up behind her as she was standing at the sink, and letting the water run until it was hot.

Candice turned to face him. 'I enjoy yours, too,' she responded in a small voice.

'You're a remarkable woman, Candice Summerville,' he said and gathered her into his arms. He bent his head. His lips touched hers gently at first, but with increasing intensity, and he kissed her until she was breathless. This was getting to be a habit – a wonderful one!

'It might be too soon to say it, but what the hell, I've always worn my heart on my sleeve,' Paul said. 'I think I'm falling for you.'

He looked so worried that Candice reached up to stroke his cheek, feeling the soft hairs of his neatly trimmed beard under her fingers. 'I think I've already fallen,' she replied.

'Oh, shit!' Paul let go of her with such suddenness Candice wondered what on earth she'd done wrong. When he moved her to one side and reached behind her to turn off the tap, she breathed a small sigh of relief.

'That was a close call,' he said. 'You don't need any more upsets tonight.' He checked his watch. 'I'd better be off. I've got an early start in the morning, replacing fence panels for an old couple in Barbourne, and I'd like to finish it before the day gets too hot.'

He wrapped his arms around her again and Candice snuggled into his chest. 'Will you be all right on your own?'

he asked her.

'Are you offering to stay?' Her voice was muffled, hiding her panic. Was she ready to take their relationship to the next level? She wasn't sure. Did he expect more from her, now that they'd cleared the air regarding the friendship thing?

'If you want me to,' he said, stroking the back of her head. 'I can sleep on the couch.'

Candice didn't know whether to feel relieved or disappointed. 'You would do no such thing,' she said, 'not when I've got two spare bedrooms. Anyway, I'll be fine. I doubt the burglars will come back. They've done their worst and there's nothing much left for them to take.'

'There is one thing,' Paul said, without releasing her. 'Your heart.'

Candice was silent for a moment, feeling Paul's increasing tension in the way he held her. Then she said, 'I think it's been taken already,' and pulled back to look at him.

Paul's answer was another deep, wonderful kiss.

It was then she realised it was true – Paul really did have her heart, and she hoped to God he'd take good care of it, because she understood that she was well and truly in love with him.

CHAPTER 23

Candice had just returned from a lovely, long, brisk walk and was still on a little bit of a high from the exercise, as she prepared her salad, before eating it on her lap in front of the telly. A David Attenborough documentary about lions was on and she watched it avidly, although she'd seen it before, until, with her meal eaten and her lone plate washed and dried, she collapsed on the sofa once more with a mug of tea in her hand.

She was almost asleep when the phone jerked her awake.

It was nearly ten o'clock; who on earth could be ringing her at this time, she wondered. Her heart did a nasty lurch. Phone calls this late in the evening could only mean one thing – trouble – and her first thought was for her children. Preston was always doing the most dangerous and foolhardy things, and she worried about him constantly. She worried about both her children, but Preston more than Ivan. She hadn't seen what Preston had been up to recently, because he hadn't posted any photos of himself hanging off a rock halfway up a cliff, or jumping off a plane, or throwing himself into a raging river with nothing but a life vest and a helmet keeping him from certain death. She prayed he was all right.

'Hello?' Her voice was quiet and tremulous. She almost wished she'd ignored the ringing. What she didn't know, couldn't hurt her, right? But that wasn't true either, was it, because not knowing could hurt very much indeed.

'Mum?'

'Ivan?'

'Yeah.'

'Is everything OK?'

'Yeah, everything's fine. Listen, Mum—'

'What about your brother?'

'What about him?'

'Is he all right?'

'How should I know?'

'You're not calling about him, then?'

'No, if you'd just listen for a minute…'

'Sorry.' Relief washed over her, making her feel weak, sick, and more than a little bit tingly, as if the adrenalin had shot to every part of her body in anticipation of some awful news.

'We're coming to lunch on Sunday,' her son announced.

Candice laughed. 'Could you say that again? I thought you said you are coming to lunch on Sunday.'

'That's right, we are.'

She dropped the phone in surprise and had to fish it out from under her feet.

'We? Okaaaay.' Candice didn't know what else to say. This was a first in her and her eldest son's history. Since he'd officially moved out, he'd never once invited himself for lunch; she'd always been the one to ask, cajole even, if she hadn't seen him for a while. Yet here he was, asking (or, to be more accurate, *telling*) her that he was coming to lunch on Sunday.

She was glad she was already sitting down, otherwise she might have fallen over.

'You said "we",' Candice remembered. 'Is your brother coming, too?'

'What's this fixation with Preston? And no, he's not coming, he's in Dubai.'

He was? That was the first she'd heard of it. What was

he doing there, she wondered. Camel wrestling, sand dune skiing (she knew there was such a thing, because she'd seen it on TV), jumping off that ridiculously high hotel? She sincerely hoped it wasn't the latter.

'I'll be bringing Sharna,' her eldest was saying, cutting into her thoughts.

'Oh, lovely.' Candice sighed with pleasure. At last, she was going to meet what she hoped was Ivan's future wife, and she was both excited and petrified at the same time. What if she didn't like the girl? Or think she was good enough for her son? What if Sharna didn't like *her*?

'How long have you been going out with her?' she asked. 'You must tell me all about her!'

'We've been seeing each other for about eight months, and she moved in about a week ago.'

Really? She'd moved in and Ivan hadn't thought to tell his mother? 'You should have brought her to see me before now,' Candice grumbled.

'I didn't want to jinx it,' her son explained. 'I wanted to make sure it wasn't a flash in the pan before I introduced her to my mother. Sharna's been nagging to meet you for ages,' he added.

'She has? What's she like?'

'Smart, pretty, great fun,' Ivan replied. 'And a vegan. Would you be able to rustle up something she could eat? But could you do one of your chicken dinners for me, please? I haven't had a decent roast for ages.'

'I'm sure I can cook both,' Candice said, already starting to panic about preparing a vegan dish, but trying to keep the worry out of her voice. Malcolm and the boys had always been meat and two veg people, so that's what she knew how to cook.

As soon as they'd said their goodbyes, Candice used her mobile phone to look up a few recipes. As she scrolled, discarding one after the other, she could hardly contain her excitement – Sharna was the only girl Ivan would have brought home to meet her, and he himself admitted it was serious.

Candice couldn't wait! As she searched through various recipes she found herself looking at hats, too. The mother-of-the-groom simply had to have a hat!

Oh, and she must call Paul to tell him, because they had planned to go out for the day on Sunday. For a second, she debated whether to ask him to lunch too, but she decided against it. Knowing he would understand, without her having to explain, that she wanted to meet Sharna without having Ivan ask the inevitable question of who was Paul and why he was there. There would be plenty of time to introduce her boyfriend (she glowed at the thought, even if the term was a bit teenagerish) later, on her own terms and when she was ready.

CHAPTER 24

Candice had been unable to sit still since the phone call from her son, and she put it down to nerves; she was possibly about to meet her future daughter-in-law and the thought filled her with a mixture of excitement and dread. What if she didn't like the girl? Or worse, what if Candice thought she was the wrong person for her son? His choice of girlfriend was up to him, but she'd heard so many stories from other women her age of daughters-in-law from hell, that she couldn't help being somewhat fearful.

She vowed to herself that no matter what she thought of Sharna, she would make her welcome. The last thing she wanted to do was to alienate the girl right from the start, and she had to respect Ivan's choice.

All day yesterday, she had been restless, so much so that even the usually oblivious Dermott had commented on it. When she'd finished work, she'd hurried to the supermarket to hunt for something (anything) suitable for a vegan to eat, coming home with a humongous pile of vegetables and little else. Although she did intend to cook Sharna a garlicky mushroom penne, with the supermarket's "free from" range of pasta, of course. She just hoped it wouldn't be free from taste too, because she wanted to make a good impression on her son's girlfriend.

Sunday morning saw Candice cleaning frantically. She knew Ivan won't even notice, but Sharna probably would, and she wanted everything to look its best. She also wanted to appear capable and in control, not pathetic and in danger of letting herself go. Ivan had a habit of coming across as the big "I am" since his father had walked out on her, and he tended to be a bit bossy at times, especially when he thought she wasn't coping. Admittedly, she hadn't been particularly good at being without Malcolm when he'd first left, but she'd had to learn to cope without him, hadn't she? She thought she'd done a pretty good job of it. She'd made sure the boys were housed and fed, and had clean clothes, and she'd carried on ferrying them to football and rugby, and extra tuition in maths for Preston, and guitar lessons for Ivan because his life-long ambition was to play in a band, an ambition he had quickly backtracked on when he realised that playing a guitar didn't come easy and that he would actually have to spend hours practising.

Anyway, now that both her children were grown, Ivan was trying to reverse their roles. As if she'd let him do that! He might be an adult, but he was still her little boy and she resented his implication that she was the one who needed looking after. She wasn't that old!

When Candice heard Ivan's key in the lock, she was standing in the kitchen basting some roast potatoes. Wiping her hands on a tea towel, she went out to the hall to greet him.

He was alone.

'Where's Sharna?' she asked, looking over his shoulder as he shut the door.

'Not here,' Ivan said. 'Sorry.' He did look very contrite. Or was that worry she saw in his eyes?

Candice didn't like to ask if they'd had a row, but she suspected they might have by the look on her son's face. She bit her lip. It really was very inconsiderate of him not to have let her know, especially since she'd gone out of her way to prepare a vegan dish. Oh well, perhaps Ivan would take it home for Sharna to eat later. Anyway, she'd suggest it after they had eaten their own meal.

'Lunch will be half an hour or so yet,' she said. 'Why don't you go into the living room and put the telly on?'

'No, it's all right.'

He followed her out to the kitchen and stood lurking as she popped the potatoes back in the oven. It made her feel slightly uncomfortable, as if he was about to do something, or say something, that she wouldn't like.

He opened his mouth and took a breath. She thought "here it comes", but all he said was, 'I'll just nip out to the garage.'

She knew exactly why he was going out there; it was to look at Jelly Bean. She was surprised, now she'd come to think of it, that he'd waited this long before he turned up to inspect her car. She was confident there was nothing wrong with it, but he'd find something anyway. He was a bit like his father in that respect – always had to prod, pick, and poke.

So it was with bated breath and a vague sense of dread that she heard him slam the garage door shut and come back into the kitchen.

Wait for it… she thought.

'It's tiny,' he said, followed by, 'I don't know how you manage to get in and out of it.'

Before he had a chance to say anything else, Candice interjected, 'It suits me very well, thank you, and I don't care if you don't like it because you don't have to drive it. If I do get stuck, I'll remember to call the fire brigade and not you. As for the boot, what exactly am I supposed to put in it? When I go to the supermarket, there's only me to buy for. When I go out anywhere, there is only my stuff to put in the boot, so just how much room do you think I need?'

Ivan shook his head. 'I was going to say that I like it,' he replied, taking the wind right out of her sails.

'You do?'

'It's a classic, and it's in good nick, too,' he added. 'I bet it's fun to drive.'

'You can have a go later, if you want,' she offered, feeling more magnanimous now that Jelly Bean had his approval.

'Maybe another time,' Ivan replied, and once again Candice got the impression something was bothering her son. Please don't let him have his heart broken, she pleaded silently, not just when he'd found someone he liked enough to ask to move in with him.

Candice removed Sharna's meal from the oven, and put it one side to cool for Ivan take home for his girlfriend. Then she lifted the chicken out and wrestled it onto a plate, leaving the roasting tin free for her to make the gravy in. While she stirred and tasted, Ivan carved the bird.

She glanced at him now and again, thinking how much like his father he looked as he held a knife in one hand and a long fork in the other, pinning the chicken in place. He even had the same expression on his face as he concentrated, minus the poking out tongue. Many a Sunday Candice had made the gravy while Malcolm had set about carving whichever slab of meat she'd roasted. Her son was a chip off the old block, all right, and it gave her a pang. If she squinted, she could almost imagine it was Malcolm standing in her kitchen and that the years had rolled back to when the children were tiny and her broken heart was still in the future.

'How's work going?' she asked, partly to break the silence and mostly because she was interested.

Ivan was a marketing executive, with his own business and several employees, and she was inordinately proud of him. Every so often, she would Google the name of the company to see how many hits it got. She didn't think much of his website, though, and knew she could make a better job of it if he'd let her, but he wouldn't, so she had to be content with making the odd helpful comment now and again, which she was certain he ignored.

'Good, yeah, really good,' he replied.

Candice waited for him to say more, but that was it, so they ate in relative silence, with only the occasional "pass the salt, please" from Ivan, and a "lovely weather we're having" from her. They simply had very little to talk about, and absolutely nothing in common. It was a shame, really, but that's the way it was. There was no law to say that mothers and sons had to be best friends.

It was only when she rose to her feet to stack the plates, that Ivan finally got around to the reason for his visit. Candice had seriously wondered why he had bothered to come at all considering Sharna wasn't with him, but it did reinforce her idea that his intention hadn't been to show off a potential bride-to-be.

'Actually, the business isn't so great,' he admitted. 'I've… erm… got a bit of a cash-flow issue,' he said, handing her his empty plate.

'Oh?'

'Yeah, it's serious. I need an injection of funds right now. Or at the latest, in the next couple of months. Even the promise of cash might be enough.'

'I don't understand. Who would you have to make this promise to?'

He shrugged. 'The bank, a few creditors, you know….' He trailed off.

No, she didn't know.

'I've… um got clients who owe me money and haven't paid yet, that's all. It's causing a bit of an issue.' He emphasised the word "issue".

'Have you asked for this money you're owed?'

'Of course I have,' her son sighed. 'They say they're waiting for some big invoices to be paid to them. As soon as those are realised, they can pay me. But in the meantime, I've got bills of my own.'

'Apply for an overdraft,' Candice suggested. 'I'm sure you can get one on your business account. What does your father say?'

'I… um… I've already got an overdraft, and it's at its

limit. Mum…' He leaned forward and put his hands on the table, steepling his fingers under his chin. 'It's like this, see. My accountant has recommended I apply for bankruptcy on behalf of the company.'

'That's ridiculous!' Candice cried. 'He can't say that.'

'He has,' Ivan replied dryly. 'Unless I can show him that funds will go into the business account shortly, the company will fold.'

'I don't have much,' she began, 'though, I've got a bit put by. It's not more than a thousand or so, but if it'll help?'

He looked so deflated, her heart went out to him. If she had more she'd give it to him; after all, that's what parents did, help their children out, but it sounded as though he needed a lot more than her paltry savings.

'Thanks for the offer, Mum,' he said. 'But it'll take a lot more than that.' He stood up and kissed her on the cheek.

'Sorry, Ivan, I wish I could help you, but I simply don't have the money.'

'I know you don't, Mum, and I wouldn't take if from you if you did. I just thought you should know, that's all.'

He left soon after, saying that he had to get back because he had some work to do. 'You never stop working when you're self-employed,' he told her. 'It's impossible to switch off.'

Then he was out of the door and climbing into his car before she could say there was jam roly-poly with custard for afters. She ate hers on her lap in front of the telly, watching the screen with a distant, abstracted look on her face and the volume turned down.

That explained why he hadn't brought his girlfriend with him, Candice realised. He'd wanted to tell his mother in private that things were looking bleak for him on the business front.

She didn't blame Ivan for not discussing his problems with his father, but Malcolm worked in a bank after all, and he knew his way around finance. It was only right

Malcolm should know, and perhaps he could do something to help. It pained her to admit it, but she needed her ex-husband's advice. Malcolm was far more experienced in this sort of thing than she ever would be. He'd know the best thing to do to help their son. Besides, she had an idea of something she could do which might help. She had a day off on Tuesday and was going into town anyway to have her hair trimmed, so she decided to pop into the bank for a quick chat beforehand.

Decision made, she turned the sound up on the telly and settled back to watch a documentary on Egyptian hieroglyphs while her lunch went down, then she'd treat Jelly Bean to a wash and wax.

CHAPTER 25

The bank was only up the road from the library, which had turned out to be both a blessing and a curse. Candice had found it a blessing when she was still married to Malcolm, because she used to pop in during her lunch break for a quick chat although he was often too busy to talk to her. He used to drop her off in the morning and pick her up after work. It had been a comfort to know he was so close, almost within touching distance, a short walk away if she ever needed him. Not that she often had, but the knowing was everything.

The knowing had become practically unbearable when he'd left her, hence the curse part of the equation.

She used to find herself standing outside the impressive old building, without remembering how she had come to be there, tears welling, her chest constricted with the pain of his abandonment. To her shame and horror, she had become something of a stalker, hanging around the jewellers opposite, with her back to the street, vainly trying to watch for him through the window's reflection. Until one day, the shop manager had confronted her. Looking back (hindsight was a wonderful thing) it must have seemed she was scoping the place out, working out how to conduct a grab and run on the display of silver necklaces and bracelets in one of the windows. The other window had far more expensive and exciting items on show, like glittering diamond rings and Rolex watches, but the angle was wrong – she couldn't see the bank's staff entrance in its clean reflective glass – so she pretended to be interested in silver instead.

As soon as a fast food place had opened up next door, she had taken to sitting in there during her lunch break, some of her attention on her sandwich and drink, most of it on the alleyway down the side of the bank and the staff entrance it housed.

She never knew whether Malcolm had been aware of what she was doing, or the way she tortured herself, but if he had been, he'd never mentioned it when he'd come to pick the boys up.

It had taken her a long time to wean herself off the habit. It had taken her even longer to accept that he was gone for good.

It felt strange to walk into the bank again. Everything was familiar, yet different. They'd moved things around. There were fewer tellers' windows for a start, and there was a kind of reception desk in the middle which hadn't been there before.

She hesitated, wondering what to do and who she should speak to.

'Can I help you?' a voice asked from behind and she whirled around.

'Erm…' Candice hesitated.

'What is it you need today?' She had her name (Michaela Hickmott) on her badge underneath the word, "Associate".

I need to speak to my ex-husband, Candice nearly said, then changed her response to, 'Is Mr Summerville available?'

'Do you have an appointment?' The woman was polite and professional, and Candice wondered if she donned her smile along with her uniform before she left the house in the morning, because it didn't quite reach her eyes.

'Um, no, but—'

'I'm sorry, you really do need to make an appointment.

Is there anything *I* can help you with today?'

If there was one thing guaranteed to get Candice's back up, it was being interrupted. Another thing was being on the receiving end of "that look", the sort that some women gave other women, the sort that swept over you from head to foot in a split-second, making a judgement according to what the looker saw.

Candice noticed the woman's glance rest briefly on Candice's feet, clad in her sensible shoes, before coming back up to her face.

'Yes, there is something you can help me with,' Candice said firmly, her hackles up. 'You can tell Mr Summerville that Mrs Summerville is here to see him and would appreciate a quick word.'

'Oh.' Michaela Hickmott's expression cleared a little, the painted-on smile becoming a little more genuine. 'You should have said you were his mother. I'll see if he's free.'

Candice's mouth dropped open, but before she could find a suitable retort, the woman turned smartly on her four-inch heels and trotted off in the direction of the reception desk.

Mother? *Mother!*

Candice took a deep breath, holding her temper in check. It was vying with humiliation in her head and she wanted the ground to open up and swallow her.

Awkwardly, she waited for Michaela and glared at her as the woman chatted on the phone for a minute, before ending the call and returning to Candice.

'I'm sorry, Mrs Summerville, but Mr Summerville isn't working at this branch today. Shall I tell him you called in?'

Candice took another breath and let it out in a huffy sound. 'Is he in tomorrow?'

'I believe so.'

'I'll come back,' she decided. 'Actually, I *will* make an appointment. Does he have any available?'

'I can check for you.'

'Good. Book me in. Anytime will be fine.' She'd

arrange to take her lunch whenever the appointment was.

'If you'd like to follow me, I'll check his diary.'

When they reached the desk, the woman pecked away at the keyboard with over-long nails, then looked up from the screen.

'He has two slots, one at ten-thirty and one at twelve.'

'Let's say twelve. Oh, and I might be Mrs Summerville but I'm not his mother,' Candice said. 'I'm his ex-wife.'

She turned on her dowdy, flat heel and stalked off, head held high. It was only when she was outside, did she register what the expression on the bank employee's face had been – shock and dismay had been there, but so had pity – and Candice guessed the woman had probably been thinking that it was no wonder Candice was the ex-wife and not the current Mrs Summerville.

That does it, she thought.

She marched outside and stomped furiously to the hairdressers. It was time she had a decent trim and colour.

CHAPTER 26

'So, are you going anywhere nice on holiday?' The girl was about the same age as Preston and wore the same bored expression as he often used to.

'Um... no. I haven't planned anything yet.' Candice never planned holidays now, not since the kids stopped wanting to go with her. There didn't seem much point or fun in going anywhere by herself.

'So, just a tidy up, is it?' the hairdresser asked.

Eh? Tidy up the house on her two weeks off? Hardly, although she might slap a coat of emulsion on the living room walls, if she could be bothered.

'How much do you want me to cut off?' the girl continued with a long-suffering sigh when Candice took her time answering. She ran her fingers through Candice's badly-in-need-of-her-roots-doing hair, lifting the ends to peer at them. Oh, that's what she meant, Candice realised and felt a bit of an idiot.

'Where's Denise?' Candice wanted to know. Denise owned the salon. Candice had been coming here for years and Denise always did her hair. She knew exactly how Candice liked it done.

'So, she broke a leg, didn't she?' the girl replied.

'Did she? I mean, oh dear, that's a shame.'

'So, I'm your stylist for today.' The girl sounded even more bored than a minute ago, if that was possible, and Candice wasn't exactly thrilled with the idea either.

'So, how much?' the hairdresser persisted.

'How much what?'

'Do you want off?' The stylist left "stupid" off the end of the sentence, but Candice heard it all the same.

'The usual,' Candice replied.

'So, what's the usual?'

'An inch or two. And my roots need doing.'

'So, Denise keeps a chart for each customer. I'll just go and check your colours.'

Candice wished the girl would stop saying "so". It really was quite annoying. She stared at her reflection in the extremely unflattering mirror, and wondered if it would be more prudent to wait until Denise was back. Denise knew what Candice liked, and she didn't start every sentence with "so" either. She also didn't bother asking her where she was going on holiday. Denise didn't speak much at all, come to think of it, which was exactly the way Candice liked it.

The stylist was back. 'So, we'll get you shampooed, then we'll start on the colour, yeah?'

'Yeah. I mean, great. Wonderful.' She was here now, she might as well bite the bullet and get this over with. Having her hair done was just another chore, like cleaning the oven, or changing the sheets on her bed. It actually gave her less pleasure really, because there was little to compare with the "ahhh" of slipping into a fresh, clean bed at the end of a long day.

The girl must have sensed her reluctance because when Candice stood, waiting to be led towards those singularly uncomfortable neck-breaking row of sinks, the stylist looked her straight in the eye, her expression earnest. 'Do you trust me?' the girl demanded.

What else could Candice say but, 'Of course I do.'

'Good. Leave it to me. You're going to walk out of here looking like a million dollars.'

Candice sincerely doubted that, but as long as the colour, cut, and blow dry didn't cost a million dollars she resigned herself to letting Miss So-So colour and trim her hair. After all, Denise would hardly have taken the youngster on if the girl didn't know what she was doing, would she?

The stylist *clearly* didn't know what she was doing Candice thought an hour later, as she stared at her reflection in horror.

No gentle caramel colour for her. Oh no. What beamed out of the mirror was a colour bright enough to bring down light aircraft. Her head bore a cap of platinum hair. Peroxide blond, her mother would have called it. Now almost white, her previously ash-blond locks also sported some silver and gold highlights. She looked like something you'd find in a cheap jeweller's window.

'What have you done?' she wailed.

'It's gorgeous, innit?' the girl replied. 'I love this colour.'

'I don't,' was Candice's sharp reply. 'Change it back.'

'Can't. If I put another colour on top of this...' The stylist shuddered theatrically. 'Let's just say, it wouldn't be good.'

'It's not good now,' Candice retorted.

'It will be when I've cut it,' the girl insisted. 'I'm thinking pixie.'

I'm thinking I need to leave, Candice thought, but she stayed where she was, staring at herself in dismay. How on earth was she going to face the world looking like that?

'Pixie,' Candice repeated, woodenly.

'Yeah, you've got the cheekbones to carry it off. See?' She held Candice's damp hair away from the sides of her face. 'So, having shorter hair will lift your look. The bob don't do nothing for you.'

'My look doesn't need lifting, thank you very much.'

'Oh, but it does. It'll take years off you. Stop you looking so grannyish.'

'I'm not a granny,' Candice said indignantly.

'So, you don't wanna look like you are then, do ya? See

how the new colour complements your complexion? So will a new cut.' The girl pouted. 'You said you trusted me.'

'I thought you were going to put my usual colour on.'

'God no! It made you look old.'

'I'm not old.'

The girl's eyes flashed. 'I mean... you *are*, a bit ... but you don't have to look it. Why would anyone want to look old, if they didn't have to?'

'Did they teach you this in college?'

'Eh?'

'How to insult your customers.'

The stylist's lip wobbled, and her eyes filled with tears.

Oh lord, now she'd made the girl cry. Candice felt a right cow, but the child had to learn that it was no good alienating the customer.

'I just wanted to make you look good,' the stylist said, a hitch in her voice.

'I appreciate that, I really do, but you simply can't do whatever you like and ignore what your clients want.'

'You said you trusted me,' the girl repeated.

'And I do, but...' Candice trailed off. Was the colour really that bad? While they were talking, her hair had started to dry a little and the shade didn't look quite so dramatic. Or maybe she was simply becoming more used to it. Either way, she was finally starting to see what her stylist had meant by "lifting her face".

She closed her eyes, counted to ten, then opened them again. 'Go on, give me a pixie,' she blurted, before she could change her mind.

She very much hoped she wasn't going to regret the impulse.

CHAPTER 27

Candice caught sight of herself in the shop window and a little jolt ran through her. The woman reflected in it looked nothing like her. She was a complete stranger, wearing Candice's clothes. Even her face was different – both the shape of it and her complexion. She actually had cheekbones for the first time ever, and her skin seemed to glow despite having no make-up on.

Now, that was a thought. What if she treated herself to some make-up to go with her new hair? She could do with buying a new mascara if she was honest; her old one was gloopy and starting to dry up.

Since she was in town, she decided she may as well pop into Boots. But when she stepped in through the door of the shop, she was overwhelmed by the choice. There must be at least twenty different stands. She had absolutely no idea where to start.

'Can I help you?'

Candice turned around to find an elderly lady by her side. A perfectly made-up, immaculately presented lady, with grey-stranded hair gathered into a bun at the back of her neck. Candice touched her own newly-shorn locks self-consciously.

'Ah, new hair-do?' the older woman guessed. 'And now you need a new face to go with it? Been there, done that.'

Candice peered at the employee name-tag. 'Er... yes,

please, Agatha.' She gestured at the stands helplessly. 'There's just too much choice.'

'Do you fancy a make-over, if you've got the time?'

'Only if I end up looking as glamorous as you,' Candice joked.

'Oh, no dear, you won't look like *me* when I've finished with you – you'll look like *you*. The best *you* you can possibly be.' She gave Candice a sympathetic look. 'Don't worry, I'll show you how to use everything I put on your face and explain what it's for. Are you game?'

Candice nodded. She certainly was, and at least make-up could be washed off if she didn't like it. Unlike hair.

'Love your hair, by the way,' Agatha said. 'Where did you get it done?' The woman did her best to try to put Candice at ease, chatting away as she led her to a make-up station, divesting her of her coat on the way.

'Right, first things first,' she said when Candice was settled on a stool. 'Do you moisturise?'

'Um, no.'

'You should, and you should use a really good quality one. You can skimp on your cleanser.' She leaned in close to whisper. 'Don't tell anyone I said this, but if you splash your face with cold water, you don't need to tone. But you do need to moisturise, firstly because as we get older, we need to nourish our skin, and secondly, because it provides a base for our foundation.'

'I don't wear foundation,' Candice pointed out.

'You do now. See that woman over there?' Agatha pointed behind her and Candice peeped around Agatha's shoulder for a better look. Then did a double-take. The woman wore so much make-up she must have used a trowel to spread it on.

'That's what we *don't* want you looking like,' Agatha hissed, and Candice let out a surprised laugh. The sales assistant continued, 'The idea of make-up is to enhance the things you want to enhance, and draw attention away from those things you prefer not to be noticed. You certainly don't want people to notice your make-up first, and you second.'

There followed one of the most delightful hours Candice could ever remember spending. Agatha was knowledgeable, and was prepared to wipe and start again if Candice didn't like something. She also wasn't precious about the cost either, presenting her client with a mix of both more expensive and cheaper items, and giving her advice like, 'Don't skimp on your foundation, but a less expensive blusher will do the same job as a top-name brand.'

Candice soaked it up like a camel preparing for a long desert trek. By the time Agatha had finished with her, she was thrilled with the results.

She was still Candice, but a fresher more vibrant (and, dare she say it, more youthful?) Candice gazed back at her out of the mirror.

'All done. What do you think?' Agatha took a step back to admire her work.

Candice was speechless, but her delighted smile and the tears welling in her eyes told the woman all she needed to know.

'I hope you don't mind me saying.' Agatha lowered her voice. 'Please don't take this the wrong way, but your clothes don't do anything for you.'

'They don't?'

Agatha shook her head, her eyes full of worry. 'I don't mean to be rude. I'm sorry, I shouldn't have mentioned anything, but with your new hair and make-up, your head is saying one thing and your clothes are saying something else entirely.'

'They are?'

Another nod. 'Looking at your face, I'd put you in your late thirties, early forties. If I was going on your clothes alone, I'd say you were seventy. At least.'

'Thank you. I think. I'm nearly fifty, so I'll take that as a compliment – not the clothes, of course, although, I always wear these kinds of things.'

'Well, don't you think it's time for a change?' Agatha leaned back against the counter and examined Candice critically, from neck to toe. 'You've got a good figure, from what I can see under the jumper and pleated skirt. Show it off, strut your stuff.'

'I wouldn't know where to start,' Candice objected, hopping down off the stool and reaching for her bag.

'Look.' Agatha caught hold of Candice's shoulders and swirled her so she was facing a mirrored column.

What Candice saw looking back at her was a bit of a shock.

Bloody hell, she really did need some new clothes!

'Go next door, they've got a sale on. Ask for Trudy – she'll sort you out, and she won't tell you fibs, either. If she thinks something doesn't suit you, she'll tell you.'

Candice was doubtful. Yes, she could do with a new skirt or two, because let's face it, the ones she had were years old, but she wasn't up for anything too drastic. She'd stick to her usual elasticated waists and pleated skirts, in whatever colours were in fashion this season. If she liked them.

Or maybe she'd stick to black and grey, and buy a couple of scarves to brighten her wardrobe up. It was the wrong time of year to be looking for scarves but someone, somewhere, would have a few in stock, surely. Lightweight fabric, pretty colours – but not too bright or gaudy…

'Give me five minutes and I'll take you,' Agatha said, to Candice's dismay. 'I'm due to go on my break and I don't fancy being cooped up in the staffroom.'

'Er, thanks, but you don't have to,' Candice objected.

'Oh, but I think I do,' the other woman replied.

Was this a conspiracy? Were Agatha and this Trudi-woman in cahoots? Had Candice found herself in the middle of some commission scam? Five minutes, Agatha said. Candice decided to wait for the woman to become distracted by a customer, then she'd sneak off. Actually, she could put some distance between them by pretending to look around the neighbouring displays, while she waited for an opportunity to make a run for it.

As if sensing she was about to lose her victim, Agatha called to one of the other sales assistants, 'I'm just popping out for my break. Keep an eye on my counter for me?' With that, she took hold of Candice's elbow and steered her out of the shop.

Candice was being kidnapped, hijacked, taken against her will. For a second, she thought about shaking the other woman off and walking away, when an image of a pair of skinny jeans popped into her head.

Jeans weren't her style at all, but she was curious to know how it felt to wear a pair. Everyone she knew owned some, including Mrs Pocock next door and she was in her seventies. What was the difference between those and a nice pair of trousers when they were on? Did they suddenly make the wearer feel more hip, more with-it, more youthful?

It wouldn't do any harm to find out. Not that she had any intention of purchasing a pair, but it would be nice to see what all the fuss was about. She could have crept into Marks & Spencer to try some on in total anonymity, with only herself to witness her dismay when she looked in the mirror. She didn't need to be forcibly frog-marched into a shop she'd never been into before and would never visit again. It wasn't her sort of place and she guessed it was hideously expensive, too.

Candice's gaze flickered from rail to rail as Agatha led her further into the shop. It all looked so chic, so well-put-together, so co-ordinated. But she was relieved to see some black among the bright summer clothes. Everywhere she looked there were little tops, shorts and bikinis on display – if they were bikinis, because they appeared to be the size of handkerchiefs, and small ones at that. Was that a *crocheted* one? Whoever bought that would be in for a shock when they went for a paddle on Weston beach. The minute the material got wet, it would sag and bag. Or maybe that was the idea?

'Trudi, this is… I'm sorry, but I don't actually know your name,' Agatha said.

'Candice Summerville.'

'Candice is here to re-vamp her wardrobe,' Agatha said, and Candice squirmed as Trudi (short, glossy hair, good figure, even better clothes) looked her up and down. She guessed the woman was somewhere in late middle-age, but it was difficult to tell.

'So I see,' Trudi murmured.

Candice felt awfully like Julia Roberts' character when she got a make-over in Pretty Woman; although Candice did prefer the idea of being Anne Hathaway in The Devil Wears Prada, being re-vamped by that guy with a roomful of samples (she never could remember his name…).

'Leave her to me. Do we know what her budget is?' Trudi spoke to Agatha as if Candice wasn't standing right in front of her or she had lost the ability to speak.

'Um…?' Candice piped up. 'Forty pounds?' That should be enough to get her a nice skirt. It certainly would be in Marks & Spencer or The Edinburgh Woollen Mill. Not that she thought they sold much in the way of woollen goods any more, but it had been a while since she'd been in one of their shops. And by a "while", she probably meant about three years. Or four.

She looked at Trudi to see the woman eyeing her incredulously. Agatha was wearing a similar expression. Yes, they undoubtedly were in cahoots, trying to get her to spend more than she needed to.

'You won't get anything for that,' Trudi said. 'Maybe a pair of lace knickers.'

Candice blushed; not at the thought of lace knickers, but at what she was wearing under her skirt and jumper. Lace wasn't the word. Her own white (OK, greyish) cotton briefs which more than adequately covered everything that needed covering from her waist to her behind, had lost some of its elastic. Her bra wasn't much better – it had once been a nude shade (best colour to wear under cream and white blouses) but had lost most of its colour and was now a non-descript, yucky, nothing colour.

There was no way on God's earth that the immaculate Trudi was going to see her in her shabby, shameful underwear!

With a squeak and a muttered, 'Must dash, things to do, someone to see. An appointment, that's it, an appointment! I'm late. Sorry.' She was out of the door and hurtling down the high street as fast as her legs could carry her.

But Agatha was right, she did need new clothes, and she knew exactly where to get them from.

CHAPTER 28

Candice usually shopped in Marks & Spencer. She felt safe there; she knew what size she was. She also knew that the quality was decent. It wasn't the cheapest shop on the high street, but neither was it the most expensive, and it certainly didn't have the outrageous prices of the shop she'd just ventured in to.

Her first port of call was the underwear department; she realised she really did need some new knickers, and a bra or two wouldn't go amiss either. But she had a bit of a shock when she secured herself safely in a changing room and tried a couple on, because her usual size proved to be too big on her. She stared at herself in the mirror wondering what she should do. None of them were any good at all – they gaped around the tops of her boobs, and she felt an insane urge to grab a couple of tissues from her bag and stuff the cups with them, until they were properly filled out.

Where had her boobs *gone?*

They'd been there the last time she'd looked, albeit somewhat droopy, but now they seemed to have shrunk.

She really couldn't be bothered to get dressed again, fetch some different sizes from the sales floor, then have to take everything back off once more in order to try them on.

She huffed loudly and was about to wrestle with the clasps, when there was a soft knock on the door.

'Do you need any help in there?' a female voice called to her.

Candice pulled a face at herself in the mirror. The sort of help she needed would probably need to come from a plastic surgeon.

'Do you require another size?' the voice continued.

Yes, she definitely did. The question was, could she be bothered. 'Erm… hang on.'

Candice opened the door a fraction and peered through the crack. 'Have you got this in a….?' In a what? She had no idea what size she needed. Should she go for the same measurement she always did, just a cup size smaller, or—?

The sales assistant pushed the door open further and Candice shrank back, her hands covering her boobs.

'Let me see what's what and we'll get you sorted out,' the woman said. 'When were you last fitted for a bra?'

Candice frowned, not liking the invasion of her privacy but realising she needed some help, said, 'Never?'

'No problem. Let's have a look, shall we?' She put her hands on Candice's shoulders and turned her so she was facing the mirror. 'Oh, goodness, this one is far too big for you around here.' The woman tugged at the material at the base of her chest where her boobs met her ribcage and inserted a couple of fingers into the resulting space.

Candice let out a squeal.

'You shouldn't be able to get any fingers under there,' the woman said. 'It's not giving you adequate support.'

To Candice's relief, she removed her hand, only to undo the clasp at the back and pull the bra tighter.

'Can you feel the difference? The bra is connecting properly with your ribcage, which means all the support is coming from there and not from the straps.' A bit more tugging followed. 'This is at least a size too big.'

The saleswoman let go and took a step back. Candice saw the woman stare critically at her chest and she felt like cringing.

'I think you're a 36C, not a 38DD. You're gaping all

over the place. Give me a minute and I'll bring some for you to try. Do you prefer a plunge, a balconette, or a T-shirt bra?'

Candice gazed at her helplessly. She'd been buying the same style bras for years, but she didn't have a clue what they were called.

'Never mind, I'll pick a selection and you can try them on. You'll probably want to wear a different bra under different clothes anyway.'

The woman left and Candice let out a long sigh. She wondered if she should take off the bra she was wearing and wait, naked from the waist up, for the sales assistant to return, but she felt too exposed, so she kept it on, even going as far as to hug her jumper to her chest. The weather was a bit too warm for jumper-wearing, but she didn't have a great many summer clothes, so she'd just grabbed the first thing out of the drawer. Naturally, it was black and so was her skirt, although the fabric of her skirt did have a grey fleck in it. She'd bought it from Marks & Spencer a few years ago and there was still plenty of wear in it.

Another knock. Candice let the sales assistant in.

'Here we go. Slip that one off, and we'll start with this, shall we?' the woman said, holding up a scrap of lace.

Candice blinked. The bra was pink. Bright pink.

Candice only ever wore black, white (although the white ones were looking a bit on the grey side these days), or nude. She wasn't sure if she could bring herself to wear such a bright colour.

'The colour's a bit… um…' she began. 'Intense?'

'Fuchsia pink, they call it. It's gorgeous, isn't it, and they do this bra in the most wonderful shade of turquoise, too. There are matching knickers to go with it. They do thongs, high-legs, and shorts.'

Candice was speechless.

Sensing her client's reluctance, the woman suggested, 'Slip it on, to give us a baseline for the fit.'

Candice did as she was told. After all, she didn't have to buy it, and she was sure there were other, more sensible bras out there.

Oh my, she thought, as the sales assistant slipped the straps over her shoulder, did the clasp up, and stood back, waiting for her reaction. Her boobs looked fantastic! If she didn't know they were hers, she would have thought they belonged to someone else!

They looked so great, in fact, that before she knew it, she'd bought the matching knickers and an additional set in the most glorious shade of blue-green. She even treated herself to a white set, too.

Candice was on a roll. Foregoing her usual Marks & Spencer tried and tested choices, on impulse she made her way to Next. Before she realised what she was doing she had taken a huge armful of assorted tops, skirts, and trousers into the fitting room, and even a pair of jeans!

She must have lost her reason, she decided, when she found herself impetuously purchasing several of the items, the jeans included, with a kind of wild abandon, and she hadn't even looked at the prices, scared she might talk herself out of it.

When she stepped outside the shop, her arms already aching from carrying so many bags, she let out a slightly hysterical giggle as she headed towards the sports shop, her mind set on something other than baggy T-shirts and oversized jogging bottoms.

God help it when her bank statement came!

CHAPTER 29

Yoga evening doesn't half come around quickly, Candice thought to herself, as she wriggled and squirmed into her new Lycra leggings and T-shirt. The rest of her purchases had been carefully hung in the wardrobe. Her new shoes were on the rack and she'd even treated herself to a new handbag. She'd had the other one since the kids were small and although it was leather and of good quality, it had seen a fair amount of action and had been looking rather the worse for wear for a long time. Her new one was also leather and had cost a fortune. If she carried on spending at this rate, she'd need to take out a mortgage just to keep herself in clothes.

The thought of a mortgage brought her mind back to Ivan and his proposal, and she grimaced, worry coursing through her. Still, she was seeing Malcolm tomorrow (although she wasn't sure how she felt about that), so everything should hopefully be sorted out soon. With that in mind, she set off for her class, determined not to think about her son or his father for the next hour or so.

There were several things she noticed between getting into her car for the drive to the leisure centre and sitting on her mat and saying "Namaste". The first was that her hair, being so short now, didn't blow around her face and therefore didn't look untidy when she arrived at her destination. A quick finger ruffle through her shorn locks ensured they looked just as good as when she'd left the house. The second was that she was slipping in and out of the driver's seat easier than she had done when Mike the Mechanic had loaned it to her, which she put down to her slowly increasing bendability. The third was the reaction of her yoga-mates.

Only Paul recognised her.

He did a comical double-take, his eyes wide and his mouth open. Then his face crinkled up into a huge smile, which was swiftly followed by a low whistle and a thumbs up.

Even Moon didn't recognise her, and welcomed her to the class and asked her if she had done any yoga before, as if she had only just joined.

Who'd have thought a new hairstyle, a bit of make-up, and some clingy Lycra could make such a difference!

Candice put everything she had into the class, pushing herself to her wobbly-armed limit as she did the downward dog, feeling the pull and stretch of muscles in her back and her legs. She bent to her limit when performing the cobra, and relaxed effortlessly into the child pose, concentrating on her breathing. For the first time in her life she felt in tune with her body, totally aware of it. After the session had ended she was surprised to find she hadn't thought about anything other than the here-and-now for the whole hour.

She was swiftly brought back to the present when several of her classmates complimented her on her hair. One even asked if she'd lost weight. She had, but not more than a pound or so since the last class, and she put the illusion down to wearing less-baggy clothes and the miracle of Lycra and Spandex. Another lady said how well she looked and asked if she'd been on holiday.

Wow! Was it this all down to make-up, because if it was, why the hell hadn't she worn the stuff before now, apart from her usual swipe of mascara and some nude lipstick? She felt as though she'd finally been let in on a secret or was now part of an exclusive club.

'You look fantastic,' Paul said, as she was rolling up her mat. 'The new hair really suits you.'

Candice ran her fingers through her hair self-consciously. She still hadn't got used to it and kept getting a bit of a shock when she caught sight of her reflection. Was that really her?

'Thank you.'

'I liked it before, mind you,' he added, diplomatically Candice thought. Bless him! 'What made you decide to change your hairstyle?' He peered at her. 'And you're wearing make-up?'

'I do wear some sometimes,' she replied, feeling a little defensive.

'Don't get me wrong,' Paul said hastily. 'You look wonderful, and I love the new outfit. It shows off your gorgeous figure,' he added, escorting her out to the car park. 'Are we going for our usual drink?'

'I don't see why not.'

He slipped his hand into hers as soon as they had dropped their mats off in their respective vehicles, and he held it all the way to the pub. His touch sent warm tingles up her arm and she was quite sorry when he released her to open the door.

Once they were seated with their drinks in front of them, Paul carried on the conversation from where it had left off.

'I was only asking about the change of hairstyle because in my admittedly limited experience, women usually make such drastic changes because something has happened. Are you all right?'

The concern on his face was touching and it prompted her to be honest with him. 'Not really.'

'Oh?'

She told him about Ivan and that her son's business was in difficulty, then she explained about visiting the bank to have a quick word with Malcolm and her humiliation at being taken for his mother.

'Maybe this young woman has met your ex's new wife and jumped to a rather silly conclusion,' Paul offered gallantly.

Candice sighed. '*That Woman*, his new wife, used to work at the same branch, so it's possible they've met,' she conceded. 'But I still felt awful at being thought of as twenty years older than I actually am.' She chuckled, as she went on to explain, 'I had an appointment to get my hair cut anyway, but when I arrived, my usual stylist was unavailable, and this slip of a girl said she was doing my hair. I don't remember how it came about, but for some reason she asked me if I trusted her and I said yes. The next thing I knew, she'd dyed my hair white blond and had talked me into this pixie cut.'

Paul laughed. 'Is that what it's called? It really, really suits you, and I'm not just saying that.' He leaned closer. 'Just for the record, and not that it makes the slightest difference to the way I feel about you, but it makes you look ten years younger.'

Candice beamed and nudged his arm. 'Go on,' she said. 'You're winding me up.'

'I'm not! Cross my heart and hope to die!'

'I haven't heard that for ages,' she giggled.

'It's true. I fancy you anyway, pixie cut or no pixie cut. You're a beautiful woman, Candice, inside and out, no matter what your hair colour. Although a curly perm and a blue rinse might be a step too far.'

She shot him an incredulous look.

'Joking! I meant what I said. I thought you were gorgeous the first time I clapped eyes on you.'

'All sweaty and red in the face?' she demanded.

'Yep. Anyway, how do you feel about your transformation, because it doesn't matter what anyone else thinks.'

Candice touched her cropped hair again. 'I'm not sure,' she admitted. 'I keep catching glimpses of myself in the mirror and wondering who that strange woman is, before I realise it's me. I'm not sure I'll get used to it, to be honest.'

'That's the good thing about hair,' Paul said. 'Give it a few months and it'll be the same as it was before, if that's what you want.'

'I'm not sure I want that either,' she said.

'I'll love you whatever you decide,' he said.

A sudden hush descended on their table. Candice wasn't sure she had heard him correctly and if she had, it might have been one of those things people said without thinking about it.

Then she caught the horrified expression on Paul's face and she understood that he'd just realised what he'd said.

'I didn't mean... um... what I wanted to say... er...' he stuttered.

'It's OK,' she said. 'I know what you mean.'

'Do you?' He shuffled a little so he could look her directly in the eye.

'Erm... yes?'

'I don't think you do,' he replied, slowly, and she stared at him, the depths in his eyes drawing her in, stealing her breath. 'I wasn't going to say anything,' he carried on. 'Not yet, not until I was as sure as I could be that you felt the same way. But I've said it now, and I don't want to take it back, or try to talk my way out of it, or pretend I meant something else. I told you before that I thought I was falling for you. I don't "think"; I know. I've fallen for you hook, line, and sinker.' He dropped his gaze to the table and took a deep breath. 'I love you, Candice, and it doesn't matter if you don't feel the same way about me, because we can carry on as we are, but I hope you might be able to love me back, just a little. I haven't really been out with anyone since Ellen died, apart from the odd date.' He took another deep breath. 'I've hardly even looked at another woman, but when I saw you for the first time in yoga, I wanted to get to know you. I'm glad I did,' he finished in a rush, 'whatever you feel about me.'

'I feel exactly the same,' Candice said after a shocked

pause, where she tried to take it all in.

'You…?'

'Love you? Yes. I believe I do.'

'Oh, my.' Paul leaned back in his seat, looking stunned. 'I'm speechless.'

The pair of them grinned at each other like a couple of lunatics, and he reached out to grasp her hand, clutching it as if he'd never let go.

'What do we do now?' she asked eventually, when her cheeks began to ache from all the smiling.

'Take it slow?' Paul suggested and he fetched them another drink.

Candice could do slow. Even though she'd already given him her heart, she really wanted to get to know him well before the next step.

For now, it was enough to know that he loved her, too.

CHAPTER 30

'Effing hell! Where's Candice and what have you done with her?' Keisha exclaimed when she walked in the office to put her coat and bag in her locker. 'You look effing great! Stand up and let me look at you.'

Embarrassed, Candice slowly got to her feet. She'd worn a pair of slim-fitting trousers (black, of course – she hadn't quite got the courage to move totally out of her comfort zone yet) but she had teamed it with a pretty, abstract-patterned top in several shades of blue and she had a new pair of sandals on her feet. She had tried on, and had seriously considered buying, a couple of pairs of high-heeled court shoes but she found she couldn't really walk in them. After a few steps they'd made the balls of her feet ache, not to mention that she felt as though she was about to topple over. She might have had a make-over, but her feet didn't appreciate anything higher than an inch or so, especially since she spent most of her day on them. There was no point in crippling herself for fashion. She'd painted her toenails instead, something she hadn't done since her last holiday with Malcolm and the boys. It was a nude shade, but at least she'd made the effort. *And* she was wearing the turquoise underwear set. Not that anyone would ever see it, but boy did she feel good, knowing she had such lovely things on underneath her clothes. If she wasn't careful, she might become addicted to buying underwear if it made her feel this good all the time. Victoria's Secret look out!

She didn't like to admit it to herself, but she'd dressed with Malcolm in mind this morning, applying her make-up with a nervous, inexperienced hand and carefully teasing her pixie cut into position, even though it had become ruffled during her top-down drive into work. A quick visit to the ladies' had soon solved that problem and now she was feeling pretty good.

'I almost didn't recognise you,' Keisha said. 'You look so different. I love your hair. It makes you look fifteen years younger.' She smirked, 'So only sixty, instead of seventy-five.'

Candice's mouth dropped open. 'Why, you little...' She picked up a stapler and pretended to throw it at her.

'Is this transformation anything to do with the bloke who came by the other day? The one you didn't want to serve?'

'It most certainly is not!'

'Well, if it is, you need to thank him,' Keisha carried on, unperturbed. 'He's done you one hell of a favour. I can't believe you look so good.'

'Thanks,' Candice said, dryly. 'Did I look so bad before?'

'Not bad, exactly, just... I dunno... unnoticeable, maybe? The way lots of old people get.'

'I'm not old,' Candice retorted, automatically.

'You looked it,' came the reply.

'Looks aren't everything, you know.'

'No, but that's what you get judged on before people get to know you.' Keisha sounded wistful. 'You can't stop taking care of yourself just because you're not young anymore.'

That's true enough, Candice thought. Looking back, she'd spent most of her adult life taking care of her husband and her family, and had paid only a token gesture to taking care of herself. She had to admit, since she'd started eating healthily and doing some exercise, she felt better than she had in a very long time; fitter, more confident, and, she was pleased to admit to herself, not so middle-aged.

When the time neared for her appointment with Malcolm, Candice's new-found confidence deserted her. What if he didn't like her hair? Or thought she looked like mutton dressed up as lamb? He never did like women who wore too much make-up – or so he'd said, although that had clearly been a lie because *That Woman* wore enough to keep a branch of Boots in profit for a year. Malcolm never liked her wearing trousers, either, although Candice had been pleasantly surprised when she found how well they suited her. They made her look slimmer, gave her a more definite shape. She was all-too-aware that they moulded themselves around her backside and legs, but she didn't look too horrendous in them. In fact, they were rather flattering. They made her legs look longer too, now she came to think about it, and she wondered why she'd never invested in a pair before. Oh, yes, because of Malcolm, that was why.

Oh, poo! What did it matter what her ex-husband thought of her? The only opinion that mattered to her was Paul's and he loved her regardless. He'd told her so.

The woman manning the reception area was the same one as yesterday, and Candice made a bee-line for her.

'I have an appointment with Mr Summerville,' she announced, then watched as the woman glanced up at her without any sign of recognition.

'What's the name, please?'

'Mrs Summerville.'

The assistant's eyes widened as Candice's name registered, and her mouth dropped open. Another swift up and down sweeping look followed. 'Um… certainly Mrs Summerville. I'll let him know you're here. If you'd like to take a seat?'

Candice sat, but not for long. In less than a minute she

saw Malcolm walk through the door which she knew led to the private area behind the tellers' desks, and stride towards her.

The satisfaction she felt when his gaze swept across the reception area and failed to come to rest on her, was tempered by the worry that she looked so different to the way she had looked the last time he'd seen her that he'd make a scathing comment when he finally spotted her.

He looked again, still not recognising her, and he went up to Michaela, who pointed at Candice.

Candice forced a pleasant expression onto her face, trying to keep the concern out of her eyes.

Malcolm turned to her and did a double-take. It was almost comical the way his head jerked back, although the frown he sported wasn't so amusing.

He strode over to her and Candice got to her feet.

'Candice?' His expression was one of shock and incredulity. 'What have you done to yourself?'

'I… er…' She hesitated. He had no right speaking to her like that, she thought, and she lifted her chin. How she looked was nobody's business but her own, and Malcolm had lost the right to comment on anything to do with her life the minute he told her he was leaving. 'I'm here about Ivan,' she said.

'Ivan?' Malcolm hadn't stopped staring and it was beginning to unnerve her.

'Our son? Remember him?'

'There's no need to be so snippy,' he said, seeming to come to his senses. 'Follow me.'

Without waiting to see if she did indeed follow him, Malcolm strode into a nearby cubicle and sat behind a desk, leaving Candice to close the door after herself and take a seat opposite him. She had a brief flashback of Paul holding the pub door open for her and pulling out a chair for her to sit on; the comparison between him and her ex-husband wasn't favourable to Malcolm. She didn't think he'd ever once held a door open for her, or anyone else, come to think of it. Not that she needed anyone to do that for her, because she was perfectly capable of opening her own doors, thank you very much, but the old-fashioned gesture spoke of old-fashioned values, plain good manners, and good breeding. Paul, in some respects, reminded her of her father, who had been a gentleman through and through.

'What about Ivan?' Malcolm asked, breaking into her thoughts without preamble.

'He needs money.'

Malcolm barked out a laugh. 'Don't we all?'

'I mean, he has a cash-flow problem with his business,' she explained patiently, but at the same time wanting to bash him over the head. He always did have an annoying habit of belittling her.

'So why hasn't he come to me?' her ex-husband asked. 'After all, I'm the banker in the family, and you haven't got any money to lend him.'

Candice bristled. This attitude was most likely the very reason why their son hadn't approached Malcolm.

'I'm thinking of mortgaging the house,' she said, 'and giving him the money.'

'You want to do *what?*' Malcolm laughed. It wasn't a particularly pleasant laugh, either. 'Tell him, no. The idiot. No one in their right mind would mortgage their house against a business.'

'He didn't ask me,' Candice said, jumping to Ivan's defence. 'I haven't even mentioned it to him yet – I wanted to talk to you first.'

'It's lucky you did, otherwise you might have gone ahead and signed the house over,' he said, his tone smug and condescending.

'If you hadn't been available, I would have obtained advice elsewhere.' Lord, she sounded like a heroine in a Victorian novel, all lofty and stiff.

'How much does he need?' Malcolm wanted to know.

'I didn't ask,' she admitted.

'However much it is, it won't be enough. You'll be lucky to get a mortgage at all on your wages. And what about the repayments?' He'd been busy tapping away at a computer as he was speaking.

She guessed he was pulling up her details. Not for the first time, she regretted not moving her account to another bank after the divorce, but her head had been all over the place and by the time she'd been back on an even keel, she'd found she couldn't be bothered.

'You can probably get a mortgage for twenty thousand on your salary,' he announced, 'but I still wouldn't recommend it, even if the loan was approved, which I doubt it would be. If you were putting the money towards an extension, therefore adding value to the house, then maybe…' He trailed off.

Would twenty thousand pounds be enough, she wondered.

'Was there anything else you needed my help with?' he asked.

'No, that's it, thank you.'

She wished she had obtained advice elsewhere. Anything would have been better than approaching Malcolm, she realised, although she was forced to admit that his counsel was probably sound.

Bugger, she'd been pinning her hopes on helping Ivan out. Maybe Malcolm could come up with something?

She was about to ask him, when he said, 'I hear you've bought a sports car.' The way he sneered the last two words made her think he was accusing her of selling her body on street corners.

'I have. A Mazda MX-5.'

'It's not got much of a boot,' he said, as if this was going to be news to her. Why was everyone so fixated on the size of her car's boot?

'Are you going through the menopause or something? You'll be taking in stray cats next.' He guffawed loudly, setting her teeth on edge. 'It's a mid-life crisis car!'

'So what if it is? It's my life, mid or not. And as for the menopause, you lost all right to comment on the state of my hormones when you had a mid-life crisis of your own. How is your new wife?' Her voice dripped sarcasm. 'Oh, and for your information, I prefer dogs to cats,' she added. 'Which shows how little you actually know me, doesn't it?'

With that, she turned on her heel, yanked the door open and flounced out, deliberately swinging her hips to make her slim-fitting trousers more obvious.

Mid-life crisis indeed! What if she *was* having one? For the first time in her life, she felt strong, confident, and in control. So there!

CHAPTER 31

'How did the meeting with Malcolm go?' Paul asked her later that evening over a shepherd's pie and chips.

Candice had rung him shortly after leaving the bank and had asked if he'd like to pop round for a spot of tea, if he wasn't busy.

He'd been delighted and had arrived with a bottle of dandelion and burdock pop to go with it. Better than wine, she thought, considering Paul would have to drive home later and they both had work in the morning.

'Not good,' she admitted. 'I suggested mortgaging the house and giving the money to Ivan, but Malcolm dismissed the idea.'

'Actually, love, I think he was right,' Paul said quietly. 'You don't want to be saddling yourself with a mortgage.' He smiled uncertainly as if he expected her to jump down his throat at his effrontery in agreeing with her ex.

'I know,' she sighed. 'I must have been daft to even consider it. I know Ivan would insist on covering the repayments, but it still leaves both of us in a difficult position if he loses the business and hasn't got any money coming in. I don't exactly earn much myself. But,' she paused, 'I have been considering something and I wanted your opinion.'

'I knew there was a reason for bribing me with pie and chips,' he said. 'And there I was, hoping you wanted my body.' He chuckled, to show he was joking.

Candice shook her head at him. 'I want your expertise,' she said.

'Fire away.' Paul mopped up the last of the gravy with a stray chip and sat back, replete.

'I've been thinking for a while that this house is too big for me. What do I want three bedrooms for? I'm just wondering how much I could get if I put it on the market?'

'You really need to speak to an estate agent. I'd love to help, but I don't want to give you any duff info.'

'I've been on the internet and checked out what other similar properties in the area have gone for, but what I really wanted is your opinion on the state of the house itself.'

'Ah, I see, now that's something I can help you with.' Paul pushed away from the table and said, 'Do you mind if I have a wander round?'

And when she began to explain what she thought the house needed doing to it, Paul held up a hand to stop her.

'Don't tell me,' he said. 'Let me take a look for myself. What you think needs doing and what I think needs doing may be poles apart.'

And with that, he got to his feet and disappeared out of the kitchen, while Candice tackled the washing up.

By the time she'd finished putting away the dishes and wiping the inside of the oven, Paul was back, holding a small notebook in one hand and a pencil in the other.

'Right, then, I'll go through it room by room, if you like?' he suggested.

Candice swallowed. Oh dear, that didn't sound good. She nodded at him to continue, and switched on her new electric kettle. This called for a fortifying cup of tea and a chocolate Hobnob, she decided.

'The small bedroom at the back needs the posters taken down off the walls, and a fresh coat of paint. The other bedroom is the same but you've also got a broken light fitting. What is that odd cupboard in the alcove used for?'

'It was there when we moved in, so Ivan just sort of used it as a wardrobe.'

'I hope you don't mind me saying, but it looks hideous. But if you put a new door on it and a new handle, it should be OK.'

She nodded. 'I'll do that, then. What else?'

'Your bedroom…' He paused and Candice's cheeks grew warm. 'Your bedroom is fine, although a lick of paint wouldn't go amiss, and considering you'll be doing the other two rooms, if you don't do yours it'll stick out like a sore thumb. I'd say all upstairs could do with new carpets, too. Or…' He paused again. 'How about, stripping them all out and sanding your floorboards down? A couple of rugs here and there should do the trick, if you want to soften the look. It'll be messy but cheaper in the long run and will bring the whole house bang up-to-date. Young couples these days love bare wood floors. Of course, it does depend on the state of your boards.'

Candice shrugged. She'd never had cause to consider her floorboards before.

'We can check that out later,' Paul said. 'Right, the bathroom needs the most work.' He took a deep breath and Candice jumped in.

'I know. New shower, retiled, new bathroom suite, and that hideous lino has to go.' She sighed. 'It might be best if I just put it on the market as it is, and price it accordingly.'

'Maybe. What if I listed everything that needs doing, to give you a rough idea of the cost of the materials and labour, and you can make more of an informed decision. I'll do as much of the work as I can, but there's some stuff I can't do, like plumbing in new shower units, and I'll only be able to work in the evenings and the weekends because—'

'Oh, no! I'm not having you do that,' Candice said. 'If you do any work in this house, I'm paying you the going rate, otherwise I'll get someone else in.'

Paul stepped towards her and pulled her close. 'We'll

talk about that when you know what you're doing, yeah?'
he suggested. 'Now, give us a kiss and make us a cup of
tea, then we'll check your boards.'

'I've never known anyone get so excited about a bit of
wood,' she said, tilting her head back and lifting her lips up
to meet his.

And for a while, all thoughts of floorboards were
forgotten.

CHAPTER 32

'I don't envy you,' Dermott said after Candice shared her intended renovations with him and Keisha. 'My old mum keeps on at me to get the paintbrush out, but—' He shuddered theatrically. 'This body wasn't built for climbing up ladders. Are you going to be doing it all yourself?'

'No chance. I don't like ladders much either, and Malcolm would never let me loose with a pot of paint.' She frowned. 'Come to think of it, he was a bit shy when it came to wielding a paintbrush too, which probably explains why so much needs doing. At least most of it is cosmetic,' she added. 'Except for the bathroom – that's a bit of a nightmare.'

'Have you sorted out a new back door after your break-in?' he asked.

'Yes, thanks, they're coming on Friday.'

'Have the police caught anyone yet?' Keisha asked, looking up from her phone.

'They've not said. Mind you, it only happened last week, so they probably haven't even done the paperwork yet.'

'Is that why you're thinking of moving? Because you're scared they might come back? I can lend you Samson, if you like.' Keisha grinned at her.

Samson was a dog. A very large, rather drooly-jawed dog who barked a lot, according to Keisha.

'No, but thanks for the offer,' Candice said.

'Dammit. I've been trying to get rid of him for years.'

'I'm sure you don't mean it.'

'Have you seen the size of him? He eats more than a team of football players would in one sitting. Can you imagine what it's like having to clean up the stuff that comes out of the other end? Ugh!'

Candice and Dermott exchanged amused looks. It was a well-known fact (because Keisha told them on a regular basis) that her dad's job was to walk the dog, her mum's was to feed it, her brother bathed and brushed it, and Keisha, bless her, had the less enjoyable task of cleaning up after it, mainly because she was the one who'd insisted on having the dog in the first place; a decision she seemed to regret on a daily basis.

'I think you're really brave to stay there all by yourself,' Dermott said. 'I don't think I could have.'

Candice had slept remarkably well; ever since Paul had let slip that he loved her, in fact.

She'd heard back from her insurers yesterday. They'd given her the go-ahead to purchase the one thing she had been lost without during this past week – a new computer. So she disappeared into the little office upstairs and spent the next hour or so studying the spec and prices of the hardware on the market.

Maybe a laptop would make a nice change? They were just as powerful as traditional static computers these days, and much more flexible. It would mean she could take it up to bed with her if she felt like it and not be confined to the office desk in the corner of the living room.

'Candice, Candice.' Dermott came hurrying through the door. 'There's a delivery for you.'

'Thanks. I'll see to it later,' she said, without looking up.

'You might want to look at it now,' he said in an odd voice, and she glanced at him to see him waggling his eyebrows up and down, reminding her of a sleazy 1970s comedian she'd once been taken to see at Blackpool Beach years ago.

'All right.' Dermott wasn't going to leave her alone was he, so she might as well get it over with and see what had gotten him so worked up. 'Where is it?' she asked, expecting him to have brought the delivery with him.

'In the staffroom.'

Candice's eyes lit up. 'Ooh, has the council finally replaced the old microwave?' she asked. She sincerely hoped so, because the one they currently had was coated with rust inside, and she was sure it didn't heat the food up as well as it should do.

'I'm not telling,' Dermott smirked, practically hopping from foot to foot.

He followed her into the little staffroom, so close behind her that she was sure she could feel his breath on the back of her recently-shorn neck (she still hadn't become used to having so much skin exposed, which had previously been covered by her trusty bob).

To her disappointment, there was no new microwave, not even a box big enough to house one. The only thing in the room which hadn't been there before, was a huge bouquet of flowers in one of those plastic water-filled bulbs to keep them fresh, and Candice wondered which of Keisha's boyfriends had forked out for such a lovely display. Whoever he was, the girl should seriously consider marrying him, because youngsters these days didn't exactly think of flowers when they made the decision to send their girl something to impress her. Selfies on Snapchat were probably more like the done thing these days, she guessed.

She whirled on her heel, preparing to give Dermott a disgusted look, when he pointed at the bouquet.

'Aren't you going to see who they're from?' he asked.

'Don't be so nosey,' she retorted. 'If Keisha wants us to know, she'll tell us herself.' Candice did want to know, actually, but not so badly that she'd invade Keisha's privacy.

'They're not for Keisha,' Dermott said, a hurt look on

his face. 'They're for you.'

Candice was astounded.

'For me?'

Dermott nodded.

'Are you sure?'

He nodded again.

'Where did they come from?' she asked.

'Interflora, I think.'

'I mean, who sent them?'

'I don't know. That's why you ned to look on the card.'

There was a little envelope attached to a plastic stick poking out of the middle of the bouquet. Tentatively, as though she expected it might bite, Candice took a step forward, then another until she stood in front of the table with the rather large and flamboyant bunch of flowers perched on top of it.

She swallowed nervously. No one had ever given her flowers before, except for the kids when they were younger; they used to pick a bunch of dandelions from the hedgerows when they were out playing. Oh, and she'd had flowers on her wedding day, of course, when her mum had presented her with a bridal bouquet of white carnations.

This must be from Paul, she deduced. How sweet and considerate of him. He knew how stressed she had been over the break-in, Ivan's news, her drastic change of image, and then the thought of selling her house, that he must have sent her some flowers to cheer her up.

Leaning closer, she inhaled deeply, letting the scent of them fill her nose. He'd chosen well, the bouquet being a colourful but coordinated mix of assorted pink, purple, and white, with green foliage for an accent. It must have cost him a fortune!

She plucked the envelope from among the stems and opened it with a big smile on her face.

She read the printed words and her smile faded.

She read them again.

The bouquet wasn't from Paul.

It was from Malcolm, and there were only two words written on the card, three if she counted her ex-husband's name:

Forgive me. Malcolm.

Candice blinked. "Forgive me"? _For what?_ Which particular bit of his behaviour did he seek her forgiveness for? Being an indifferent husband? Being a less-than-hands-on father? For not loving her enough? For not loving her at all? For leaving her and their children? For being an insufferable, pompous git yesterday?

She was tempted to give him a call to clarify the situation.

'Well, who are they from?' Dermott wanted to know. 'Have you got yourself a gentleman friend? You have, haven't you? You're a dark horse. You never said, but it would explain the new look.'

'Give it a rest, Dermott,' she said.

'Oh.' He looked crestfallen.

Candice could tell he wanted to pursue the matter, so she stuffed the card in her trouser pocket and stalked to the door.

'I don't want them,' she said over her shoulder. 'Give them to your mother.'

She went back to her computer, her mind whirling with a mixture of anger, regret, and sorrow.

CHAPTER 33

Paul bent down and examined the door frame. 'They've done a good job,' he stated, referring to her new back door. 'The plaster needs repairing in places, but I can do that now for you, if you like.'

'There's no need,' Candice replied, feeling a little awkward. She didn't want him to think she only wanted him for his handyman skills. To be fair though, he had popped around out of the blue to make sure the door was fitted correctly, so it wasn't as if she'd called him.

'It'll only take half an hour. I've got some plaster in the van. Then I thought, considering it's such a lovely evening, we could take a little drive to Upton-on-Severn, have a stroll by the river, and a bite to eat out. I'll drive,' he added. 'As long as you don't mind getting in the van.'

'I don't mind at all,' she said. 'What I do mind, is you doing work on my house without letting me pay you for it.'

Paul turned to face her. 'I want to do it,' he said. 'I'm not too good at the romantic stuff like flowers. I'm better doing something practical. This is my way of showing you I care.'

Guilt flooded her veins at the thought of Malcolm's flowers. She'd done nothing wrong and she certainly hadn't encouraged her ex-husband to send them, but she still felt as though she was doing something underhand. Maybe she should have told Paul about the bouquet. But she'd been so taken aback and, she had to admit, rather cross, that she'd not said anything and it was too late to mention it now.

'OK, but I'll drive and let *me* buy dinner,' she said.

Paul scrunched up his eyes. 'You drive, we go Dutch on dinner?'

'Deal.' Candice held out her hand, expecting him to shake on it, but instead he pulled her close and held her tight, his arms encircling her, his lips in her hair.

'You just don't want to be seen in my van,' he teased.

'You got me,' she admitted. 'Jelly Bean is much classier.'

'I can't argue with that,' he said, leaning back a little so he could gaze down at her. 'Not as classy as you, though.'

She gave him a gentle push. 'Flatterer.'

'It's true!'

'Get away with you. I've never been called classy in my life.'

'Then it's about time you were,' he said. 'And I mean it.' Then he stopped any further discussion on the subject by kissing her soundly.

'Right, get your glad rags on and we'll get going,' he said, coming up for air far too soon for Candice's liking. She could have carried on kissing Paul all evening, and then some. 'I'll sort this bit of plastering out, then pop home to change, and I'll be back by 6.30. Is that OK?'

It certainly was. When he left, she dashed upstairs to rifle through her wardrobe of new clothes, humming to herself. Life couldn't get much better than this, could it?

Dressed in jeans (she actually found the courage to wear them) a pair of leather pumps and a pretty summer top, with a cardi slung around her shoulders just in case it cooled off later, she was waiting outside, leaning against Jelly Bean's bonnet, with her legs crossed at the ankle, when he pulled up in his van.

Paul got out and wolf-whistled. 'Don't you look nice,' he said, and she positively glowed at the compliment. 'If I wasn't so hungry, I might just waltz you back inside and up those stairs,' he joked.

Joke or not, his words made her tingle all over. If she wasn't so scared of ruining what they had, she thought, she might just let him. The idea brought a flush to her cheeks, and she hid it by scrambling into the car and fussing with her seat belt, all fingers and thumbs.

Trying to get the conversation back on an even keel, to a point where she didn't feel like a hormonal teenager, Candice said, 'I've got an estate agent coming round the day after tomorrow to value the house. At least then I'll have some idea what I'll get for it. Once I know that, I can look for something smaller. I just hope it won't take too long to sell, and there will be enough left over to help Ivan.'

'You do realise that you might not sell it in time to help him, don't you?' Paul said, gently.

She did, but it wasn't going to stop her trying. Even the promise of cash might keep her son's creditors away for long enough for him to get back on his feet again.

'I know, but I've got to try,' she sighed.

Ivan and his problems were still on her mind as they were shown to a table and sat down. The pub was lovely, right on the river, with great views along the banks.

'Fancy going for a stroll afterwards?' Paul asked, and she agreed happily, her mood lifting as she tucked into her food.

What a perfect evening, she thought later, as they sauntered along the river bank. Full of Hunter's chicken and raspberry Pavlova, a walk was just what she needed to help her food go down.

Hand in hand, they wandered down the grassy path, the river lapping gently at the sides, seeing dog walkers and parents out with their children. It was still warm enough not to need her cardi, and by the time they'd returned to the pub car park and Jelly Bean, the sun was setting in glorious shades of pink, orange, and purple.

With the wind ruffling her hair, Paul singing along to

the radio by her side, and the car eating up the miles, Candice couldn't remember the last time she had been as happy.

And, no matter what anyone said, Candice was convinced it was all down to Jelly Bean.

CHAPTER 34

'Ivan? It's me, Mum. I've got some news,' Candice said into the phone.

'I hope it's good, because I don't think I can take much more of the bad stuff.' Her son's tone was light-hearted and jokey, but she could tell he was putting it on.

'It is. I'm putting the house on the market.'

'Oh.'

'What do you mean, "oh"?' she wanted to know.

'I just didn't think you'd ever consider moving,' he said. 'You and Dad bought that house before us kids were born.'

'And that's one of the reasons why it's time to sell up and move on,' she stated. 'You and Preston have got your own places now, so I don't need such a large house. I'm rattling around in it on my own. Besides, there's another reason I'm selling it. I'm going to use a big part of the money to buy something smaller, but I want you to have whatever is left. It should be enough to help you keep the wolves from the door until you get your finances sorted.'

'Oh, Mum.' He sounded so sad, Candice wanted to cry – she thought he would have been pleased!

'That's so kind of you, but there's no way the sale will go through in time to save the business.'

It was Candice's turn to say, 'Oh.'

'And, anyway, I don't want you to sell your home

because of me. It isn't right and it's not fair on you. I can't let you do that.'

There he goes again, she thought, trying to manage her life as if she was the child in this relationship.

'It's not up to you. If I want to sell the house, I will.'

'Mum—'

'I don't want to live here anymore, Ivan,' she interrupted. 'I want to move on, have a fresh start. I've vegetated in this house for long enough. It's about time I cut my ties with the past. This was your father's house and mine. Now that I'm on my own, I want a house that isn't anything to do with him.'

'Fair enough,' her son said. 'I can see the sense in that.'

'Don't worry, I won't go for a one-bedroomed flat. There'll always be a room for you if you need it, you know, if the business goes bust and stuff.'

Ivan laughed. 'I'm not going to lose my house, if that's what you're worried about. It's totally separate to the business. I'm not going to be homeless.'

'As long as I have breath in my body, you'll always have a home with me,' she vowed.

There was an odd kind of choking noise on the other end of the phone. Candice took it away from her ear and looked at it for a second, before putting it back. 'Hello?'

'I'm still here,' Ivan said, although he sounded as though he'd suddenly developed a cold. 'Look, thanks Mum, but I've got to go. Speak soon, yeah?'

And with that, he ended the call. Candice looked at her phone again, wondering what all that was about, then a thought struck her. Had he been crying? She strongly suspected he had, and her heart went out to him.

Feeling emotional herself, but at a bit of a loose end, she decided that now was as good a time as any to make a start on sorting the house out. She'd have to do it anyway, if she was going to decorate, so she might as well begin now.

She decided that Ivan's old bedroom would be the first

to be blitzed, but when she stepped in through the door, her son's teenage presence wrapped itself around her, refusing to let go.

Aw, look, there was his little bookcase, with his school books sitting on the shelf, together with a wooden box he had made in Year Nine. Candice picked it up, tears gathering in the corner of her eyes. How could she bear to throw all these memories away? Perhaps she should concentrate on the things which she'd have no qualms about parting with, like his old football boots which had been stuffed into a plastic carrier bag and shoved in the bottom of his wardrobe. He wouldn't be wearing those again, nor the clothes hanging on the rail above.

She had come upstairs armed with several black plastic bags, and she methodically began to take everything off their hangers, fold them, and place them inside. Some of Ivan's old clothes were in very good condition, and she intended to take them to the charity shop tomorrow. The rest would be put in the bin.

When the wardrobe was empty, she turned to the chest of drawers, but after she'd finished with that and had stripped the bed, she was once again faced with the bookcase and its contents. And she hadn't even looked in the drawers underneath his desk yet.

This was awful, almost as bad as when he had told her he'd signed the contract on a property and was moving out. Talk about empty-nest syndrome!

Shakily and feeling rather emotional, she heaved one of the bulging plastic bags and made her way downstairs. She'd only just put it by the front door ready to be squashed into Jelly Bean's boot (she'd have to take the bags one at a time, she realised) when the phone rang.

It was Paul. 'I've just called for a chat. What are you doing?' he asked. 'I'm babysitting Barny.'

'That's nice. I've just started sorting out the boys' bedrooms.' Her voice cracked towards the end, and she swiped at her face, annoyed at the tears trickling down her cheeks. Get a grip, she told herself, you're being pathetic.

'Are you all right?'

'I suppose.'

'You don't sound too sure.'

'It's just that it'll be hard to leave all the memories behind. I was trying to sort out Ivan's stuff, but practically everything I touched had some meaning.'

'I understand,' he said. 'It's OK to be upset.'

Of course he understood, she realised. He understood far, far better than she hoped she ever would need to. At least she still had her boys – Paul's wife was gone for good.

'I wish I could come round and give you a cuddle, but I can't leave Barny. He's fast asleep and I wouldn't want to wake him.'

She wondered if Paul was about to suggest she go to his instead, so she cut him off at the pass by saying, 'That's OK, I'm done for tonight anyway. I'm going to have a hot bath and an early night.' She really wasn't in the mood for company, no matter how lovely that company was.

'How about doing something tomorrow?' he asked instead. 'I'll have Barny with me, though.'

'That'll be wonderful,' she said, meaning it.

There was nothing like a good man and a small boy to chase the blues away.

CHAPTER 35

West Midland's Safari Park was the perfect place for kids, Candice decided, especially big ones like her and Paul – the pair of them seemed more excited about the trip than Barney himself.

Paul picked her up in his van, with Barny in tow.

'Can I see Jelly Bean?' the boy asked before they left, and Candice rolled up the garage door to show him.

'I'd love to have a go in it,' he said, wistfully.

'I'll take you out in her, one day,' she promised. 'But not today, because there are only two seats.' She turned to wink at Paul. 'I could pop you in the boot, if you wanted, though. You're just about the right size.'

It was a shame that Jelly Bean was only a two-seater, because it meant that Barny couldn't join in the fun. She did love this car, she thought to herself, but maybe it really wasn't all that practical. Not if either Ivan or Preston were to present her with grandchildren.

She gave herself a mental shake – if that were to happen she'd deal with it when the situation arose. For now, she was going to enjoy her little car, because one never knew what the future might hold.

Even if Barny hadn't been with them, Candice wouldn't have been able to take the soft top into some areas of the park where the big cats roamed free. Or into the enclosure where the monkeys were. She wouldn't have felt safe going through some of the other safari areas either, she realised when a giraffe's enormous head appeared right next to the van window. It's odd-coloured tongue waggled about in search of more of the pellets they had purchased before they went through the gates.

Then there were the rhinos. What if one of them had a tiff with its neighbour and Jelly Bean was in the way? The poor little car wouldn't stand a chance – at least the van offered some protection from these giant semi-wild beasts.

She loved watching Paul with his grandson as they walked around the petting zoo, visited the insect and the reptile houses, and sauntered around the bird displays. He was so patient with the boy, and clearly adored the child. It was hard not to adore Barny, she acknowledged – he was such a sweet, polite, inquisitive little boy, and she smiled with delight when his small hand slipped into hers.

'Shall we have a look in the gift shop?' she suggested, after they had seen everything there was to see, had been on all the rides in the amusement park, and had eaten a burger and chips each while perched on a bench opposite the meerkats' enclosure.

'Yes, please!' Barny's eyes lit up.

It was while they were wandering around the shop, picking up and putting down assorted cuddly animals, fridge magnets, masks, and all the things guaranteed to appeal to children, that Candice spied something she simply had to have – jelly beans!

She bought a bag for Barny (silently apologising to his grandfather for the inevitable sugar rush) and encouraged him to open them.

'Find a purple one,' she urged.

He dug around in the bag and brought one out.

'Look at the colour. That's why I call my car Jelly Bean,' she told him, laughing when the little boy giggled loudly.

By the time Paul pulled up on her drive a couple of hours later, all three of them were exhausted, but happy. It had been a thoroughly lovely day out and Candice didn't want it to end.

'Do you fancy a salad for tea?' she offered, as she got out of the van. There was little else in the fridge, but after eating junk food for lunch a salad would do them all good.

'I'd love to, but I need to get Barny home because his mum is due back at five o'clock. She will want something to eat, and to spend some time with Barny. Besides, he has school tomorrow; his bedtime is half-past seven.'

He leaned out of the window and kissed her on the lips, both of them smiling when Barny made pretend gagging noises. Paul was about to drive off, when he stopped the van and leaned out of the window again.

'Barny wants to know if you're my girlfriend,' he called. 'I told him "yes", if that's OK with you?'

'It most certainly is,' she replied, with a big smile. Paul smiled back and Candice opened her front door and went inside, feeling happy and contented.

Deciding to do a bit more sorting out, she went upstairs to change her clothes and remove her make-up. This taking off of make-up every night was a bit of a pain, but she did it religiously, although she was finding that she wasn't wearing quite as many of the products as she had been sold. Besides, she mused, checking her face in the somewhat unforgiving light of the bathroom mirror, there was nothing short of plastic surgery that could iron out the encroaching lines around her eyes or her mouth. Anyway, underneath her foundation her skin had a glow from being out in the sun so often, so she didn't feel the need to wear as much as the sales assistant, Agatha, had suggested.

Maybe, when it was time to have Jelly Bean's top up permanently, Candice would have to put more on. For now, though, she was content to wear a little bit of foundation to even out her skin tone, a spot of blusher, and some mascara. She'd even left the lipstick off today – Paul's kisses tended to make it disappear!

She heard her phone buzz, signifying a text. Wandering into the bedroom still swiping at her face with a cotton wool ball saturated in cleanser, she reached for it, expecting it to be from Paul.

Malcolm's name was on the screen.

Candice hesitated, unsure if she wanted to read it. There'd been no contact from him since she'd received the flowers, which, by the way, she hadn't thanked him for and had no intention of doing so. She really had nothing to say to him – it had all been said long ago, and mostly by him. She had lost count of the number of times he'd told her that he didn't love her anymore and to stop bothering him. Unless it was about the kids, he didn't want to speak to her.

Wait, maybe that was why he was contacting her now…?

She steeled herself and opened the text.

Can we meet? I'm at the Worcester branch tomorrow. How about the coffee shop opposite at 1pm?

That was it. Nothing else. No indication of how he was going to help Ivan. She texted him back.

See you there

She wasn't looking forward to meeting Malcolm one little bit, but if it helped their son, she'd do it.

CHAPTER 36

Malcolm was late. Nothing changes, she thought, checking her watch. He had always been late when she was married to him. It used to drive her mad, as it tended to make her think that his time was so much more valuable than hers. She'd give him another ten minutes; if he didn't show by then, she'd go back to work. He could tell her what he wanted by text.

She'd picked a table by the window when she saw that Malcolm wasn't already there and waiting for her, and now she watched him as he scurried across the road in his sharp suit, looking all self-important and busy. He'd always been good at displaying an air of confidence, she mused, thinking that it had added to his appeal for her. It came as a bit of a shock to her now, to realise she no longer felt the slightest bit attracted to him and hadn't felt that way for quite some time. When she delved deeper into her heart, she came to the conclusion that she'd stopped loving him some years ago but hadn't had the courage to admit it to herself.

She'd loved this man so desperately and for so many years, that she'd clung to the idea long after the emotion had faded away. To her surprise, she understood that actually Paul hadn't had anything to do with this new-found detachment – he'd simply been the catalyst to make her see that Malcolm was her past and that was where he should stay.

Malcolm hesitated by the café door, shooting his cuffs, and sneaking a glance in her direction. For a second Candice wondered if he'd been watching her from one of the bank's windows, making sure she had arrived first before he went to join her. It was exactly the kind of thing he'd do, she knew. He used to like playing subtle little games. It looked like he still did.

Candice narrowed her eyes as he slid into the seat opposite her and glanced around to catch someone's attention.

'It's self-service here,' she informed him when no one came over for his order, and she almost smiled as he huffed, got to his feet again, and strode off to the counter.

He came back. 'Did you want anything?'

Typical – she had always been an afterthought. Why should that change now?

'I'm fine thanks,' she replied, gesturing to her berry smoothie. It was far too warm for a coffee and she had no appetite for food. She simply wanted to get this meeting over with and leave.

He returned with a cappuccino in his hand and a smile on his face. She recognised it as his professional smile, the one that was all shark-teeth and calculating eyes. She had an awful feeling that he was going to pitch something to her that he knew she wouldn't like; but she couldn't for the life of her guess what it might be.

'Did you get the flowers?' he asked.

'I did.'

'I thought they might have gone astray, because you didn't call me or anything.'

Candice looked at him over the rim of her glass as she sucked on her straw, and said nothing.

'Did you read the card?' he persisted.

She wished he'd drop the subject and move on to why he was really here. She'd wasted enough time on this man over the years; she wasn't prepared to waste any more. Besides, her lunch break was half over, thanks to his tardiness.

'Yep.' She knew she sounded dismissive and flippant, but she didn't care.

For Malcolm, her tone was clearly unexpected, and he blinked owlishly at her. 'Well?' he demanded after a second, recovering his equilibrium pretty quickly.

'Well, *what?*' she countered.

'What did you think of it?'

Oh no, did he really want to go there right now? Surely not...

'Not much,' she replied, keeping her unexpected and slowly burning anger under control. She had no intention of quarrelling with him in public. In fact, she had no intention of quarrelling with him at all. He simply wasn't worth getting all cross or upset about.

'What do you mean, *not much?* I bare my soul to you, and that's all you can say.'

'Huh! The only thing you bared was your credit card.'

'That's harsh, Candice. I never thought you would speak to me like that. You've changed.'

Yes, I have, she realised, and for the better, too. Over the course of the summer she had finally crawled out from under the shadow of her marriage, and was now basking in the sunlight and enjoying every minute of it. She felt reborn, renewed, free. Free from the old emotions, the old guilts, the old bonds and restrictions, and she was astute enough to realise that they had been of her own making. She had wallowed in the despair and grief at Malcolm walking out on her for far too long, when she should have been out there living life to the fullest, not simply existing from day to day, trudging through the weeks and months as if life was a chore and not a precious gift. She had been a shell of a person; but not any longer, and she wondered what had happened to bring her back to life.

Then she smiled to herself – Jelly Bean had happened. Ever since she'd bought the little Mazda, her simple joy at owning it had turned her life around. She was going to get a tattoo, she decided abruptly, and she knew exactly what it was going to be…

'What are you smirking at?' Malcolm demanded, bringing her out of her thoughts with a jolt.

'Nothing…'

'You think my apology is something to be laughed at, do you?' Malcolm kept his voice low, but he almost hissed the words at her, and she recoiled a little at his vitriol.

Not too long ago she would have been beside herself at the thought of upsetting him, but now she simply shrugged. 'It was a bit ridiculous,' she said.

Malcolm's mouth dropped open and he stared at her in shock. 'I can't believe you said that, Candice. You've become really hard and bitter. It's not very attractive, if I'm honest. Are you going through the menopause, or something? It would certainly explain the hair and those clothes.' He gave her a scathing look.

Candice was wearing a pair of capri pants in navy, a pretty cream top which fitted in all the right places, some strappy sandals, and a lovely chunky necklace in the most glorious shade of coral. She'd thought she looked fairly good when she'd checked herself in the mirror before she left for work that morning; she still thought she looked OK, despite Malcolm trying to put her down and belittle her.

'I was going to tell you how nice you looked,' he said, contradicting himself. 'But I shan't bother now.' He leaned forward, resting his palms on the table, then snatched them back off again with a scowl as his fingers came into contact with the sticky residue of the previous drinks to have rested on the Formica surface. He sat up straight instead, giving her his most intense, calculating stare.

'Right, I'll come straight out with it,' he said, and Candice thought thank God for that. She was eager to hear what he was going to suggest to help Ivan. Time was of the essence, as they say; Ivan needed the money now, not in a few weeks' time.

'I think I've made a mistake,' Malcolm said.

'Eh?'

'We had a lot going for us, didn't we?' he continued. 'I see that now. I don't know what I was thinking.' He looked at her expectantly.

Candice stared back at him. What on earth was he talking about? What did this have to do with raising funds for Ivan's business? She shook her head slowly in confusion.

'It's no greener, really is it?' he said.

'What isn't greener? I don't understand.'

'The grass. On the other side.'

'Now you've lost me.' Candice peered at him, frowning. Was he having some kind of breakdown? Or was the reference to "green" referring to greenbacks, like Americans sometimes called their dollars? Could he be referring to some kind of international financial deal?

'Marriage,' he huffed. 'Keep up.'

Candice squinted at him, still confused. She had no idea what he was on about.

'I should never have left you,' her ex said in a rush. 'I'm not happy, Candice.'

She winced at the sound of her name on his lips, having forgotten he had an annoying habit of using her name more often than was necessary. 'I'm sorry to hear that,' she said, noncommittally. 'About Ivan—'

'I'm saying that I want to come back,' Malcolm interjected abruptly.

'Come back where?'

'To you, of course. Tianna is too demanding, always wanting this or that, always complaining about my golf, nagging that I don't spend enough time at home. What does she expect? I work all day – when I get the chance, I like to play a couple of rounds, just to unwind.'

Candice didn't believe what she was hearing. He wanted to come back? After all this time?

'You were never like that,' he was saying, his tone

reminding her of a petulant child. In fact, he sounded exactly like Preston, when she used to tell him he couldn't play on the swings or stay out late.

'I want to come back, Candice. Can you understand that?'

Of all the patronising, supercilious, arrogant, selfish—! She ran out of words – clean ones, that is. There were plenty of sweary ones rushing through her mind right now, ones that even Keisha probably wouldn't use.

'What do you say?' Malcolm asked.

Her mouth opened and closed a couple of times – to say that she was gobsmacked (not an expression she liked using but it suited these circumstances perfectly) was an understatement.

'No,' she said, after a moment's pause.

'No? But Candice!' It was Malcolm's turn to sound astounded. 'I still love you, you must know that. You can't just say "no" without even thinking about it? After everything I did for you—'

'Right. It's time for a few home truths,' she hissed, trying to keep her voice low so the whole café didn't hear, 'although I honestly don't know where to start. One,' she held up a finger. 'You don't love me. I don't think you ever did, otherwise how could you have left me and the boys?' Two—'

'Do you know why I left?' he interrupted. 'I was having some kind of mid-life crises, just like you are now. I wasn't in control of my actions.'

Candice growled at him and he shrank back. 'Two,' she repeated firmly. 'You have a wife and a child. I'm not going to help you abandon them the way you abandoned us.'

'I'll support Tianna, of course I will, and I'll still see Felix when I can. You'll like him,' he added. 'You'll enjoy mothering him.'

'I don't believe you, I really don't. You've got some cheek, I'll give you that. "I'll see Felix when I can", indeed.

Your *son*,' she emphasised the word heavily, 'deserves more from you than the odd trip to the park every third Saturday, *if* you can be bothered, or *if* something better hasn't come along. What in your tiny, pathetic, little mind, makes you think I'd be a party to that, after seeing the way you treated Ivan and Preston? *And*,' she continued as Malcolm tried to speak, 'I don't need another child to mother, thank you very much. I doubt if his real mother would appreciate it, either. When I wanted another baby, you point-blank refused. Yet here you are, offering me your new wife's child as some sort of consolation prize?'

'Shh, keep your voice down,' Malcolm muttered. 'You don't want the whole world to hear you screaming like a fish wife.'

'I don't care what they hear,' Candice stated. 'It's about time people realised what a little shit you are. I'm just sorry that I didn't work it out sooner.'

'Well, if that's all the thanks I get for laying myself on the line, then maybe I don't want to move back in with you after all.'

She shook her head. 'Even if you did, I wouldn't have you back. You were right when you said the grass isn't greener on the other side – it hardly ever is. It's just a pity you had to break my heart, walk out on your kids, and have a baby with another poor woman for you to realise it.' She glared at him. 'I know what's brought this on; it's because you can see that I'm finally moving on with my life. I bet you loved it knowing that I was still pining after you, but now that I'm not, you think you can waltz back into my life and pick up exactly where you left off. Well, let me tell you something, Malcolm Summerville, that's not going to happen. Ever! I'll tell you something else, too – the reason why you're not happy isn't because of me or Tianna, it's you, and if you can't see that, you'll never be happy.'

She slid out of the booth and stood up.

Malcolm, eyes wide, stared at her incredulously, his

mouth hanging open.

She lifted her bag onto her shoulder, spun on her heel, and marched out of the door, her head held high.

It was only when she slipped inside the library doors and into the staff only area, that the trembling began. It started in her hands, then her legs became wobbly, until she shook so much she had to lean against the wall to prevent herself from sliding down it.

If anyone had told her she would ever speak to her ex-husband the way she had spoken to him just now, she would have thought they were mad. Yet, that's exactly what she'd done, and she was so shocked she could hardly stand up.

She worked her way slowly to her tiny office and dropped into her chair.

Malcolm wanted her back. He wanted to come home and— *What?* Divorce Tianna? Candice couldn't even bring herself to call his new wife *That Woman* anymore. In fact, she actually felt sorry for her, and wondered if the woman had any inkling that the man who had so blithely left his wife for her, had been planning on doing the whole leaving thing in reverse.

It was Felix who Candice felt the sorriest for. She knew what her own boys had gone through, what they were still going through, after their father had left. She certainly didn't wish that on another innocent child.

Now that she had given Malcolm a piece of her mind, she guessed he was unlikely to simply walk out on Tianna, not without somewhere (or should she say *someone*) else lined up first, so he would probably be playing happy families with Tianna for a while yet.

She wondered what had made Malcolm decide he wanted to come back to her. She doubted he'd have heard about her and Paul, so it probably wasn't a dog with a bone situation. Had it been the new hair, the make-up, the clothes? When she'd met with him to discuss Ivan's situation, had he realised that she'd moved on with her life?

A wry smile played on her lips. All this new-found confidence had stemmed from when she'd bought Jelly Bean. Not that the car was responsible, per se, but her impulsive purchase of it had awakened something in her. Since Jelly Bean had come into her life, she'd become healthier, had had a make-over of sorts, had met Paul...

Her life was good now. With the benefit of hindsight, she could see that Malcolm leaving her had been for the best, although she certainly hadn't thought so at the time, and not for years afterwards. Looking back at her life with him, she understood that she had been down-trodden, subservient, a push-over and that, perversely, Malcolm had encouraged her to be like that. She'd believed that was what he'd wanted, that was how a good wife should behave, and which was why it had been such a shock when he'd waltzed off with her complete opposite.

She had lost herself in the marriage, and she had found herself again now. It might have taken her a long time to get there, but she had finally become the person she was meant to be.

CHAPTER 37

Should I say anything to Paul, Candice wondered, unsure how he would take the news that her ex-husband had made a play for her. He might be OK with it, but on the other hand… Maybe saying nothing was best. After all, she had dealt with Malcolm herself and had told him in no uncertain terms that she wasn't interested.

She signalled left, changed gear, and turned the corner. As usual, she had the top down because it was another glorious day and the lovely, tantalising smells of summer flew past on the breeze. Aside from the slight worry about Malcolm, and her much greater worry over Ivan, she felt very content, happy even. Paul was coming over later to help her paint the kitchen, and she'd bought new blinds to brighten the room up, plus some stuff to refresh the grouting around the tiles on the floor.

Candice knew her hope to sell the house quickly was a long shot. Of course, she could always set it at a low price for a quick sale, but she was aware that she needed to realise enough from the sale to enable her to afford a much smaller place and to give Ivan enough to make the whole thing worthwhile.

She checked her mirror as a car came up behind her, fast. What was the point of that, she asked herself. Driving like a bat out of hell, just to have to slow down once he caught up with her. She couldn't go any faster anyway, because there were several cars in front of her. It did make her a little nervous, though, to have some idiot on her tail, who couldn't wait to overtake, and she wondered what made people behave like that. All that angst and hassle, just to get a few more feet up the road. It was pointless and stupid.

Instead of fretting, she turned the radio up, and tried to ignore the car which was following too near to her rear bumper. She was on her way to another library halfway across the county because they had an IT issue which they couldn't sort out themselves, so she'd been sent to see if she could help, and she was really glad she was outside on this lovely morning. Actually, she felt as though she were truanting; she had only ever truanted once, because, after the initial excitement – much like she was feeling now – it had become rather boring. Sitting in the park on a slightly drizzly day in March, when she could be in a warm, dry classroom, hadn't been Candice's idea of fun. Plus, she'd had to copy up the lessons she'd missed; so all in all, bunking off school for most of the day hadn't been worth it.

This journey was worth it, though, because it was sanctioned; although she suspected the joy she currently felt at being out on the road on a summer's day, driving an open-topped sports car, would soon transform into something more akin to frustration as she tried to get the library's computer system up and running. If she took her time, she might stretch the job out for most of the day, then it wouldn't be worth going into her own branch for an hour, so she might as well go straight home.

With a laugh, she turned up the volume on the radio as she heard the first few bars of the next song, Gloria Gaynor's *I Will Survive*, which was so apt under the circumstances that she almost cheered.

Then a movement in the rear-screen mirror caught her eye. What was the idiot in the car behind doing? He was almost bumper-to-bumper with Jelly Bean and had half-pulled out into the middle of the road, trying to overtake her. The rural road itself was only two lanes wide, with hedges on either side and sharp bends. Although seventy miles an hour was the speed limit along it, only a total moron would consider doing anything more than forty; fifty at the most along one of the straighter stretches. As well as the unexpectedly sharp bends, motorists ran the risk of encountering farm traffic such as tractors or, and this was highly likely at this time of year, heavily-laden hay lorries.

Instinctively, Candice slowed, trying not to let the guy behind intimidate her into going faster than was safe, or at a speed she didn't feel comfortable driving at. An extended blast of his horn made her jump. He clearly wasn't impressed and was intent on letting her know it.

Thank God, she thought, as another straight piece of road came into view. Please let him overtake her. She dropped back further from the car in front, opening up a wide gap between her and it, for the idiot to slot his vehicle into after he had overtaken her. If it wasn't illegal and dangerous, she'd have been tempted to get her phone out and film his reckless behaviour. She wondered if he'd try the same bullying tactics with the rather solid-looking Range Rover in front. Perhaps he had a thing about little sports cars, she mused, dropping even further back and glancing in her mirror.

'If you're going to go, go,' she muttered, desperate to have him in front of her, rather than practically sitting on Jelly Bean's little boot.

Finally, she heard the engine behind roar and guessed he'd dropped down a gear to give his car an added boost of power.

As he drew alongside, she glanced at him.

The man glared back at her and waved his fist. She was shocked to see that he wasn't a silly youth who'd only just passed his test, as she'd assumed, but was in his forties at least, and wore a suit and tie. He was old enough and experienced enough to know better, but there was no accounting for a lack of manners or bad driving, was there?

Without warning, the Range Rover in front slowed dramatically.

Candice slammed on her breaks, trying to leave enough distance for the idiot behind her to pull in, but he'd pulled ahead and was now almost alongside the Range Rover, clearly not having anticipated the rather abrupt deceleration.

Heart pounding, Candice watched the idiot fall back as the Range Rover swerved out into the opposite lane, and time seemed to slow down.

Oh, my God, she thought – there was an enormous, chestnut-coloured bull standing on her side of the road. It lowered its head and turned on its haunches to swing its horns at the Range Rover.

The idiot blasted his horn again as he, too, applied his breaks and swerved violently in front of Candice to avoid the Range Rover, then swerved again to avoid the bull.

The animal let out a mighty bellow and charged.

The last thing Candice saw before her world turned into a screaming, churning mess, was the red-rimmed whites of the bull's eyes.

CHAPTER 38

Noise, too much noise; sirens, metal screeching, someone shouting.

Candice fought to open her eyes. Only one of them seemed to work, and horrible bright light stabbed through her pupil and into her brain.

She groaned.

'It's all right, love. You've been in an accident. Lie still. I'm a medic and I'm going to check you over. Is that OK?'

Candice had no idea if it was OK or not.

God, but she hurt. It was her chest mainly, although her head pounded and throbbed with every beat of her heart, and somewhere below her left hip, her leg screamed in agony, the pain shooting from her toes to her groin. She whimpered.

'Let's get a line in,' the same voice said.

She hardly felt the sharp scratch on the back of her hand.

I'm going to be sick, she thought, as nausea swept through her, and she tried to turn her head. It wouldn't move.

Oh God, oh God, oh God, her mind gibbered – she was paralysed. Her neck must be broken. Please no, please…

CHAPTER 39

It was the smell that Candice became aware of first, clinical and antiseptic, with an underlying odour of something far less pleasant. Blood?

'That's right, Candice, open your eyes for me, there's a good girl.' Someone was tapping her hand.

She wanted to tell them to stop, to leave her alone. Let me sleep, she tried to say, but her mind appeared to be disconnected from her body.

The tapping continued. 'Come on, my lovely, we need you to wake up for us.'

'I need you to bugger off,' Candice muttered. Or she thought she did, but the words stayed in her head.

She moaned instead. God, she hurt all over.

'Let me go back to sleep,' she murmured, and she heard herself say the words out loud this time.

'You can in a minute, dear, when you've opened your eyes for me.'

Tap, tap, tap.

Candice opened one eye. The other still didn't seem to want to cooperate. Would the tapper be content with just the one?

'There's a good girl.'

The tapping thankfully stopped. Candice did her best to focus, but her world was blurred and fuzzy. She groaned again, as the vague hurt from a few minutes ago grew into a sickening ache emanating from her leg, travelling up through her body until it reached her throat, making her whimper.

She tried to take a deep breath and agony sliced through her chest.

'Please make it stop,' she whispered. Her breathing sounded ragged and uneven, her voice hoarse and scared.

'I'll sort out some pain meds for you.'

Candice concentrated on the figure hovering over her, until it gradually became that of a young woman dressed all in green. She was fiddling with some kind of tube.

'Do you know where you are?' the young woman asked.

'Hospital?' Candice croaked.

'That's right. You've had an operation on your leg. You've got a couple of cracked ribs and some other more minor injuries. We'll get you settled on the ward, then give you something for your pain. The doctor will come around later to explain everything. OK?'

Candice nodded weakly, the movement sending bolts of thundering pain through her head, and she gasped at the force of it.

'There you go,' the young woman said, fiddling some more and Candice could have wept as the pain subsided and she sank into blessed oblivion.

CHAPTER 40

Voices, specifically Malcolm's, penetrated the fog in Candice's brain. she lay there, listening to the familiar cadence, wishing he would either shut up or go away. She didn't care which. She'd been dreaming, she realised, and part of her wanted to return to it, where she had been happy and warm on a beach somewhere. Someone (*Paul?*) had handed her a cocktail and told her if she drank it, all her dreams would come true. She wanted to stay in it, because she knew deep down that reality wasn't going to be anywhere near as pleasant.

She screwed her eyes shut tightly, the light making the inside of her eyelids glow in shades of pink and orange, like a sunset.

Malcolm was still talking, using his loud whisper-voice and a supercilious tone, the one he used when he wanted to put people down and assert his authority.

'I don't know who you think you are, but you have no right to be here. She's my wife and—'

'Actually, she isn't, is she?'

The second voice belonged to Paul. Despite the pain (if she thought about it, she had been aware of it for a while now, but since she'd woken up the pain had decided to crank up a notch) she smiled. He was here – *Paul* was *here*. He cared enough to come to the hospital. Which one was she in anyway?

Fully awake now and wishing she wasn't, she opened

her eyes, relieved to discover that the one which had refused to budge previously was now playing ball, and she could see out of it a little.

'I think you lost that privilege when you walked out on her,' Paul added.

'I'm still her next of kin,' Malcolm blustered.

'No, you're not; that will be Ivan and Preston.'

'But they're not here are they and I am, so I'm asking you to leave. Candice won't want you here when she wakes up.'

'I will,' Candice whispered, too softly for either man to hear.

'I'm not going anywhere unless Candice tells me to,' Paul stated, firmly.

'I'll get the doctor to throw you out,' Malcolm threatened. 'And, I'll have you know, Candice and I are getting back together. Ah ha! She didn't tell you that, did she? She said she wanted me back the day before the accident.'

Malcolm sounded so smug, Candice wanted to thump him.

'No,' she cried, her voice weak and thin.

Malcolm didn't hear her, but Paul did, and he hurried to her bedside and sat in one of the chairs next to her.

Oh-so gently, he took her hand, stroking the back of it, his fingers warm on her skin. 'Do you want me to stay?' he asked.

He looked anxious and there were lines around his eyes which hadn't been there the last time she'd seen him. He looked exhausted, too.

In comparison, she could see that Malcolm was as fresh as a daisy. 'I would have brought you flowers,' her ex-husband said, hanging back slightly, the expression on his face more cunning than concerned. 'But they don't allow flowers in hospitals anymore, so I brought you a balloon.' He pointed at it. It hung jauntily in the air in a corner by the window.

Candice ignored him. 'I want you to stay,' she said to Paul. 'Malcom is lying,' she added with a sigh.

'Are you in pain?' Paul asked, worriedly. 'Do you want me to call for a nurse?'

'Yes, please. But get rid of him first,' she pleaded, her voice so low he had to lean in closely to hear her. She suspected her ex-husband was making her feel worse, and she felt bad enough as it was. The simple act of breathing hurt like the devil, and talking was a step too far. Her head wasn't quite as achy, but her face felt all odd and her leg was becoming a sheer misery.

Paul gave her hand a soft squeeze and got up. 'She wants you to leave,' he said to Malcolm.

'I'm not taking orders from you—' Malcolm began.

'You're going to take orders from *me*,' a nurse said, bustling into the room. 'Out, both of you. My patient needs to rest. You can come back at visiting time, if Candice wants to see you,' she added.

'When is that?' Malcolm blustered. 'I've got something on this evening, and—'

The nurse shut him down with a steely glare. '6pm to 8pm. No exceptions.'

Malcolm huffed and went to walk out of the ward, but when he realised Paul hadn't made any move to leave, he halted.

Candice wished she had the energy to tell her ex where to go, but the only thing she was capable of concentrating on right now was not crying.

Paul stood up. 'I'm not going anywhere,' he said to her. 'I'll be in the cafeteria if you need me, and I'll pop back at six.'

'Promise?' she croaked.

'Promise. Now, concentrate on getting better. I'll see you in a couple of hours.'

'He's been here more or less since you were brought in,' the nurse said, after he'd left. 'Here, take these.' She handed Candice a tiny plastic cup with two white tablets in it. 'Painkillers,' the nurse said, giving her a cup of water with a straw in it to wash them down.

The nurse helped Candice lift her head and she swallowed them with difficulty before sinking back into the pillow. Just that small movement exhausted her.

'You get some rest – that's what will help you recover quicker,' the nurse advised.

'What happened?' Candice asked her.

'You had an accident.'

'I know, but what actually happened?'

The nurse moved closer and smiled. 'I believe it had something to do with a cow…?'

Ah, yes, the bull. She remembered an idiot of a driver, seeing a bull in the middle of the road, then – nothing.

'Was anyone else hurt?' she asked.

'No. Not even the cow. You came off the worst apparently.'

Thank God for that. Candice let out a small sigh, a breath she hadn't been aware she had been holding. 'My leg?'

'The consultant will tell you more when he does his rounds, but for now all you need to know is that you had an operation on your leg to pin it, you sustained a couple of cracked ribs, and you suffered a blow to the head. Everything is healing nicely, despite how you're feeling at the moment,' the nurse reassured her.

'My son?' she croaked, tiredness dragging her down towards oblivion.

'He was here yesterday and said he was coming back again this evening. He rang earlier to see what sort of a night you had. His girlfriend is pretty, isn't she?' The nurse chattered on for a minute longer, but all Candice could think about before sleep claimed her was that this total stranger had met Sharna before she had.

CHAPTER 41

'Oh God, Mum,' I've been so worried.' Ivan bent down to kiss her lightly on the forehead and Candice winced.

'Sorry.'

'It's OK.'

'How are you feeling?' he asked.

'Like I've been trampled by a cow?'

Her son smiled at her feeble attempt at a joke. He looked as tired as Paul had done (speaking of Paul – where was he? He said he wasn't going to leave the hospital).

'You're going to be moved to a proper ward soon,' Ivan told her. 'Now that you've come round, you're going in with the other sickies, so don't get too used to this luxury.'

'I take it I'm in Worcestershire Royal?'

He nodded.

Good. It would make visiting easier for people.

She had woken up in time for the evening meal, had managed to eat some of it, had been issued with more painkillers, and was starting to feel more like herself, although she was under no illusion that the effect was only temporary. She realised she would go through cycles of feeling better, then feeling worse again. Right now, she still felt like she'd been steamrollered, but the pain had reduced to a dull ache with only the occasional stab of agony if she moved too suddenly. Her head was far less woolly than it had been earlier, too.

'I've brought you a couple of pairs of pyjamas and some toiletries,' Ivan said, holding up a bag.

'Thank you.' That was very thoughtful of him.

'Actually,' he said, 'it wasn't me who packed it, but Sharna. I hope you don't mind.' He delved inside the bag and came out holding a pair of PJs, her best pair, the ones she'd been saving for… what, exactly?

Just such an occasion as this, she realised. Not that she had expected to have to stay in hospital, but here she was, and for goodness knows how long.

'I don't mind,' she said. 'The nurse said she was here yesterday?'

'Yeah.' He looked sheepish. 'I know it wasn't the best circumstances to meet, but…'

'We didn't actually meet,' she pointed out.

Mother and son stared at each other. Lordy, but this was awkward, Candice thought. Since when had she not known what to say to her own child?

'Does Preston know?' she asked, eventually.

'Yes. He's on his way back from Bolivia, or somewhere. He should be here tomorrow.'

'He doesn't need to come all this way,' Candice said. 'I'm not dying or anything.'

Although she was delighted she was going to see her youngest son after so long, she was worried that she'd put him out.

'Mum, you've had a serious accident,' Ivan said. 'Of course he wants to see you.'

'I want to see him, too,' she said, and her eyes filled with tears. Damn it, she didn't want to cry.

'Oh, Mum.' Ivan stood up and leaned in, holding her awkwardly.

She realised he was trying to avoid hurting her.

Actually, one of the reasons she didn't want to cry was for precisely that fact. It hurt enough to breathe, without adding sobbing and snivelling to the mix. She took a couple of shallow breaths (all she could manage without sending bolts of agony through her chest) and she fought to compose herself.

After a few moments, she said, 'I'm OK,' and Ivan released his hold and sat back down.

'You can let it all out, you know,' he said.

'No, I can't. It hurts.'

'Oh, I thought you meant you had to be strong for me. Or something. Because you always have been. Strong, I mean. Capable. Confident. It's humbling seeing you like this.'

Eh? 'Strong? *Me*?'

'Yeah, Mum. You.'

'I'm not strong or capable.'

'You are.' He reached out and grasped her hand. 'You're the strongest woman I know. I love you.'

'Stop it. You'll make me cry again. I wasn't joking when I said it hurts.'

'Sorry.'

'Well, is she here?' Candice demanded.

'Yes?' He seemed uncertain and she guessed her son was nervous about the meeting.

'Bring her in, then,' Candice said. 'I'd prefer to meet my future daughter-in-law for the first time, when I didn't have my leg in traction, but I'm not prepared to wait until I'm up and about again.'

'Before I go to get her, there's some guy in the corridor. He says he's visiting you? I told him I wanted to check with you first.'

'His name is Paul, and he's my... I suppose you'd call him my boyfriend, if it didn't make us sound like a pair of teenagers,' she explained, her heart swelling with love at the realisation that Paul was still here, just like he told her he would be.

'My, you're a sneaky one. How long has this been going on?'

Candice studied Ivan's face as best she could through

one and a half eyes. He didn't look put out or annoyed. In fact, he appeared to be delighted for her.

'A few months. Since the beginning of the summer, in fact. We met at yoga.'

'You didn't tell me you did yoga,' Ivan said.

'I don't tell my son everything I do,' Candice replied primly.

Ivan laughed. 'Clearly not.'

'Go and fetch Sharna, and ask Paul to give us a few minutes, would you? I'll say hello to your girl, then you two can bugger off. I'm sure you've got better things to do with your evening than spend it in a hospital.'

Her son halted, half in, half out of his seat. 'Oh, Mum? I've got something to tell you. It's important.'

She tried to sit up a little more and grimaced.

'You don't need to sell the house,' he said.

'I do, and I want to.'

'No, I mean, there's no need.' He grinned. 'Sharna's dad has invested in the business. He now owns part of it, enough to turn it around financially.'

'But it's *your* business. What happens if you and Sharna split up? Don't take it the wrong way, but things like that happen, don't they?'

'Wait there,' he said to her. 'Er, I mean, I'll get Sharna,' he added, seeing her quizzical expression.

Candice kept her gaze on the door, eager for her first sight of Ivan's girlfriend.

She was certainly pretty, was Candice's first thought, as a slender girl followed Ivan into the room. Dark hair, dark eyes, a heart-shaped face, and an uncertain smile sat above a small, high bump.

Sharna was pregnant.

'We wanted to tell you face-to-face, but the day we were supposed to come over for lunch, when I told you about the business, Sharna felt really unwell, and, you know…' he trailed off.

Candice stared and stared, hardly daring to believe what

she was seeing.

'Mum, say something,' Ivan pleaded after the silence had stretched a little too long.

'What?' Candice jerked awake. She'd been half asleep, lost in a dream of rocking a tiny baby, smelling that delicious infant scent, and feeling the solid, precious weight of the newborn in her arms.

'I think that's the most wonderful news I've heard in a long time,' she said, then cried out as a fresh jolt of pain shot through her.

'We'll go,' Ivan offered. 'Let your... er... Paul visit for a while. I'm glad you're pleased.'

'So am I,' Sharna said, stepping forward to lean down and kiss Candice on the cheek.

Candice resisted the urge to feel the girl's baby bump. There would be plenty of time for that when she got out of hospital. If she had been able to, she'd have squealed with joy – she was going to be a grandma!

CHAPTER 42

Candice watched as Paul stuck his head around the door. He looked a little better now than he had done earlier, she noticed, not quite so grey and drawn, although he still looked tired.

'Have you been home at all?' she asked him, motioning for him to come in.

'Not really.'

'That's a "no", then. Promise me you'll go home and get some sleep.'

'I promise. I'll go now that I can see you're on the mend.' He sat on the chair which Ivan hadn't long vacated. 'So, they've told you? Ivan and his girlfriend?'

'I could hardly miss it, could I?' She tried to laugh and instantly regretted it, holding a hand to her side to support her ribs.

'Look, I'll leave,' Paul suggested. 'Let you get some sleep. I'll be back for visiting hours tomorrow afternoon.'

'Don't go,' Candice pleaded. 'Not until they kick you out.'

He nodded and smiled at her. Despite feeling worse by the second, she smiled back. It was good to know that someone cared enough to stay with her, even if she hadn't been aware of it at the time. She was aware now, and that's what mattered.

'I didn't even ask how far along Sharna is. She looked to be about five months, but she's so slim it's difficult to tell.'

'You're delighted, aren't you?' he asked.

'I am. And,' she grinned although she had an inkling her smile was more a grimace. 'Ivan says that her father has invested in the business. Isn't that marvellous?'

'It's wonderful. You must be so relieved You don't have to sell your house now, either,' Paul pointed out.

'I think I still might. Anything left over will be a nice little nest egg.' She shifted again, trying to ease the pain, but nothing seemed to be working.

Paul noticed her discomfort. 'Can I get you anything? There's a shop downstairs,' he offered.

'A bottle of juice and don't forget a bunch of grapes. Isn't that what you give to patients?'

'Green, black, or red? Seedless or don't you care?' he grinned.

'Green and seedless, although I'm not sure I'll actually eat any of them. I've never really taken to grapes. I wouldn't mind a tangerine or two.'

'Tangerines, it is then. I'll get the easy-peeler variety, shall I?'

Candice loved how he was so much on her wavelength. Paul understood her in a way Malcolm never had. If she had still been married to Malcolm he would have brought her something he liked, and not something she liked, because he'd be the one to sit there eating it during visiting hours. That is, if he thought to bring her anything at all.

'If they don't have them in stock,' he said, looking anxious, 'can you wait until tomorrow?'

She nodded carefully. Her headache was coming back. The consultant had told her she'd suffered a small concussion and, by the way her eye and surrounding skin had swollen up, she guessed she probably had a black eye to go with it. Not that she'd looked in a mirror yet, which was probably a good thing. By the time she would be able to get to the bathroom, hopefully the swelling and bruising might have gone down a bit.

'Anything else?' he asked.

She was about to say "no" when a thought occurred to her. 'What about Jelly Bean?' she asked in a small voice.

Paul dropped his gaze to the pale-yellow bedcover, and she knew the news wasn't good. 'I'm sorry, my love, but she's a write-off.'

She suspected as much. Poor little car; she hadn't deserved such an end. 'Where is she?' Candice asked.

Paul looked surprised at the question. 'I don't know. I can find out for you, if you like?'

'Yes, please.' She welled up, the sting of tears making her blink.

'Come here,' he said, moving closer and wrapping his arms around her as best he could without hurting her. 'It'll be OK. You'll get the insurance money and maybe even compensation for your injuries. It will be enough to buy another car.'

'I don't want another car,' she sniffled, sounding more like a lost child than a grown woman, which made her cry even harder because she was being so pathetic. 'I want Jelly Bean.'

'You can have another MX-5. I'll find you one just like Jelly Bean,' he promised.

'You don't understand. Jelly Bean has done so much for me, and now she's gone.'

Paul pulled back slightly, reached for a tissue off the stand by the side of her bed and gave it to her. 'Don't try to blow your nose,' he warned. 'Not unless you want to feel as though your ribs are about to explode.'

She gently wiped her eyes instead as Paul stroked her hair.

'What has Jelly Bean done for you?' he asked gently.

'Everything. Before her, I was in a rut – home, work, bed; home, work, bed. I felt lost, invisible and lonely, and I'd forgotten what it was like to be me. I was nobody. Not a wife. Not a mother. Nothing.'

Paul cupped a rough, calloused hand around her

undamaged cheek, his forehead almost touching hers. He didn't say anything, letting her tell the story in her own time and her own words. She loved him for that, too.

'Then the Ford died, and I fell in love with Jelly Bean. It was because of her that I started to eat healthily and go to yoga, and people began to talk to me. OK, it was usually about the car, but that was fine. It was better they talked to me about the car than ignore me completely.' She shook her head slightly. 'It was because of her that I met you.'

'Actually, I met you before I knew you even had a car,' he pointed out. 'And I asked you out for a drink *before* I knew what you drove. Candice, look at me.' He lifted her chin with his finger, and she allowed him to bring her head up. 'It was you I fancied, not your car. I think I fell in love with you from the minute I saw you in your baggy T-shirt and leggings, standing on your mat, looking all lost and worried.'

'I didn't, did I?'

'You did. The only thing I wanted to do was to pick you up and tell you it'll be all right. It will be all right, you know,' he added.

'But Jelly Bean…?'

'Was just a car, a very cute car I admit, but still only a car. It was because of what's in here,' he touched her lightly on the forehead, 'and in here,' another touch, this time to her chest above her heart, 'that has been responsible for you coming out of your shell.'

'But what about the hair and the clothes?'

'All you,' he assured her. 'It was *you* who had the confidence to do those things, not the car. Another thing – I fell in love with you before you went all glam on me. I'll love you no matter what you look like, Candice, because it's what's in your head and your heart that matters to me, not what colour your hair is.'

CHAPTER 43

'Can I get you another cup of tea?' Paul had fussed around her from the minute the hospital had allowed him to bring her home. She was enjoying the attention, even if she wasn't enjoying being less-than-mobile and something of a burden. He'd actually moved in for the duration, staying in Ivan's old room, at least until she could get about a bit better. On his insistence, her bed had been moved downstairs, with Ivan and Preston doing the donkey work, before Preston had flown back to deepest, darkest Peru, or wherever it was he was headed off to. She had loved having both her boys around her, and had been like a dog with two tails for a while. But now Preston was gone again, leaving her with the knowledge that he was healthy, happy, and living life to the fullest. The only thing she asked of him was to be more careful. He'd laughed, assuring her he was always careful. She still had her doubts, though…

'No thanks,' she said to Paul – she'd drunk enough tea recently, to last a lifetime. 'But you could pass me the post. I just heard the letterbox go.' She moved her crutches to the side and waited eagerly. It had come to something when the postman's visit was one of the highlights of her day. She was sick of daytime TV, had read so much that her eyes hurt, and with Paul having to work she was often on her own during the day. He popped back when he could (like today) but it depended on where he was working and what the job entailed.

'Here you go, love.' He put a couple of letters and flyers into her outstretched hand.

Casting one of the letters aside (help with funeral costs? No thanks. She wasn't ready to pop her clogs just yet), she turned the other over curiously.

It was from the insurance company regarding the car.

'Oh. My. God,' she breathed as she read it.

She already knew from the police that the Idiot Driver had been charged with driving without due care and attention, plus a couple of other offences (apparently the car behind him had a dash cam fitted and had filmed it all, so Idiot Driver hadn't had a leg to stand on) but she hadn't taken much notice, apart from being glad he was being punished.

But this? She read the letter again; she hadn't expected *this*.

'What is it? I've got to get off in a minute, so if you're sure you don't need anything…' Paul trailed off when she thrust the letter at him, and he began to read. 'Oh, my God.'

'Exactly!'

Candice couldn't believe the amount of compensation she was being awarded because of her injuries, plus the cost of the car. It was a small fortune.

'It's only what you deserve,' Paul told her, his eyes wide as he read the figure again. 'After everything you've been through; are still going through.'

'I know, but what am I going to do with it all?'

'You could buy a new Mazda?' he suggested. 'Jelly Bean, version 2?'

Candice shook her head, thinking furiously. 'There'll never be another Jelly Bean. She came into my life when I needed her, but now it's time for another sort of car.'

Her gaze went to the little framed picture resting on the mantelpiece. It was of the Mazda, and underneath it was the car's badge. Paul had tracked down the garage where

Jelly Bean had been sent to be assessed, and had begged them to take the Mazda badge off the front of it. Beside it, was a tiny die-cast figure of a Mazda MX-5 in the exact same shade of purply-blue as Jelly Bean. Candice had cried when he had presented it to her.

'What with the baby coming and Barny, I think I need a car more suited to a family than a couple, don't you?' she asked. 'If we want to take the children out, we can hardly do that in a two-seater or in your van. We need a proper car, for a proper family.'

'Is that what we are, a proper family?' Paul knelt by her chair, taking hold of her hand.

'Yes. We are,' she replied firmly. 'I love you so much and I want you to marry me.'

'Eh?' Paul's eyes nearly popped out of their sockets and his eyebrows practically disappeared into his hairline.

'That is… if you want to… Oh, no, have I gone and spoilt everything?' Candice bit her lip, tears threatening.

'Of course I want to. I'm just shocked, that's all. Isn't it supposed to be my job to ask?' Paul tightened his grip on her hand.

'I'm a modern woman,' she replied loftily. 'There's nothing in the rules that says a woman can't do the asking. Besides, I know you. You wouldn't ask me now anyway, would you, because you'd hate to think that I might get the impression you were only asking because of that.' She jerked her head at the letter Paul still held. 'So, what do you say?'

'Yes, but there's something I have to show you,' he said, clambering to his feet awkwardly.

She was right to ask, she decided, watching him walk out of the living room and into the hall. Neither of them were old as such, but they weren't getting any younger, either. Candice had come to realise so abruptly over the last couple of weeks, that life was far too short not to seize it by the scruff of its neck and squeeze every second of joy and love out of it. Why wait, when she was sure this is what she wanted?

He came back looking sheepish, one hand behind his back.

Candice guessed what it was and she laughed.

He got down on one knee, brought his hand out, and presented her with a small black box. When he opened it, a beautiful solitaire diamond sat inside.

'I'll marry you, if you'll marry me,' he said.

'Yes, yes, a thousand times yes. But,' she hesitated, a gleam in her eye. 'On one condition.'

'Oh?'

'I get to pick the car! Oh, and I'm getting a tattoo…'

Liz Davies writes feel-good, light-hearted stories with a hefty dose of romance, a smattering of humour, and a great deal of love.

She's married to her best friend, has one grown-up daughter, and when she isn't scribbling away in the notepad she carries with her everywhere (just in case inspiration strikes), you'll find her searching for that perfect pair of shoes. She loves to cook but isn't very good at it, and loves to eat - she's much better at that! Liz also enjoys walking (preferably on the flat), cycling (also on the flat), and lots of sitting around in the garden on warm, sunny days.

She currently lives with her family in Wales, but would ideally love to buy a camper van and travel the world in it.

You can find her on:

Website: elizabethdaviesauthor.co.uk
Twitter: lizdaviesauthor
Facebook: LizDaviesAuthor1